Die Laughing
A Cape Cod Mystery

by

Arlene Kay

Dedication

*For absent friends
who shaped my life*

Arlene Kay

Published in the United States of America

Also by Arlene Kay:

Intrusion
The Abacus Prize
Swann Dive
Man Trap
Gilt Trip

One

Nicole Nelson trudged up a hilly street toward the Goodhaven Town Hall, pulling her muffler tight against her skin. Brisk April winds straight off the ocean had cooled down the entire waterfront. Might as well enjoy the chill while she could. Once she entered the political arena, things would warm up in a hurry. When the verbal fireworks started, the town's heating bills would plummet.

Tonight's community forum should be a doozy. Doozy. That was Grandma Duffy's word, old-fashioned but spot-on for these proceedings. There was a whiff of the Roman Coliseum about them, too, and Nik wasn't sure where she stood: observer, martyr or rapacious lion. She felt certain of only one thing. A fierce and bloody battle was likely with casualties on both sides.

The agenda, boldly posted on the town's website, provoked a tsunami of protest. Mayor Morgan Haas had really done it this time. By proposing a one-time special assessment on every residential property owner, he'd put the cat squarely among the pigeons. His reasoning was flawless. Goodhaven's Cultural Center needed a quick infusion of cash. If roof repairs weren't made, the spring recital, not to mention the sacred summer tourist season, would be imperiled. The town counted on income from the plays, poetry readings and private functions to subsidize other activities, like the food pantry, children's story hour and after-school clinics. It made sense except for one thing: Shelby Whitholm.

Nik's relationship with Shelby was complex. Since they'd met at Lifelines, the no-kill animal shelter, the woman had shown her limitless kindness combined with an odd sort of maternal interest. When she'd needed a cheap place to roost, Shelby offered Nik her old carriage house for a paltry sum. It was a generous impulse that meant the world to a penniless grad student. Her new digs weren't large, but the cleverly renovated space became Nicole's sanctuary. Shelby housed her old Jeep in one of the garage bays, converting the remaining two into a comfortable family room and office. Nik's living quarters, two bedrooms, bath and kitchen were upstairs.

Shelby's nephew Jarrod had chided his aunt, reminding her of the outrageous sums she could extract from summer renters. Fortunately, he had no influence with Shelby, an ardent environmentalist who'd banished him one day when he'd appeared in her driveway, flaunting a shiny black Hummer.

Nik was a loyal soul, but gratitude didn't blind her to Shelby's eccentricities. You couldn't ignore them if you tried. Shelby Whitholm was a seething, pulsating mass of contradictions even in a Cape Cod town that celebrated the bizarre. An environmentalist who smoked like a chimney? A crusty scold with a soft spot for pets and vagrants? Nik was both puzzled and intrigued.

To many, Shelby was a virulent pest, a strident voice at every public function, who couldn't be appeased or silenced. Kinder folks termed her a gadfly and political activist. Everyone agreed that her constant presence at Goodhaven events was the stuff of local legend, a type of free entertainment to wile away the winter months. When even the most mundane items piqued her interest, she'd stage a show brimming with a dramatic monologue spiked with vitriol.

Every citizen was entitled to five minutes of airtime at township meetings. Shelby never missed the chance. She arrived at the podium armed with statistics, surveys and clippings, making her point with devastating accuracy. Everyone knew the drill: mismanagement, fraud and municipal waste were her constant refrain. When the buzzer rang, Shelby nodded politely and shut up. No fuss, no muss, end of chapter. Her age helped a bit. After all, a seventy-four-year-old woman got some deference in the court of public opinion, even a curmudgeon.

Nik chuckled as she recalled Shelby's latest letter to the *Goodhaven Times*. She'd likened Morgan Haas to King Louis XVI, whose wife's profligate spending had cost him his head. As a scholar Nik knew that was an overstated, somewhat misogynistic view. Historians had given the luckless Marie Antoinette a bad rap. Morgan's wife, who had probably never cracked a history text in her over-privileged life, was not amused by the simile. She was a transplant, a Manhattan product who couldn't or wouldn't adjust to New Englanders' sly wit and understated appearance. Amanda Haas bustled about town like affronted royalty, railing against Shelby as if the first amendment didn't exist.

Small town drama was more grist for Nicole's mill. After all, that's why she'd left the urban jungle for Goodhaven's placid streets. If all went well and the stars aligned, she'd finish her dissertation, get her Ph.D. and become solvent by next year. Hallelujah! They'd chuckled at Boston College when she announced her plan. Her thesis advisor had actually chortled. Nobody leaves Boston for the lower Cape in search of original material. Nobody with sense, that is, especially during the winter. When Nik persisted, he'd shuddered, wished her well and washed his hands of her.

Undaunted, she'd packed up her ancient Jeep and headed south, envisioning the looks of shock and envy when her tome, *Impact of Local Activism on Social Mores*, hit *The Journal of Politics*. Optimism was a genetic quirk of the entire Nelson clan, one that Nik embraced. After all, she was only twenty-four. Time was her ally.

She shook her head, fanning long black hair around her shoulders. Nicole was proud of that hair, a legacy from her Italian forebears. It contrasted nicely with the sapphire eyes and ivory skin bequeathed by the Duffy side of the family. An act of sheer willpower let her ignore the mirror nestling in her purse. How many times had the nuns lectured her about vanity? Too many, she told herself. There's nothing wrong with taking pride in your appearance. Still, she recognized that beauty was fleeting, outlasted by intellect every time. Brains, not beauty, would ultimately set Nik free.

She'd done the research The data suggested that Goodhaven was an incubator for citizen activism. The perfect spot for her research. The permanent population was small. Well under five thousand intrepid souls braved the frigid climate and fierce winds that buffeted the lower Cape in the winter. They were a tough, independent lot, better educated than most and big believers in citizen activism. Nik saw the living proof of that every time Shelby opened her mouth.

"Yo, Nicole! You're walking around in a fog." Mayor Morgan Haas patted her shoulder. He grinned as he looked around him. "Don't see your mentor anywhere. What are you, the scouting party?"

"Maybe she won't show up." Amanda Haas appeared at her husband's side, clutching an outsize leather purse. "Honestly. That woman has some nerve." She shivered despite the thick shearling coat she wore. "Can't you do something, Nicole? It just isn't right."

Amanda often said that civilization began and ended at the East River. Goodhaven was her husband's dream, not hers. He'd been somebody in New York, a god of finance, master of the universe. That made her somebody, too. By selling his holdings and trading arbitrage for seashells, he'd robbed her of that lofty perch. Amanda didn't fit into the cozy Cape Cod hamlet. Even she knew that. The town wags sneered at her clothes, called her a name-dropper and an airhead because she cared more for Armani than Aristotle. She, in turn, scorned most of them. Women without makeup, manicures and leg waxes were a curious breed to Amanda. She hibernated until the arrival of the summer people, that horde of outsiders who actually understood her. Flocks of them came from New York or Connecticut each year with priorities that matched Mandy's.

"I've been working at Lifelines all day, Mandy, so I haven't seen her. Shelby's probably busy checking her data. Don't worry. She'll be here." Nik ducked her head to hide the grin that peeked out. No sense in alienating anyone, especially the mayor's wife.

Shelby was definitely up to something. She'd sounded mysterious this morning when they'd shared their daily toast and espresso. "Get a good seat tonight. You don't want to miss the fireworks." That's all she'd said except for her daily quote from The Bard. "Check your *Macbeth*, Cookie. You'll see what I mean." Shelby Whitholm, superannuated Shakespeare groupie.

"Come on, hon." Morgan steered his wife toward the door. "We'll get you the best seat in the house." He pivoted, winked at Nik, and disappeared through the heavy oak portal, leaving her to ponder the laws of attraction. There was something rather sexy about Morgan even though he was old, fifty at least. She'd never had a daddy complex. No Electra here, no sir. But Morgan's shaggy brown hair and twinkling eyes were engaging. Maybe it was the shreds of bravado that clung to him like a monarch's cloak. Money and power, the ultimate aphrodisiacs. Hadn't Kissinger or some other luminary said that? No man made big bucks in the City without having sharp elbows, a nimble mind and steely nerves. Morgan needed that forbearance to deal with Shelby. Why else, short of a sick streak of masochism, would he endure her taunts and still act as her attorney? For free, no less.

Mandy was another thing entirely. She epitomized the social x-rays so famously described by Tom Wolfe. Any day, Nik expected an ocean wind to lift the woman's frail frame aloft until she floated, kite-like, back to home base.

"Joining us tonight, Ms. Nelson?" Harris Goldman's reedy voice cut through the frigid air. "You've been our guest for eight months now, so I suppose that dissertation's almost done."

Nik's hands balled into fists. Something about this wizened professor made her skin crawl. Calm down, she told herself. The guy's older than your grandpa, for heaven's sake.

Goldman's lips stretched into an unnaturally tight grin as he adjusted his muffler. Dr. Harris Goldman, retired professor of philosophy, had a slew of academic credentials and limited social skills. Under that veneer of civility was a flawed human with a dim view of his fellow creatures. Nik was positive about that. Since her arrival in Goodhaven, she'd observed him at a number of meetings and social venues. Each time, he waited until others took a risk before committing himself with a weasel-worded sentence that said nothing. Shelby loathed him, especially after he'd called her an atheist. "Watch out for him, Cookie. He's a sly one." Nik recalled Shelby's puckish grin. "Still as the grave. The Bard got Goldman down pat."

She checked her watch before answering him. Five minutes 'til show time. "I'm still plugging away, professor. I just may take you up on your offer to help." She gave him her most winsome smile. Most men came close to swooning when Nicole Nelson turned on the charm. The guys at B.C. called her an intellectual bombshell, someone who could lure admirers to their doom like Circe. Harris Goldman reacted differently. He recoiled, stepped back as if he'd been propositioned.

"Any time." He scrambled up the stairs. "I'll just go take my seat."

In the background someone snickered. A stocky young man with round glasses, wispy beard and an impish grin stepped into the light. Jett Hall had been eavesdropping, and he made no attempt to hide it. He bared a set of gleaming teeth as he approached Nik.

"Another conquest, Ms. Nelson? Hmm. Guess I'm too young for you if octogenarians turn you on."

"What makes you think that age is the only reason?" Nik tossed her curls. "Shouldn't you be tending your bookstore or something, Jett?"

He squeezed her shoulder, nudging her toward the welcoming warmth of the hall. "Don't be snippy, my beauty. When your opus is published, you'll sing another tune. Independent bookstore owners can make or break you. For sure, Barnes & Noble won't give you a tumble." He thumped his chest. "But I, on the other hand ..."

"What's this about a tumble? You have sex on the brain." Danielle Stevens brushed past them with a silken swish. Nik deflated like a child's balloon as she eyed the svelte form of the real estate broker. Danielle Stevens, mistress of the night, was beautiful, a constant vision in splendid blonde on black outfits. She exuded a chilly blend of hauteur and scorn that made Nik shrink into her worn Gap pea coat and rough wool scarf. Some day, she told herself, I'll have nice things, too. When I'm finished with school and too old to care.

"Let's get this show on the road," Jett said. "I plan to leave right after Shelby's speech. Wouldn't miss that for the world." He raised his eyebrows in a pathetic imitation of Groucho Marx. Both Jett and Danielle were star players in Goodhaven's community theatre, and Jett never missed an opportunity to test his skills.

Danielle risked a mini-frown. As Jarrod Whitholm's fiancée, she couldn't afford to badmouth his Aunt Shelby, no matter what the provocation. She pasted a faux smile on her face and said nothing.

"Come on, ladies. Hubba, hubba. Half the town's already in there." Jett made a sweeping gesture and sprinted up the weathered wooden steps. He was Nik's only friend in this small, cliquish town, closer in age to her than most of the others. Shelby tried, she really did, but she couldn't shake the need to mother her lodger and ply her with unsolicited advice. The bits on local politics were worth remembering, but not Shelby's acerbic take on everything else. Life was too short for unrelenting cynicism.

Nik loved the town hall with its gnarled mahogany pews and sculpted spire. Speakers used the old pulpit to address the gathering, lending their remarks a perceived link to the Almighty that was quite undeserved.

Tonight's gathering, the community forum, was one of six special sessions convened each year. It was a stroke of genius and the product of sheer desperation. A decade ago Goodhaven had been torn asunder by political disputes so rancorous that the town threatened to implode. To avert disaster the Forum was established, giving each citizen the chance to learn about and comment on issues. Original democracy at work. Nik savored every bit of it. The link between the forum and town government was the key to her dissertation, the jewel in her academic crown. She crossed her fingers, praying that Shelby wouldn't disrupt the proceedings too much.

Turnout was exceptionally high that evening despite the winter chill. Money or the prospect of losing it seemed to pump life into even the hardest hearts and arteries. Nik flipped open her iPad, ready to record every *bon mot*. She never took sides; that would be unprofessional. She was an observer, not a participant. As such, that accorded her a neutral status akin to a U.N. peacekeeper. A few hardliners groused at her association with Shelby, but most folks in this academically inclined town applauded the effort.

Three other council members sat at the dais, counteracting Danielle's insolence and Morgan's hubris. They were forgettable town fixtures, providing the small community with continuity and peace of mind.

The imposing walnut grandfather clock chimed seven times. Nik loved the beautiful antique, a relic from a long-ago sea captain's house. Several townspeople craned their necks as if waiting for the fireworks to start. Waiting for Shelby, of course. Dramatic entrances weren't typical of her, but she did enjoy the element of surprise. Harris Goldman leaned forward in his seat, looking pointedly at his watch. He glared at the mayor and heaved an exasperated sigh.

After Danielle elbowed him Morgan gave a startled yelp and gaveled the meeting to order.

"Great turnout tonight," he said. "I'll read the proposal aloud and allot thirty minutes for comments and questions. Let's see," he fumbled through a sheaf of papers, "We've got eight speakers. That's forty minutes."

Danielle's pained expression spoke volumes. She seemed jumpy, eager to dispense with the nonsense.

"Check out Amanda," Jett whispered. "Is she in a trance? Maybe she hypnotized herself."

"Hush," Nik said. "We'll get thrown out of here if you don't shut up." She had to concentrate in case Morgan made some salient point. If he succeeded in winning over the town, he'd score a major *coup*. Shelby would be apoplectic, but that was one of the dangers of living in a democracy. You made your case, and sometimes you lost. Speaking of which, where the hell was Shelby? She was always punctual to a fault. Her front row seat stayed empty, adding to Nik's growing anxiety. After all, Shelby was no kid. What if she'd had a stroke or something? Even worse, she might have had an accident and be lying out in the road somewhere, freezing. Shelby insisted on pedaling all over town on her ancient Schwinn despite the impenetrable New England darkness and the hint of ice. She activated her venerable Jeep Wagoneer only in emergencies.

"Where is she?" she hissed to Jett. "Shelby always speaks first."

His shrug said he didn't really care. "Chill, for Christ's sake. It would take the entire Sixth Fleet to derail her. She just wants to make an entrance."

Morgan droned on, cataloging the repairs needed for the cultural center and their cost. In a clever counterpoint he also listed the revenue stream that a fully functioning facility could generate.

"We're talking about a self-sustaining venture for Goodhaven," Morgan drawled. "All you merchants can get on board with that, I bet. With the right inducements our tourist traffic will double."

Amanda Haas sprang to life, startling them all by clapping her hands like a child. Danielle was too sophisticated to cheer, but she brightened as Morgan discussed revitalizing the moribund real estate market. Business had stalled during the recession, even for the high-end properties she represented.

Nik stole a glance at Amanda. Her eyes looked unnaturally bright in her otherwise pallid face as she stared up at her husband. How odd to see that look of adoration. Did the wives of even minor politicians acquire it by osmosis, or was it a cool, calculated piece of theatre? Mandy's pupils looked dilated, but Nicole couldn't really tell. Maybe the woman just needed a good meal instead of another pill.

"Okay. Let's start our citizen commentary." Morgan hesitated and pushed a paper toward Danielle. She shook her head, whispering a reply into his ear.

"I'm going to ask our esteemed professor, Harris Goldman, to lead off."

The crowd stirred as townspeople craned their necks. Probably looking for Shelby, Nik thought. Speaking slots were assigned impartially on a FIFO basis, but somehow, Shelby Whitholm's name always surfaced before any of her fellow citizens could even blink. Her absence tonight upset the natural order of things.

Goldman trotted up to the pulpit like a racehorse at the starting gate. Even Nik had to admit that he was spry for his age. There was no Mrs. Goldman. Rumor had it she'd decamped to Florida with her chiropractor the year before. That humiliation should have made Harris a sympathetic character, but most of the town still rooted for his wife.

Nik understood betrayal, even though she considered Harris Goldman an insufferable insect. Her fiancé, Mark Murray, had unceremoniously dumped her last year for the heiress to a German munitions fortune. Nik managed to behave reasonably well every time they encountered each other, even though she longed to claw his eyes and throat. Three months ago Mark had suddenly appeared at her front door. Instead of proclaiming his love, he'd begged for a hookup. Just sex, no emotion. His fiancée, Hilda or Helga or something equally banal, was spending the semester in

Berlin, and Mark was lonely. Horny, more likely. She'd sent the bastard packing without shedding a tear, and the next morning, Nicole Nelson escaped to Goodhaven.

The ping of an iPhone signaled that Goldman's five minutes were over. Nik elbowed Jett in a panic. "Where *is* she? Now I'm really scared." She gathered her things and inched toward the edge of pew. That's when everything fell apart.

The hall door opened, admitting a new player. Sheriff Bob Fuselli entered the room, accompanied by a long, lean stranger with masses of unruly black hair and tons of attitude. The audience sat in stunned silence as a scene played out in a thousand horror movies became real. Fuselli strode toward the podium, exchanged a few words with the mayor and took the microphone.

Two

Robert Fuselli inspired confidence. There was something in the set of his broad shoulders and steady blue eyes that channeled lawmen across the generations. Elliot Ness with a touch of John Wayne, that's how Nik always thought of him. Tonight as she watched him calmly adjust the microphone and survey the crowd, she felt no comfort. Abject terror turned her body into an iceberg incapable of movement or sensation. *Shelby.* The name bounced through her brain like a rabid ping-pong ball.

Oh God, Shelby. What have you done?

"Ladies and gentlemen. I have an announcement to make."

No one said a word, not even Morgan Haas. Everyone froze, immobilized by the prospect of impending tragedy. Amanda moved forward, swaying back and forth in some arcane ritual. Nik leaned back in the pew, feeling Jett's arm around her shoulders, steadying her.

"I'm sorry to report that our friend and neighbor Shelby Whitholm is dead."

There were gasps and a few cries but very little outward grief. After all, in a town filled with the elderly, death was a constant visitor. Nik felt the salty sting of tears on her cheeks. She gripped the sturdy arm of the wooden pew to keep from fainting. *Poor Shelby. I hope it was quick. No pain.*

Fuselli's face was set in grim, unwavering lines. He was a newcomer, barely six months out of Washington, D.C., unused to confronting the grim reaper in this tight-knit community.

Morgan pounded the desk with his gavel. "Out of deference for Shelby, I'm going to adjourn this meeting. I'm sure you'll want to share your memories of our friend."

Fuselli clenched his jaw and held up his palm. "Excuse me, Mayor. There's more." His clear eyes grew flinty. "Ms. Whitholm's death was no accident. We're conducting a murder inquiry."

"Murder!" Mandy tented her hands, closed her eyes and swayed.

Danielle reached surreptitiously into her leather tote, extracting her phone.

"What happened?" Harris Goldman's eyes were bright, energized, more voyeur than grieving friend.

Fuselli stared at him a moment before answering. "Ms. Whitholm was found in her home. We got a call about a fire and found her. That's all I'm prepared to say at the moment. I'll interview most of you over the next few days."

Fire! Shelby loved her old brick Tudor. It stood out in a block of cottages and Capes with well-manicured yards and a view of the ocean. One of a kind, just like Shelby. Nik thought of the yellow irises that ringed the curb near her mailbox and the small but emphatic sign stating Friends for Peace. Fire! Oh, my God. Her pets! What happened to Atticus and Annabel? The cats always stayed indoors, but Confucius, her shepherd-collie rescue had a fenced yard.

Nik turned toward Jett, thankful for his presence. She was dumbstruck, unable to form a coherent thought. Hysteria was out of the question. She owed it to Shelby to see this awful thing through. She had to do something, anything.

"Steady, girl," Jett whispered. "Here he comes."

The sheriff moved purposefully toward them, followed by the stranger. Fuselli laid his large hand on Nik's shoulder and patted it.

"Let's talk, Nicole." He nodded toward the alcove at the back of the room. Jett helped her up, gathered her things and prepared to follow. "Not you, Mr. Hall. Not yet." Fuselli held his arm outstretched. "We'll talk tomorrow."

A deputy gently herded stunned citizens from the room as Nicole followed the sheriff.

Morgan Haas lingered at the podium. "I was her attorney, you know," he said. "Shelby's, I mean. Maybe I should sit in on this."

Fuselli gave the mayor a patient smile. "Thanks anyway, Morgan. I'll speak to you first thing tomorrow." He pivoted toward the stranger. "Same goes for you, Dr. Lee. I assume you're staying at the Lion Inn?"

The stranger narrowed his eyes and nodded. They were strange eyes. Nicole couldn't help but notice that. Amber, slightly slanted and fierce, rather like a hawk's. His long, thick hair was raven black, adding to the avian illusion. She'd never seen him before. In fact, she'd never before seen any man who looked more like a film star or a model.

Despite the blast from the room's radiators, Nicole couldn't stop shivering. She retrieved her gloves and hunkered down into her coat.

"Her pets. I have to get them, sheriff. Please." Tears flooded her cheeks as she recalled them. They were her real family, more giving than Jarrod Whitholm had ever been.

"Hey, Nicole. Don't worry. They're fine. My deputy took them over to my place. You can pick them up tomorrow."

Nik searched her pockets for a handkerchief. "Okay," she said sniffling.

Fuselli pulled out a clean linen square. "Here. Blow."

It was a curiously gentle gesture from such a big man. Nik had never quite figured out the sheriff. He'd come from the Treasury Department, highly decorated, a senior special agent, no less. At least that's what his official bio said. Plenty of those guys came to Boston, settling into corporate security jobs. Only a few, like Fuselli, chose real police work in a town with a modest budget.

"There are questions, Nicole, about Shelby. I need to ask them now." Fuselli clicked on a small recorder. My office is stone cold, or I'd take you there." He patted the seat of a sturdy oak chair. "Come on. Sit down for a minute and take it easy. I know Shelby was your friend."

Nik closed her eyes, taking a series of full yogic breaths. The air filled her abdomen and chest. A fellow student had taught her the practice, and it worked like a charm to dissipate tension. In and out. She did it for twenty breath cycles before opening her eyes and facing Fuselli. There. At least she wouldn't throw up or sob hysterically.

The sheriff moved closer and touched her shoulder. "Everything okay? Thought for a moment you were in a trance."

She blinked and in a low, barely audible voice said, "How can I help you?"

Nik was fairly certain that his days chasing tax cheats and counterfeiters hadn't prepared Fuselli for this one. She also sensed that Fuselli found her appealing. She'd overheard him chatting with Jett Hall one day as she passed by.

"She's young, way too young for me." His eyes had been glued to her backside. "Sure is one sexy babe, though. Brightened up this old burg by a hundred percent." Fuselli and Jett shared that male-to-male grin she'd seen so often.

"Last time I fell for a pair of spectacular tits, I married them ... her."

"How'd that work out for you?" Jett's laughter rang out.

"Still writing checks every month."

Nik reluctantly brought herself back to the present. She owed it to Shelby to focus.

"Right now we're just having a discussion." Fuselli switched off the recorder. "Unless you plan to confess. That would change everything."

Nik bolted upright, forgetting everything else. She clutched her chest as her heart rate soared to stratospheric levels. "Confess? I would never hurt Shelby. What happened? How did she ... how do you know it's murder?"

"Easy." Fuselli lowered his voice to a near whisper. "It's not pretty, Nicole. Looks like she died from a head wound, a massive one."

"It still could have been an accident. Maybe she fell." Nicole willed Fuselli to give her a crumb of hope, something to mitigate the awful sting of violence.

Fuselli patted his pocket as if searching for the comfort of a long ago pack of smokes. "She was tied up. Someone used a rope, the kind that anchors boats. Pretty common around here."

Rope! It didn't make sense. Shelby kept some kind of rope in the garage. They all did around here, but not in the house. Someone had to bring it in—deliberately. Her throat closed, causing Nik to swallow convulsively. She coughed until Fuselli gave her back a resounding thump.

"There's more," he said. "Feel up to hearing it?" He looked down at a folder in his lap. "I won't show you the pictures. Apparently this sick bastard had a warped sense of humor: He used red, white and blue strands of rope to bind her."

Nik's voice quivered as she processed the tragedy. "Oh God. Shelby used rope like that for the parade, Fourth of July floats and such. Half the town helped with that." She put her head between her knees. That helped somehow. "Why would anyone hurt Shelby? She was harmless."

"Really? Ms. Whitholm had quite a bite to her. Words sting too, you know."

Nik shivered again as Fuselli observed her. Now her teeth were chattering.

"Listen," he said. "Unless you know something specific, we'll wait 'til tomorrow for an interview. Are you okay at that carriage house?"

Nik frowned as she considered the question. "I hadn't … I'm not sure. Shelby was the only woman in Goodhaven I really knew. I could ask Jett, but he might misinterpret. Infer things, you know." She looked down as a blush stained her cheeks. The last thing she needed was a mercy fuck from Jett Hall. She'd have to scrape him off like day-old gum.

"How about this?" Fuselli asked. "I'll station a deputy outside Shelby's place tonight. That way you'll have some protection. Our forensic people will be there all night anyway."

"I'm not in danger." Nik wound her muffler tighter. "I'm nobody." She'd lived alone for a long time without having a meltdown, and tonight was no time to start. She laughed, closer to a sob. "Maybe those karate lessons will come in handy after all."

Fuselli ignored her ramblings and held out his arm. "Come on. I'll drop you off. We can stop by and get her pets, if you'd feel better. That dog made quite a racket today. The neighbors complained and tipped us off."

Nik recalled how Shelby proudly paraded Confucius back and forth. Her trophy pet. He was fearless, a valiant guard dog who seemed grateful just to have a home. If he'd been inside the house, no one would have touched Shelby. Why was he outside? Shelby always babied him, called him Foo Dog and kept him indoors once it got chilly. That required some serious thought.

"Thanks," Nik said. "I'd like that. I'll feel safer with Confucius than any deputy. I need to hug the cats, too, have them purr me to sleep tonight."

"Let's head out." Fuselli gathered his things and led the way.

Nik finally crawled in bed after midnight, cuddling up under Grandma's down quilt with Atticus and Annabel on each side of her, purring madly. Confucius was restive. He patrolled the carriage house, sniffing the air and whining softly. *You miss her, Foo Dog. I know that. So do I.*

Money was tight, but she kept the lights on anyway. She'd moved chairs under each of the doorknobs and propped Shelby's old Louisville Slugger against the wall for a weapon.

In her dresser drawer Nik found a gift from Shelby: a half-filled bottle of Ambien. Every student she knew had that and a matching bottle of uppers. Student housing was a drugstore during exam week. Everyone pooled their pharmacological resources in a unified battle against the study gods. Nik eased back on her pillow, hoping to rest her eyes.

The sharp b-r-ring of the door chimes made her leap out of bed. Shards of bright morning light assailed her as she searched her bedside table for the alarm. *Eight o'clock. What the hell? At least she'd gotten some sleep.* Nik grabbed her thick wool robe, easing into old shearling slippers. L.L.Bean outlet. Not designer duds but a cheap, sensible choice for New England's chill.

The persistent ring launched Foo Dog into a hysterical spate of barking. If he kept that up, he'd rouse half the neighborhood. Nik had no doubt that every door in Goodhaven had been bolted last night, some for the first time. Shelby's murder marked the death of innocence and complacency in the little town. Things would never be the same. She was sure of that.

Nik tucked the baseball bat inside her robe and crept toward the front door. Maybe it was one of the deputies. She brushed aside the heavy silk drapes and peered out. *Shit! Just what I need.*

She stared into the patrician features of Jarrod Whitholm, Shelby's nephew and putative heir. He'd never said more than a few words to her. Probably considered her a serf intruding on the liege lord's property. Her stomach clenched as she realized that the arrogant prick was likely to be her new landlord.

She gripped Foo's collar and slowly opened the door. Jarrod was tall, with pale blue eyes and a sharp, aquiline nose. She'd never seen him smile, although Danielle probably knew how to coax that and more from him. He'd look okay then, not handsome, certainly, but better than average. A fair replica of her father's hero, William F. Buckley, Jr., absent the devastating wit and snarky charm.

Jarrod gave her a curt nod, dismissing Nik's tatty robe and scuffed slippers with a glance. Despite the hour, he was flawlessly attired in a tan Burberry and matching plaid cravat.

"Morning, Nicole." Jarrod shifted from foot to foot. "Look. I found out something important, something you need to know. Can you spare me a few minutes?"

Nik hesitated, immediately suspicious. Why was he being polite? Jarrod Whitholm was never polite. He thrived on controversy, made his living from it. She'd seen him on that reactionary cable channel, throwing barbs or brickbats as the subject warranted. Jarrod Whitholm, defender of the Constitution, Yale graduate and ardent neocon. She had to admit that she admired his mind. Some of his writing was quite brilliant, actually, but his derision of the less fortunate sickened her. He probably pegged her as some sort of charity case, too.

"Come in," Nik told him. "I'm so sorry about Shelby. She was very kind to me." Tears slipped unbidden down her cheek as she recalled her friend.

Jarrod stepped gingerly around Confucius and surveyed the living room with the practiced eye of an investor. "This place is nicer than I thought. Aunt Shelby wasn't much on décor."

Nik had always had a sense of style. She'd managed to cobble together auction and flea market finds that made her space both warm and chic. Jarrod couldn't sneer about that. She was proud of her little home. After waving him toward a wing chair, she headed for the kitchen.

"You've got her ... animals ... I see."

"The sheriff brought them over last night."

She could tell by the stiff set of his shoulders that Jarrod wasn't a pet person. When Atticus jumped into his lap, he deftly fended him off by crossing his legs.

"You mentioned something important. I have to admit that makes me curious." Nik summoned her party smile. "I assume you're my new landlord." She placed mugs, cream and sugar on a vintage tole tray and carried them in. Confucius stayed at her heels.

"He doesn't like me," Jarrod said, pointing at the dog. "Animals never do."

"Hmm. Foo Dog is pretty mellow, but after yesterday ... "

"Look Ms. Nelson—Nicole. I ran into the Mayor last night, and he told me something important. Something you should know."

Nik felt a strange sensation tiptoe up her spine. It was odd, surreal, to sit here in Shelby's carriage house and speak dispassionately about her death, her murder, with a man that neither of them had liked.

"He was her attorney. Morgan, I mean." Jarrod stammered a bit, just enough to arouse Nik's interest. How strange to see the preternaturally calm Mr. Whitholm lose his cool. Strange and satisfying. Nik forced herself to use silence, the ultimate weapon. She smiled at him and said nothing.

"It was about my aunt's will. You should know, too," Jarrod said. "Fuselli already mentioned it, and he'll probably ask you about it."

Nik glanced down at her tatty robe and slippers. "Wait until I get dressed. I won't take long." She sped toward her bedroom without waiting for his response. No way would she let anyone, especially the male population of Goodhaven, see her half naked and without makeup. It was personal pride, not vanity.

She hopped into the shower and did her ablutions. To hell with Jarrod Whitholm. Let him cool his heels.

It took half an hour, but Nik was more than satisfied with the results. Despite her modest wardrobe, she filled out a sweater better than most women, even the elegant Danielle. As she applied makeup, Nik glanced at a photo of Shelby taken at the animal shelter. Jarrod was right about one thing: Shelby wasn't much on decor or personal style. She'd been a plain, rather lumpy woman who made no excuses for herself. When Nik suggested trimming her shaggy mop of gray hair just a touch, Shelby bristled. "I am who I am, pumpkin. God never gave me good looks. Not like you. I accept that. Hell, I'm grateful for it. I earned every one of these wrinkles, believe me." Shelby pushed her heavy, horn-rimmed glasses high on her head and smiled. "Besides, life is simpler when you buy T-shirts from K-mart." She shrugged. "I just throw 'em out. No muss, no fuss."

What happened, Shelby? Who did this dreadful thing to you?"

When she walked back into the living room, Nik caught Jarrod prowling through the papers on her desk. "Find anything interesting?" she asked.

His flushed face gave her pleasure. "It's a bad habit of mine, curiosity. Killed the cat, as they say."

"Yes, they do. You had something to tell me?"

"Morgan will do a formal notification, but this is important. Shelby made both of us her heirs or co-legatees, as we lawyers say." Jarrod's pale blue eyes never left Nik's face. They were hard, predatory eyes. "That surprises you? I thought Shelby would have discussed it with you."

Nik eased onto the sofa, feeling unsteady. "I guess that means the house and furniture. I don't think she had much else."

He shrugged. "Probably. Morgan said that she left me the main house and you this place." A faint smile lightened his face. "Makes me wonder if you got the better part of that deal."

Nik barely heard him. Her mind was cluttered with untidy memories of Shelby Whitholm, her friend and now her benefactor. She couldn't even process what had happened. She was just too sad.

"There's more to it." Jarrod assumed his television persona, bland but full of guile. "You and I are now Fuselli's number one suspects. *Cui bono?*" He repulsed another advance by Atticus. "Before you ask, you get full custody of her animals. I'll gladly concede to that."

Any man who disliked animals was Nik's natural enemy. Now she remembered one of the reasons she disliked Jarrod.

There were plenty of others, of course, like his reactionary political beliefs, sense of entitlement and general unpleasantness. He'd asked about her academic pursuits just once. When she mentioned Boston College, his eyes flickered with distain. He didn't even try to hide it. Nik had learned to read people quite well during her short life. Obviously, in Jarrod Whitholm's world only Ivy League colleges counted for anything. Maybe it wasn't Yale, but Boston College was a well-respected institution. Nik knew that. Her family wasn't wealthy, and she was thrilled when B.C. offered her a full scholarship. A doctorate was her ticket to independence. Screw Jarrod Whitholm and his contemptuous views.

"You're overreacting," Nik told him. "I have nothing to hide. Of course, you and Shelby had that falling out …"

Jarrod struck like a cranky rattler. "Wait just one minute. I'll have you know that Shelby and I were close. We sparred, of course, quarreled occasionally, but remained close. Blood. It's thicker than most people realize." He squinted at her. "Think twice before you blab that to Fuselli."

Nik shivered, recalling the sheriff's description of the crime scene. Plenty of blood had spilled there, and the house hadn't been broken into. She'd known her murderer. Shelby was a soft touch for anyone with a hard luck story, but she was no fool. Confucius would have been there, right by her side, if she'd had any doubts. Someone who disliked dogs, someone like her nephew, might have persuaded her to put him in the yard.

"Don't threaten me. I won't volunteer any information." Nik met Jarrod Whitholm's eyes. "I won't lie either. If the sheriff asks me something, I'll tell the truth."

"Look. I'm telling you this as a lawyer. Watch what you say to Fuselli. He's in way over his head."

A sharp rap on the door interrupted them. As if on cue, Bob Fuselli stood on her doorstep, poised to knock again.

"I'm sorry, Sheriff. Please come in." Nik opened the door, watching as Fuselli patted Foo Dog's glossy fur. "Mr. Whitholm just stopped by."

Despite having very little sleep, the lawman looked sharp, his uniform crisp, trousers creased. He hadn't come alone. That stranger from the night before was nipping at his heels.

"Who's this, Sheriff? Introduce us." Jarrod met the amber stare of the newcomer without flinching. They were both tall men with hard, serious eyes.

"This is Alejandro Lee, a business associate of your aunt. He's the one who found her yesterday. Risked his life to extinguish that fire. Saved her pets, too."

The stranger gave a modest shrug. "Alex, please. My condolences to you both. Shelby and I spoke often on the phone, but I really didn't know her. Charming lady. A great loss."

"Hmm," Jarrod said. "I didn't know my aunt had business contacts. She was a retired librarian, for God's sake. All she cared about was the animal shelter and the town government. Furthermore, very few people would call her charming."

Nik studied Alejandro Lee closely, wondering why he'd lied. Maybe he was just being polite, or maybe even Shelby wasn't immune to a man who looked like an underwear model. Nik had learned more than once that age was no barrier to desire.

His plaid sport coat and fawn-colored slacks fit Alex like a sleek second skin. Nik knew they were expensive, probably cashmere or some other exotic material. She'd bet that outfit was Italian, too. It had that exclusive, custom-made look that she aspired to but couldn't yet afford.

He was handsome, no doubt about that, with sculpted features and masses of wavy black hair. On more than one occasion, her passion for great hair had blinded her to less savory traits in men. Her ex-fiancé, the faithless Mark Murray with his silky blonde curls, immediately sprang to mind, just one in a long line of male mistakes she'd made before forsaking romance. From now on Nik intended to focus laser-like on one thing: her career.

"Have we met?" Alejandro Lee's mocking eyes pinned her to the wall like a lab specimen. "You must be Nicole, Shelby's protégé. She often spoke of you."

Protégé! She flushed to the roots of her hair. Damn. He'd caught her staring at him.

"See here, Sheriff. Do you intend to take our statements or not?" Jarrod fingered his shirtsleeve like a put-upon monarch. Another Ivy League memento, the elegant Yale monogram, *Lux et Veritas*, graced the face of his gold cufflinks. Like everything else about him, they reeked of privilege, class and good taste. No wonder Jarrod scoffed at her tatty robe.

With three big men pumping testosterone into the air, Nik could have lowered the thermostat in her living room by ten degrees. They stood facing each other like alpha wannabes in a nature video.

"Please sit down," she said, waving them toward two leather club chairs. "I have coffee."

"Great," Fuselli said. "How about you, Alejandro?"

The stranger nodded, giving Nik a bright smile with a side of attitude. He followed her as she entered her Pullman kitchen and got to work grinding beans, measuring espresso and carefully spooning it into the Bialetti. Coffee was serious business here.

"Excellent," he said with an easy grin. "I love espresso." Ignoring the murderous glare Nik sent his way, he held out his arms. "I'd never expect a lady to carry all that by herself. Let me help."

"Thanks, I can manage." There was something disquieting about him, something that activated all her defenses. To her horror Nik felt a slight tingling in her nether parts.

His eyes never left her face. "You don't like me very much, do you?"

"Nonsense," Nik said with a snort. "I don't even know you."

"But I know you. At least I know what Shelby told me. Nicole Nelson, ABD, Boston College. Smart, hardworking. Finishing her dissertation in political science." His smile showcased a set of dimples. "For some reason, she didn't mention how beautiful you are."

Nik considered flinging espresso into his self-satisfied face but summoned a smile instead. "Hmm. You know a lot about me for someone who never met Shelby. Play fair, Mr. Lee. Tell me about yourself."

He sighed. "Alex, please. That would take some time, and the Sheriff and your boyfriend are waiting for us."

"Boyfriend! Why I'll have you know ..." Yoga, self-discipline. Just in time, Nik controlled herself. "You're wrong," she said. "I barely know Mr. Whitholm. We're not even friends."

The light on the Bialetti said that the espresso was ready. Nik busied herself with filling the tray and handed it to him. "Thanks so much for the help," she said. "I couldn't have done it without you."

Three

Alejandro Lee suppressed a chuckle. Despite the grim circumstances of Shelby's death, simple human emotions had seeped into the little coach house, noxious fumes that could poison all they touched. Fuselli and Jarrod Whitholm were jousting for dominance like two stallions in rut. He fully expected that any moment one of them would paw the ground or mark his territory. Meanwhile the lovely Nicole lounged gracefully against the wall as if she were above such things.

Nicole Nelson. He liked the sound of that name. Alliterative. Easy on the tongue. Alex gave himself a mental shake. *Stay focused, brother. Take care of business.*

Besides, she was much too young. Just a kid really. A beautiful, sensuous kid with generous curves, eyes to die for and something else. Vulnerability. It lurked just beneath the surface despite her efforts to be tough. She could easily be hurt if a guy mistreated her. Alex saw the blinking red lights and the big Keep Out sign that surrounded her.

He turned away, focusing his attention on Fuselli. Interesting man, not your typical bumpkin. No sir. Alex knew the type and resolved to be wary around him. Jarrod Whitholm was another story. Alex looked beyond the façade: East Coast preppy, old money, stodgy Ivy Leaguer. Jarrod Whitholm was all those things and more. He had a first-class intellect, freely displayed every Sunday on his talk show. As part of his research, Alex had watched a few episodes, gotten hooked.

With the preliminaries over, Fuselli sprawled on the sofa and stated his agenda. "Dr. Lee asked to meet you. He'll answer any questions and be on his way. Then we'll have that discussion, Mr. Whitholm."

Jarrod pointedly looked at his watch. It was expensive, a Cartier Tank with alligator band. That didn't surprise Alex one bit. Only the best for a Whitholm.

"How long will this take?" Jarrod huffed. "I have other commitments."

Fuselli went all cop on him. Alex figured he'd probably reeled in far bigger fish than Jarrod and wasn't intimidated at all. "We'll be here until I conclude my interview, unless, of course, you'd prefer to go to my office. That can easily be arranged." Fuselli flashed a bland, nice guy grin that fooled no one.

Alex used his coffee cup to mask a smirk.

Nicole did the same.

"I suppose it'll have to be." Jarrod set his jaw like a petulant juvenile. "Perhaps I should consult my attorney while I'm waiting."

Fuselli affected surprise. "Oh. I thought you were an attorney, Mr. Whitholm. My mistake."

"Of course I am. Don't they have cable news in this rural outpost? I'm a scholar. My specialty is constitutional law, not criminal."

"Fine. That's settled then. Let's get on with it, shall we?" Fuselli nodded to Alex.

Before anyone else spoke, Jarrod barked out a question. "Bottom line, Mr. Lee. What was your business with my aunt? Remember, she was elderly. We have strict laws in this Commonwealth against bilking senior citizens."

Fuselli gave Jarrod a look sharp enough to slice steel. This whole charade was probably a set-up, Fuselli's idea of a trap. Alex was amused, not alarmed. One of the values his dad always stressed was self-control, no matter what the provocation. He punished any signs of weakness, making Alex an outstanding card player and a contained, somewhat somber man.

"I came here to consummate a business deal with your aunt," he said. "When her estate is settled, I'll make the same offer to her heirs. I presume that means you, Mr. Whitholm. Perhaps not."

"It's no big secret," Nicole said. "Jarrod and I share Shelby's estate, but it's puzzling, Mr. Lee. I recently helped Shelby sort through her attic and clean her house, and I don't understand your interest. Are you some sort of real estate speculator?"

Fuselli and Jarrod exchanged glances. After a nod from the sheriff, Alex spoke up.

"I represent a very motivated buyer, Ms. Nelson, who was prepared to pay Shelby Whitholm a large sum of money for her collection. We'd been negotiating online for some time. I'm sure the sheriff can track our e-mails."

Jarrod's face flushed an appalling shade of fuchsia. "Well, for Christ's sake, spit it out, Lee. What collection?"

"Her comics, of course. Graphic novels are prized by collectors."

"Comics!" Nik and Jarrod spoke in tandem.

"Exactly." Alex smiled broadly. "You really didn't know? Either of you?"

"Certainly not," Jarrod said. "You're joking, right? My aunt, a connoisseur of comics? That's ridiculous."

"Have you seen this collection, Mr. Lee?" Nik asked.

"Yes. Well, mostly photos of it, actually. Shelby sent me a representative sample on e-mail. Very impressive. She'd been collecting since the '60s, you know."

Jarrod Whitholm snorted. "No, I don't know. Where's your proof? My aunt was old, delusional probably. What made her confide in you?"

"If Sheriff Fuselli will let us check her computer, we'll verify things." Alex knew his demeanor infuriated Jarrod Whitholm. He looked ready to burst a gasket or lead a lynch mob. Either one would prove interesting.

Three pairs of eyes turned toward Fuselli.

"There's a problem," he said. "If Ms. Whitholm had a computer, it's not there now. Someone must have taken it."

"Not someone, Fuselli. The murderer stole her things. She had a computer, all right, one of the few luxuries she allowed herself. I set it up for her personally." Jarrod zeroed in on Alex and cut back to the sheriff. "Tell me this. Did you find this collection when your people searched my aunt's house?"

"Not yet," the sheriff said. "We're being very, very cautious. Dr. Lee tells me those things are fragile."

Alex nodded. "Collectors are quite fussy, as you can imagine. Your aunt was very savvy. She used museum-quality materials for storage." He rose gracefully to his feet. "I know you're all busy, but my offer still stands, assuming the collection wasn't damaged in the tragedy, of course. I'll be at the inn for the next week if anything develops."

He handed each of them his card and glided out the door.

Jarrod Whitholm stalked over to the window and watched the stranger. "That's it? You're just letting him walk away, Fuselli? He probably murdered my aunt, for God's sake." He studied the stranger's business card: Dr. Alejandro Lee, Esquire, Buyer's Representative. "Too vague. Sounds suspicious to me."

"Don't worry. He's not going anywhere," Fuselli said. "Now, I need to interview you and Ms. Nelson—separately. You decide. Who goes first?"

Nik gave Jarrod a syrupy sweet smile. "Jarrod's a busy man. I'm only a student. I can wait." She grabbed Confucius's lead and headed outside with him. "We'll take a walk while you two talk. Okay, Sheriff?"

"Sure. Go ahead." Fuselli winked. "We'll be a while."

Jarrod protested as she walked away. "Oh, for pity's sake."

Nik headed seaward, allowing the slap of salt air to bring her back to reality. Shelby Whitholm, her friend and supporter, was more complex than she'd appeared to be. Clever enough to play the town crank, subsisting on a librarian's pension while sitting on a potential fortune! That explained some things that had nagged at her. Shelby's property was modest, but its location was prime. Anything close to the ocean translated into some serious cash. Nik had wondered how a pensioner could afford such a treasure, and now she had her answer.

Confucius strained toward the water, jostling her for his beloved tennis ball. The dog had a major identity crisis. He thought he was a retriever, not a herder. Nik eased gingerly down the wooden steps toward the public beach, focused on maintaining her balance. When Foo Dog made a sudden leap for freedom, she lost her footing and began to tumble.

"Whoa. Hold on." A strong arm gripped her from behind. "Good thing I was here. You might have hit your head." Alejandro Lee released Nik and grabbed the lead. "You know what the proverb says. Since I saved your life, we're linked forever."

"Don't worry," Nik said, "you're absolved from that burden, but thanks anyway for catching me. I'm terribly clumsy."

She clutched the tennis ball as Confucius did his frenzied dance.

"Hey, wait a minute. Mind if I join you?" He held out his hand for the ball and threw it far across the sand. "Dogs and balls. Gotta love it."

He was persistent. She'd have to give him that. But Nik wasn't naïve. He probably thought she was some hick who'd soak up attention from a hot, big city guy. *Think again, Buster.*

"I promise to answer your questions," he said. "Ask away. Anything."

"Okay. I read your card. What field's your doctorate in, and where did you get it?"

His grin was sheepish. "Kind of dull. Economics. Not exactly a babe magnet. I went to Stanford." He managed a sunny smile, full of promise. "And before you ask, yes, I'm a lawyer too."

Nik rolled her eyes. "Yeah. I figured that when I saw Esquire on your card. What'd you specialize in? Entertainment law? It fits. California and all."

"Wow, you must be some kind of seer. I'd say witch, but you're much too beautiful for that." His dancing eyes sliced through her defenses like a Ginsu knife.

Fortunately, Confucius broke the spell by dropping his sodden, sandy tennis ball at her feet. Nik bent down to retrieve it, giving herself a mental pinch.

You're a professional, not some kind of silly schoolgirl. Act like it. This guy just might be a murderer. At the very least he's trying to use you.

"California ... wait a minute. San Diego is the site of Comic-Con. Is that how you got interested in them?"

Nik read *The New York Times* every day. It was her lifeline, a tangible connection to higher level thinking. Last spring she'd read an amusing piece about the freak show these comic book fans put on every year at their convention. Costumes, music, the whole enchilada.

Shelby's reaction surprised her. "Don't fool yourself, Cookie," she'd said. "They may have fun, but Comic-Con is big business. Million-dollar deals go down there every day."

At the time Nik dismissed those comments as yet another Shelby-ism, further proof that the ex-librarian seldom missed a trick. Now everything made sense. Last July Shelby disappeared for a week. She asked Nik to watch the pets and took off without giving any reason other than "personal business." Jarrod Whitholm had gone ballistic. His ranting could be heard up in Provincetown. Naturally, he held Nik responsible for his aunt's mysterious departure.

"Why didn't you call me?" he raged. "You should have stopped her. If anything happens to that old woman, you're responsible."

Shelby returned a week later without mentioning one thing about her trip. Nik now realized that Shelby's trip coincided with Comic-Con. As a political scientist she'd been trained to view coincidence with a jaundiced eye, especially when big bucks were at stake.

Alex wagged his finger at her. "You'd make a great prosecutor, you know. But to answer your question, I did attend Comic-Con this year. My client has plenty of disposable income, and he's obsessed with golden age comics. That's how I got wind of Shelby's collection."

Before she could continue, Nik's cell phone vibrated with a text message from Fuselli. "You'll have to excuse me," she said. "Time for the inquisition. Thanks again for the assist." She extended her hand to him.

Instead of a handshake, he gently brushed her knuckles with his lips. It was unexpected. Hand kissing was a courtly gesture she associated with Camelot and knights errant, not West Coast lawyers. Without releasing Nik's hand, he trained those amber eyes on her.

"May I call on you tonight? Dinner, perhaps?"

She felt the flush all the way to her toes. "I … not tonight. Perhaps tomorrow?"

"As you wish." He helped Nik up the beach steps, waved and glided gracefully toward town without even a backward glance.

Alex strolled slowly back to his car, feeling confused and uncertain. That wasn't like him. All his life he'd valued control and a firm sense of purpose. Since coming to Goodhaven, he'd lost touch with that part of himself. It was both disquieting and exhilarating.

The Shelby phase had been easy. She'd liked him from the beginning, doted on him, actually. She was no pushover, of course. She'd teased him about that comic collection until he agreed to fly up and see it for himself. The reality was far better than anything he could have ever imagined. Her hints about the Ashcan inflamed him. Funny. He sounded like a randy lover, not a businessman. Hell, no woman had ever stirred him like the thrill of that collection. Until now.

He'd only met Nicole twice. Two times. Hardly enough to make a difference, until it had. It wasn't her beauty. The world was filled with beautiful women, and he'd had more than his share of them. There was something different about her, something dangerous and potentially lethal to a man who valued independence. Better to leave Goodhaven, cut his losses and run while he still had the strength to do so.

Run? Fuselli might have something to say about that. The sheriff was no country bumpkin, not by a long shot. Most lawmen went by simple math: vicious crime plus sinister stranger equaled major suspect. That equation made sense in a small town that touted its reputation for safety.

Alex sighed. He was in a real pickle now. He couldn't leave Goodhaven even if he wanted to. And he wasn't sure that he wanted to.

Jarrod Whitholm snarled goodbye as he brushed past Nik on the walkway. He turned up the collar of his Burberry and stalked toward the Hummer, giving Confucius a very wide berth. The dog didn't growl, but his rigid body and raised hackles sent a clear message. *Jarrod certainly got that right,* Nik thought. *Foo Dog really doesn't like him.*

She hesitated for a moment until she came to her senses. She was behaving like a fool. After all, the carriage house was her home, not a police substation, and Fuselli was the intruder.

He sat hunched over the dining room table, surrounded by a neat pile of folders. When the door opened, Fuselli looked up and beckoned to her.

"Sorry to clutter up your place, Nicole. Come on. Have a seat. Then you'll finally get rid of me."

His wide smile was a shade too warm for comfort. Nik liked Fuselli, but she had no intention of encouraging any personal contact with the man. No time, no way. Old men didn't do it for her, especially poor ones. She had big plans for the future that didn't include settling down in a quaint seaside community with great charm and no career opportunities. Not after all her hard work.

"Jarrod didn't look happy just now," she told Fuselli. "What'd you do, give him the third degree?"

Fuselli raised his eyebrows. "You know, I've never seen Mr. Whitholm look happy. It's tough to grill somebody in this place. Way too relaxing." He glanced around and nodded. "Subtle but elegant. Nice."

She could feel that flush again. Damn! Good thing she'd abandoned thoughts of being a diplomat. Transparency was a major liability in that field.

"Do you have any leads? Have they done the autopsy yet?" Nik closed her eyes and shuddered. The thought of Shelby laid out on cold steel sickened her. Some evildoer had ripped the life from her friend as casually as if he were swatting a fly. Shelby, who had worked tirelessly to save even the sickest kitten, didn't deserve that contemptuous end. Nik felt a surge of anguish coupled with a hint of steel. Someone would pay for this crime. She'd make sure of it.

Fuselli kept his voice steady and matter of fact. "They have preliminary results. No blood work yet, of course. Not much of a surprise, really. Ms. Whitholm died of blunt force trauma. Weapon unspecified but probably a baseball bat or some kind of wooden club." He patted Nik's arm. "I'm sorry you have to hear this, Nicole."

Her voice shook as she answered. "I guess I'm a suspect now. *Cui bono.* Right? I want to do whatever I can to help find her killer. Ask me anything. I have nothing to hide."

"Okay. Let's start with the last time you saw Shelby. Anything unusual happen? Was she nervous or upset?"

Nik forced herself to focus. "Shelby was always ... well, you knew her too. She was high-strung, emotional. It didn't mean anything."

"What bothered her yesterday?"

"The tax increase, of course. Shelby said ..." Nik suppressed a sob. "She said she had something special planned for the meeting."

Fuselli's brand of the third degree was surprisingly gentle. "Any hint about what she meant?"

"No. She liked to keep me guessing. Part of the fun, I suppose." Nik felt Foo Dog's cold nose nudge her hand. The dog's sense of timing was uncanny. She needed some canine therapy right then, and he seemed to know it. Stroking his silky fur grounded her, bringing her back to reality. Nik sighed and trained her eyes on Fuselli.

He gave her a hard stare. "Jarrod. Mr. Whitholm. He was close to his aunt?"

She couldn't lie, but Nik had no intention of accusing anyone, even Jarrod Whitholm. "Well, they were both strong personalities. Jarrod is kind of a know-it-all."

Fuselli laughed out loud. "I noticed. Someone told me they argued about politics a lot."

Nik snorted. "Shelby was no bleeding heart, but she abhorred some of Jarrod's positions. To tell you the truth, I think she enjoyed needling him. Ruffling his feathers, she called it."

"He's pretty well fixed, I guess. Went to Yale and all."

Nik had finally gotten wise to Fuselli's technique. He dropped conversational breadcrumbs, waiting for his victim to follow them to the truth.

"I don't know anything about his family situation," she said. "All Shelby said was that he was her brother's only child. I know she helped out with his schooling, sent him spending money when he was at Yale. Jarrod doesn't confide in me." She poured Pellegrino into a crystal tumbler. Nik loved beautiful things, lusted after them, actually. Thanks to Shelby, she'd now be able to indulge herself a little.

"He's a lucky man," Fuselli said. "Got it all. Big job, beautiful fiancée, the works. How close are you to Ms. Stevens?"

Nik shook her head. "You've got it wrong. I'm invisible to most of these people. Danielle thinks I'm a peasant. Old clothes, weathered jalopy. Nothing she'd identify with. No girlish confidences exchanged, believe me. Shelby rarely mentioned her. Just made fun of her airs, as she put it."

Danielle had a nasty habit of looking right through those she considered social inferiors. Occasionally she nodded at Nik as she swept by in her Mercedes, but that was it. Danielle drove one of the best cars in a town where millionaires weren't uncommon. High-end real estate demanded it, she said, but Nik had her doubts.

Fuselli drummed his fingers on the table in a rare display of impatience. Nik realized that he was waiting for something.

"I'm sorry, Sheriff. I missed your last question."

His guileless eyes were deceptive. He'd zeroed in on something big, and he knew it.

"Simple question. Did Shelby ever discuss her child with you?"

Nik gulped. "Child! You're mistaken. Shelby never married. Jarrod was her closest relative. She told me so herself."

The silence in the little room felt oppressive. She clamped her jaw shut, determined not to say a thing. Let Fuselli play his little games without her. She'd sounded so naïve, as if you couldn't have a child without having a husband.

He slowly flipped through one of the folders and extracted a fax. Nik saw what looked like some kind of official seal at the bottom. She held her breath, not even daring to exhale.

"Coroner in Barnstable is thorough. I'll give him that. Gnarly old bastard but rock solid." Fuselli donned reading glasses and stared at the sheet. "According to this Shelby Whitholm had a child. Some time ago, of course, but still."

Nik forced herself to stop gaping like the village idiot. *A mistake. It must be an error. Probably confused Shelby with some other corpse.*

Fuselli was a bulldog. He wouldn't let it go. "You see how that could complicate things, especially with a sizable estate. Dueling claimants. Might tie everything up for quite a while." He leaned forward. "Might even be a motive for murder."

Four

At first Nik was speechless. Visions of Shelby swirled in her mind, obscuring any rational thought. Had she really known Shelby? Like everyone else, she'd automatically accepted the comfortable fiction presented by her landlady. It fit the stereotype so perfectly: spinster librarian, squeezing every nickel until it yowled in pain. It was hard — nearly impossible — to envision her as a pregnant young woman with all the normal fears and aspirations, who took the secret to her grave. *Why didn't she confide in me?* Nik wondered. *I'd have understood.*

"I take it this is news to you," Fuselli said with a shrug. "Hmm. Kids and comic books. Wonder what else Ms. Whitholm kept to herself?" He patted his shirt pocket, finding his pen. "Let's take it nice and easy, Nicole. Tell me everything you remember about her last week. Any quarrels, something out of the ordinary?"

Nik cleared her mind, resurrecting every particle of information. "Shelby was sort of prickly, you know that. I thought that tax hike would enrage her, but come to think of it, she took it in stride."

"How so? You just said it upset her."

"It did, but not by her usual standards. I expected her to take Morgan's head off, but she just laughed and said not to worry. She had some kind of data — called it her neutron bomb — that would scuttle his plan. 'It's foolproof, Cookie,' she told me. 'Morgan will run out with his little tail between his legs.'" Nik recalled that mischievous smile Shelby got just before a major coup.

"Anything unusual that week? You know, different from her normal routine?" Fuselli's eyes flicked toward his notebook as he waited for Nik's response.

Unusual? Nothing about Shelby was really normal. Nik wracked her brain for something, anything, that might be significant.

"There was one thing, just a chance remark she made. It probably means nothing." She heard Fuselli's patient sigh.

"Shelby looked at the Goodhaven website the day before she died. I mean really scrutinized it. Then she started laughing and said, 'Good thing I know where the bodies are buried, Cookie. Literally. Makes things a lot easier around here.'"

Nicole shrugged. "It doesn't sound like much. I realize that, but if you'd heard the way she said it, almost as if she meant actual bodies. Corpses."

"Ms. Whitholm was a scholar, wasn't she? You academics love using allusions, metaphors and the like." Fuselli shook his head. "If she had acquired a taste for blackmail, Shelby probably knew where plenty of secrets were buried." He spoke casually, as if he were arguing with himself. "Still, I'd better check out that website just in case. I don't suppose you recall what was on it last week."

"Nothing special," Nik said, "just the topic for the evening's forum and the list of speakers. Shelby's name was first. It always was." Nik wondered how the town would have voted that night if the agenda hadn't been interrupted. According to Jett, a number of people supported the tax assessment, even naysayers like Harris Goldman and Danielle Stevens.

"What about this collection of hers?" Nik asked. "Have you found anything yet?" She knew almost nothing about comics. Didn't care. She was far too immersed in the books, periodicals and papers of her own trade to intrude on another's space.

"We're still looking," Fuselli said. "So far we've searched the house, garage and that old Wagoneer. No dice." He cocked his head. "Got any ideas? I'm not proud. I could use the help."

Nik shrugged. "No clue, I'm afraid, but I'll bet Dr. Lee could tell you."

Alejandro Lee knew plenty, she was certain of that. The way he hovered around Goodhaven suggested that he didn't know the whereabouts of Shelby's collection either. If he had, Nik suspected he'd have been long gone, lolling on a beach somewhere with a sultry temptress. He was too handsome, too smooth, for an impoverished academic like her. Even at twenty-four, she had very few illusions when it came to gorgeous men. Misadventures had taught Nik an immutable truth: They broke your heart and made you bleed every time.

"I can research it for you, find some information." Her eyes filled, but she met his gaze without flinching. "If I can help, I'd like to. Shelby was good to me."

"Be my guest," Fuselli said. "Just watch your step. I'm not trying to scare you, Nicole, but whoever murdered Ms. Whitholm was brutal." He patted her arm again and gathered his things. "Don't put yourself at risk."

Jett Hall crouched behind the counter at Mindbender doing his daily inventory. The bookstore closed at six o'clock, and only one straggler still browsed the neatly arranged shelves.

"Hey," he said as Nik barreled into his store. "Come over here, Dr. Nelson. You look frazzled." He attended to his customer, ringing up the sale of yet another paranormal romance.

"Vampire love is big business, even on the Outer Cape," he said, winking at Nik. "Leaves me cold, but those bloodsuckers sure help my bottom line."

"Pays better than Dickens," Nicole said with a laugh.

"So true. Those fangs and claws just may help me survive another year." He crossed his fingers. "One slim ray of hope. One more winter of profit gives Mindbender a stay of execution."

Jett bustled to the front door, key in hand, and flipped the closed sign. "Let me lock up," he said, "not that I can afford to offend a paying customer these days, what with Shelby gone. She sent a lot of traffic my way from her librarian days."

"Shelby was generous," Nik said, thinking of her bequest. She wrapped her arms around herself in a futile attempt to get warm. On most days Jett's store was a cozy refuge, but today an arctic chill assaulted her. Mindbender had always reminded her of a set from Masterpiece Theatre. In fact, Jett had chosen the décor with that in mind. He'd installed a gas fireplace in the reading area, ringing it with puffy down sofas and a large, sun-faded Kashan. The overall effect was homey enough to encourage customers to curl up and read or flex their mental muscles by playing chess. He even had Fagin, a friendly feline greeter who served as goodwill ambassador. Tourists called it quaint. Residents knew that Jett brought informed discourse to their town by recreating the literary salons of a bygone era. Local authors and visiting luminaries did readings there all winter long, followed by spirited debates. If it didn't go bankrupt, Mindbender might well become a Goodhaven institution.

"C'mon," he said. "Looks like you could use some of my special cocoa."

"Make mine tea," Nicole said. "Calories, you know."

Jett sped back to the tiny kitchen, talking nonstop all the while. "The view from here looks fine. Don't worry about calories. It's info I'm hungry for. Tell me everything. I mean, if it's not too tough for you. Fuselli hasn't spoken with me yet. Guess I'm not important enough."

"What are you talking about?" Nik sounded peevish, and she didn't care. She'd expected comfort from Jett, not a scoop for the *National Enquirer.*

"Touchy, touchy. The beauteous Danielle graced the premises today. She told me about the will." He gave Nik a mock salute. "Congrats! I mean, it's tragic and all, but at least you came out of it okay."

Nik stood and pointedly turned her back on him. "Is that what they taught you at Amherst? Guess you flunked Empathy 101. I'd rather have Shelby around than get an inheritance any day, especially when it means sharing things with Jarrod Whitholm."

Jett powered down and busied himself making cocoa. "Sorry, superstar. It was insensitive of me. Guess I've been cooped up in here with dead authors too long. You're right. Jarrod is a real piece of work. Every time I see him on those news panels, I positively retch." He poured the steaming brew into two mugs, set them on a tray and walked cautiously into the reading room. "Come on. Sit down and tell me what's on that brilliant mind of yours." He fumbled with a napkin. "Here. Take these marshmallows before they spill all over the floor."

Nik knew enough to discount most of the flattery Jett sent her way. Oh, he wanted her, she knew that; but he was essentially harmless, more like the chaste medieval knights. Courtly love, that's what it was. Longing looks and steamy poetry. Jett was a romantic, a creature of the mind. Whether his body went along for the ride was another matter. He wasn't repulsive, just curiously asexual with his rimless glasses, snub nose and curly brown hair.

Some serious gym time might transform him, but even then Jett Hall wasn't Nik's type. *Not that I have a type*, she thought. *I'll probably end up as an old maid college professor.* Suddenly she felt more alone than at any time since her parents' plane crash. That horrible day had made her an orphan. Now violence had again robbed her of someone special. Nik took a deep breath and regrouped. Self-indulgence was a luxury she couldn't afford. Not now. She'd come to Jett for information, and she intended to get it.

"I need your help," she told him, parceling out a dollop of charm. "What do you know about comic book collecting?"

Jett Hall's jaw dropped. "A bit. I had a modest collection myself as a kid. Nothing major, fortunately. My mom threw it away when I went to college. But honey, this isn't the time to start squandering your money on something like that."

She sighed. "Not for me. It's about Shelby. Apparently she was a major collector. I had no idea she was into that stuff. Neither did Jarrod, or at least that's what he says."

It was tempting to demonize Jarrod. His demeanor, a combination of hubris and arrogance, practically begged for it. But he was Shelby's nephew, and Nik had to deal with him somehow.

"Did Fuselli send you here?" Jett asked. "It's not like him to be so lazy. He's typically one of those macho guys who tries to do it all."

"No. No. Listen. This is for me. If Shelby had a valuable collection, someone might have murdered her for it. The sheriff hasn't located anything yet, but that stranger, Alejandro Lee, is all over it."

Jett stared at her. "Hmm. The way he looked at you last night, I thought he'd be all over you. Danielle thinks he's gorgeous, her very word. What would Jarrod make of that, I wonder?" He drained his cocoa and placed his cup back on the tray. "Hold on. I have something that may help you. Get you started anyway." Jett sped over to the specialty racks and selected two paperbacks. "Listen up," he said. "If you want to learn about collecting, Overstreet is the bible. That's Bob Overstreet. His grading and pricing guides are the industry standard." He handed them to Nik. "Here. Take them. Don't worry about paying. It's just a loan."

She quickly flipped through a thick volume. "I can see I'll have to study this thing. Tell me. Did Shelby talk to you about this ... this hobby of hers? She was so devoted to great literature, I just can't see her with this stuff."

His shrug said it all. "Hey, don't knock it. Shelby was into survival, making money. She was a pretty shrewd old trout, come to think of it. Never mentioned a comic collection to me, but that's no surprise. Why spill the proverbial beans if you don't have to?"

Nik scooped up the books and stuffed them into her backpack. "Thanks, Jett. We'll talk again after I read everything. Maybe then I can ask intelligent questions." A sudden wave of lethargy swept over her as she forced herself to rise.

"Hold on. Wait just a damn minute." He held out his arms, crossing-guard style. "It's dark, dank and deserted out there." A broad smile split his face. "Pretty good alliteration, wouldn't you say?"

"Impressive. I'll know who to call if I'm mugged by a poet."

"Not so fast, smarty pants." Jett chucked Nik under the chin. "I plan to escort you back to your place personally and check it out. No arguments. There's a depraved killer loose, in case you've forgotten. He may still be around."

Hyperbole aside, Jett made sense. Nik told herself she was wary, not frightened. Maybe a little male company wasn't such a bad idea. After all, the killer was probably still searching for Shelby's collection. If so, the carriage house might be next on the agenda.

"How do you know that a man did it?" she asked. "Women commit horrific acts too, you know." That bit of feminist wisdom didn't comfort her, but it triggered a thought. Shelby would have opened her door to a woman, especially one with a hard luck story. She wouldn't have feared a female guest.

"Hello, is someone alive in there? Did you even hear my answer?"

Nik ducked her head, embarrassed at her rudeness. "Sorry."

Jett extinguished the indoor lights and set his burglar alarm. "Okay, but come follow me." He shined his flashlight on the icy steps, guiding Nik down the bricked path toward Main Street. "I heard that killer tied Shelby up and beat her head in. That sounds more like a masculine crime to me."

"What? No one mentioned that." She covered her mouth to stifle a scream. "Oh, my God! Poor Shelby. If only I'd checked on her that afternoon."

Jett stopped under the streetlight and pulled Nik close to him. "Jesus, I'm such a clod sometimes. Just ignore me, and stop punishing yourself. You might have ended up just like Shelby."

They walked silently toward the carriage house, buffeted by the fierce ocean breeze and the unsettling memory of murder. Shelby's English Tudor, now Jarrod's, stood in splendid isolation, stoically facing the sea. Fire damage had been minimal, mostly smoke confined to the living room. Nik recalled the old horsehair sofa Shelby insisted on keeping there. Its worn velvet, stiff and unyielding, was hardly welcoming. "That's just the point, Cookie," Shelby had told her. "Put these busybodies in the parlor and let 'em suffer. They won't stay long that way."

When she'd paid a duty call, Danielle couldn't wait to escape. Her exquisite facade didn't intimidate Shelby one bit. She'd peeled it back, layer by layer as if she were skinning an onion. Nik had almost felt sorry for Danielle that day. Almost.

"You're awfully quiet, Double N." Jett had any number of pet names for her.

"Sorry, I'm bad company, I know. It's just that ..." She grabbed Jett's arm and pointed toward the outer door of the carriage house. "Oh, God! Someone's prowling around in the bushes!" Her heartbeat skyrocketed. "Quick. Call the sheriff. Please, Jett. It might be the murderer."

He pushed her behind him, shining his torch on the bushes. "Hey! Who goes there? Show yourself, or we'll call the cops."

Nik loathed cowardice, especially her own. She stepped alongside Jett and stood, legs apart, in a Wushu fighting stance. She had never actually tried it out, but she'd been a prize pupil at Master Chen's dojo.

The figure stepped out of the dark with his hands up. "Okay. Don't shoot. You got me fair and square." The snarky, New York voice of Morgan Haas rang out loud and clear.

"Morgan! What in the world are you doing here?" Nik forgot that he was a dignitary, someone whose support she badly needed. She reacted like any surprised homeowner confronting an intruder.

Jett switched off his torch. "Man, you gave us a start, creeping around in the bushes like that. What's up?"

Haas quickly regained his dignity. "First of all, I wasn't lurking, creeping or skulking. I was waiting to see Ms. Nelson about ... personal matters." He tapped his big clunky Rolex.

"For Christ's sake, it's barely seven o'clock. That's early even by Goodhaven standards."

After fishing keys out of her backpack, Nik walked upstairs and unlocked her front door. "Come on in, you two. I have some wine somewhere." She stepped inside and screamed. An uninvited guest with a mean streak had destroyed her home.

Five

She was speechless, numbed to any normal reaction. Every pillow and sofa cushion had been savaged; downy stuffing spilled out like road kill. The floor was littered with papers, and the drawers had been ripped from her antique desk and commode.

"The cats! Where are Annabel and Atticus? Oh, my God!" She'd read about vicious thugs who tortured pets when they burglarized a house. If that happened here, Nik wasn't sure she'd survive. She rushed to the backyard to check on Confucius. Thank goodness she'd left him outside. He wouldn't pose a threat to anyone out there.

Morgan whipped out his cell phone. "I'm dialing Fuselli right now. Go step out on the porch, Nicole. We may not be alone." He gave Jett one of those caveman looks that relayed a message.

"Forget it," Nik said. "I'm not leaving 'til I find those cats." She called their names, tiptoeing through the kitchen to the bedroom. Her coverlet, pillows and blanket had been tossed in a heap in the corner. Dresser drawers were slung on the floor amid splinters of aged walnut. Nik ignored the pile of lingerie heaped on the chair. *I refuse to consider what that pervert might have done with those.* Under the bed. Sometimes they hid there when they were scared. Nik flopped down on the floor and peeked. Empty. She had the same result in the guest room. As her options dwindled, Nik checked the closets. Bedrooms first, then the laundry area. "Atticus, Annabel, come out. Please." Her voice quivered with weariness and despair. Suddenly she heard a faint meow coming from the utility closet. She flung it open and found both felines, big-eyed and frantic.

"They're okay," she shouted. "Oh, thank God!" At least the burglar wasn't a complete monster, just a vicious murderer. In the back of her mind Nik heard a niggling voice of doubt. Jarrod Whitholm hated animals. He'd gladly have stuffed them in the utility room. On the other hand, it was hard to picture Jarrod, that meticulous lawyer and political seer, rifling through her undies. The elegant Danielle was an even less likely culprit.

"Everything all right, Nicole? Fuselli is on his way." Morgan put his arm around Nik, squeezing her shoulder. Fortunately, his touch was paternal, not a vulgar attempt to cop a free feel. She'd fended off plenty of married men in her time, and that made her wary. They usually came with a host of baggage and a vengeful wife, to boot. Amanda Haas would take a hatchet to anyone who threatened her comfy lifestyle. Nik was certain of that.

"Come on. Let's go wait for the sheriff." Morgan led her into the small living room where Jett was petting Confucius.

"Look who I found sleeping out in the yard. Funny he didn't raise a stink. Not much of a watchdog, is he? Zero for two this week." Jett gave the dog a disgusted look.

Nik buried her face in Foo Dog's silky coat. "That's unfair, Jett. He only barks when there's trouble. Right, boy?"

"What would you call this?" Jett asked, pointing at the debris. "If that's not trouble, I don't know what is."

Nicole ignored him, focusing instead on a siren that whooped its way down the street to her door. In a flash a deputy appeared, followed by Bob Fuselli. His voice was calm, but his hand stayed close to his side. Nik suspected he had ready access to his gun that way.

"Whew, what a mess." Fuselli did a quick survey of her apartment. "I'm sorry, Ms. Nelson. I should have anticipated this."

Morgan Haas had a somber look on his face. "Someone's pretty desperate, wouldn't you say, Sheriff? How could he even know that Nicole would be gone?"

"Maybe whoever it was didn't care," Jett said. "After all, Shelby was home the other day."

Fuselli must have noticed Nicole's pale face. "Can it, will you? Ms. Nelson has enough to contend with as it is." He lowered his voice and spoke softly to Nik. "I'll send someone over here in the morning to help you with this. Meanwhile, maybe you should check into the Cliff House for the night. Make you sleep better."

Money wasn't the issue any more. At least it wouldn't be in the future. Nik was more concerned about salvaging her possessions and comforting her pets than sleeping. "Thanks, Sheriff, but I'll stay here."

Jett Hall leapt to the rescue. "Not a problem, Fuselli. I'll stay with Ms. Nelson tonight. She'll be safe with me here." He ignored the incredulous looks that both men gave him.

"I need to speak privately with Ms. Nelson. In fact, she's welcome to stay with me and my wife until this blows over. I'm the executor of Shelby's estate." Morgan's master-of-the-universe smile was clothed in rank and privilege.

Nik walked unsteadily toward the kitchen. "Very kind of you, Mayor, but I intend to make some coffee and start cleaning up this mess. Is that a problem, Sheriff? Fingerprints or something?"

"It's not like television. No CSI to find clues and solve the case. My deputy will dust everything for prints. Shouldn't take too long. By the time you make coffee and speak with the Mayor, everything should be over."

He was being kind; they all were. Nik knew she was more resilient than any of these men suspected. She'd been on her own since her parents died, and events had forced her to toughen up in a hurry.

"Thanks," she said. "A jolt of caffeine will fix me up just fine. Don't worry."

Jett folded his arms and gave her his alpha frown. "I'm staying, Double N. No debates."

She nodded, too weary to argue. "Okay. Let's see if we can find some cups that aren't broken. I'm afraid I don't have any food in the house. Shelby … she and I always did our food shopping on Fridays."

Morgan grabbed his iPhone again. "No problem. I'll order take-out. Chinese okay? I think Wong House is still open."

As Nik arranged the coffee pot with a mismatched array of cups and saucers, she could hear him issuing brisk instructions to the restaurant. Morgan Haas, man of action, strikes again.

They assembled in the first floor family room. Oddly enough, it looked as if nothing had been touched. Nik sank down on the sofa, greedily sipping her coffee, inhaling the potent brew as if it were a magic potion.

"Perhaps we should do this alone," Morgan said, glaring at Jett. "It involves confidential matters."

"Stow it, Haas," Jett said. "I already know about the inheritance. I'll leave only if Nicole asks me to." He wiped his glasses on a tissue and turned toward her.

Nik had neither the energy nor desire to mediate a dispute between two horn-locking rams. "Thanks, Morgan, but it's okay. Jett's been a lifesaver for me. I think he can help us."

"Your choice. Jarrod told you about some of it. You get the carriage house and furnishings, and he gets the Tudor.

Oh, yes, Shelby also wanted you to have her old Wagoneer and that Schwinn bike." Morgan shook his head. "I can't imagine anyone riding that relic anywhere, but it's yours."

Nik did her best to staunch the tears. "I'll always keep it. It was such a part of Shelby." Suddenly, Fuselli's words about the autopsy rang in her ears. "Tell me this. Are there any other claimants? You know, other relatives?"

"Not according to Shelby. She was somewhat of a recluse, as I'm sure you know. Anyhow, you're also the beneficiary of a small insurance policy. Nothing spectacular. Of course, there's a double indemnity clause in there." Morgan's voice dropped. "Funny thing. I laughed when she chose that provision. Goodhaven and violence tend to be strangers."

"Huh," Jett snorted "Tell that to Shelby." His eyes narrowed. "Anything else for Nicole? You know, hidden treasure or whatever." He didn't say the words, but Nik knew he meant the comic collection.

Morgan bristled. "That's the same thing that stranger asked me."

"Alejandro Lee?" Nik felt the flush creeping up her neck. What was it about that man that made her tingle?

Morgan spread his hands wide. "Anything else except those things I specified will be split down the middle between you and Jarrod, fifty-fifty."

"I don't know how to ask this," Nik said, "but is there any problem with my staying here for a while? I mean, while the will's in probate?"

"None. You'd continue paying rent to the estate, which in essence is you and Jarrod, unless you two plan to sell the place. You'd have to come to some kind of agreement then."

"What about your future, getting your Ph.D.? I can't see you sticking around Goodhaven once that's finished." Jett tried to act disinterested. He failed.

Nik shrugged. "*Quien sabe*?" She poured everyone coffee with a splash of Brandy. "Here. I think we've all earned this," she said.

"Does that include me?" Fuselli asked joining them. He held out his cup. "My deputy's finished with the fingerprints. Maybe we'll get lucky, but I'm not optimistic. This guy is pretty damn slick." He leaned back against the sofa cushion and closed his eyes. "Can you think of anything Shelby left here that might interest a burglar?"

Nik shook her head. "I've been wracking my brain, presuming that it all relates to this comic collection. That's the only thing of any value except for the real estate." She bent down and brushed her lips over Annabel's ears. "And her pets, of course. They're priceless."

"I know a little bit about comics, Sheriff. You can't just store them anywhere, not if you expect to sell them someday. Shelby must have squirreled them away in some secure space." Jett furrowed his brow as he considered the local options. "I bet they're in some kind of facility near Boston. Might be worth checking out."

Fuselli's smile was more grimace than grin. He nodded briskly at Jett and turned back to Nik. " Mr. Whitholm said he knows nothing about it, but I was thinking maybe you found something. A scrap of paper, business card, anything? My deputy did a preliminary search. Over two hundred fifty storage facilities in the Boston area." He spread his arms wide. "That'll take some time for a five-man force to cover. May not even mean anything. Frankly, I could use some help. Maybe I'll take you up on your offer, Nicole."

She knew what he wanted, but Nik had issues of her own. Damn Jarrod Whitholm! Shrug off responsibility, and scoop up the proceeds. He'd never appreciated his aunt, not really. Jarrod acted like Shelby was a nuisance, an embarrassment to him and his fancy-pants girlfriend. That's why—Nik gulped—Shelby counted on her so much. A wave of guilt swamped her. She owed something to the woman who'd befriended her. Maybe she could help in some small way to find the murderer. After all, research was her forte.

"Okay, Sheriff. Just give me a little time to get this mess cleaned up."

Fuselli's smile transformed his solemn face. "Terrific! I'll swing by late tomorrow to discuss specifics. Don't worry, I'll call first." He tipped his hat to the three of them and strolled out the door.

Jett wrinkled his nose. "Thank goodness he's finally gone. That guy acts way too interested in you, Nicole. Watch your step. Might be some kind of trap."

Morgan scoffed. "Fuselli's interest is more of a personal nature, unless I'm way off base. Guess you can't blame a guy for trying."

"Really, Mayor?" Jett puffed up like a banty rooster. "It's disgusting. That guy's old enough to be her father."

"Older brother, maybe." Haas drained his coffee and faced Nik. "Sure you don't want to stay with us tonight? Mandy would love the company."

I'll just bet she would. Nik took the Mayor's hand. "No, but thanks anyway. I really appreciate it."

She walked him to the door, bolted it and wedged a chair under the knob. Tomorrow those locks would have to be changed. The intruder hadn't forced his way in or broken a window. Nicole shivered at the realization. Someone used a key to access the carriage house. Had the same person used a key on Shelby's door and murdered her? That explained a lot, but it also widened the suspect pool. She suppressed a yawn and reached for the phone. Damn it all. Jarrod deserved to know about this even though he was an arrogant creep. It wasn't safe for him to prowl around Shelby's Tudor without first changing the locks.

She fished his card from her wallet and dialed.

Jarrod's telephone etiquette was sadly lacking. Maybe he skipped that course at Yale. His brusqueness faded when she mentioned the break-in.

"What? Anything destroyed?"

"Just my possessions, and I'm fine, thank you for asking. So are the pets."

He stammered. "Sorry. Didn't mean to sound insensitive. Can I do anything for you? Bring you something?"

Nik was basically a pacifist. She saw no need for a blood feud. Not yet anyway. "Thanks, no. Look, I just wanted to warn you. I'm getting the locks changed tomorrow, if you want the Tudor included. It's not safe going in there."

Jarrod harrumphed a bit, playing for time. "This … it's quite upsetting. My aunt was unconventional, annoying even, but she was good to me when I was a kid. I owe her."

A woman's voice sounded in the background. *Probably Danielle,* Nik thought sourly. *Shrew!*

"Listen Nicole, we need to meet, discuss this situation without Fuselli and all the other hangers-on, especially that foreigner."

"Foreigner?" She was genuinely puzzled.

"That Lee person. You know who I mean."

"He's from California, Jarrod. He's an American."

"California! Might as well be a foreign country. Bunch of weirdos. Anyhow, I'll stop over tomorrow morning. Nine okay?"

"Sure," Nik said. "I'll make coffee." She paused before hanging up. "Shelby wouldn't give just anyone a key, would she? I mean, she seemed pretty suspicious of most people."

"Are you kidding?" Jarrod grew testy again. "I had to force her to give me a key, her own nephew. She wasn't credulous like most of these Outer Cape types. Shelby had real trust issues."

"I thought so," Nik sighed. "See you tomorrow."

The moment she hung up, Jett attacked. "What was that all about?"

"Nothing. Just Jarrod."

Jett's scowl made him look like a garden gnome. "I bet he's got a key, doesn't he? Makes sense. I never did trust that guy."

Nik grabbed her broom, sweeping broken crockery into a pile. "Cool it, Jett. Haven't we had enough excitement today? Either help me with this mess, or leave now. I can't stand any more fighting." She tiptoed around Atticus and gave the trash can a vicious kick. "Stupid thing. Always in the way."

"Geez, I'm sorry." Jett draped his arm over her shoulder. "Come on. I'll get the vacuum. We can clean this stuff up in an hour."

Two hours later, they finally called it a day.

Six

Nicole was no social butterfly. Despite her good looks she loved libraries, not luxury spas, and Proust more than Facebook. When four reasonably attractive men started buzzing about, she had no illusions. It was nothing personal, just a tribute to the power of inheritance.

The fun began promptly at eight the next morning with Alex's rich baritone wafting through the wires.

"Are you still available for dinner?" he asked. "I made an eight o'clock reservation at the Cliff House just in case."

She thanked heaven this was the lower Cape, where Skype was rarely used. Since he couldn't see her, she could at least pretend that her hair was combed. What was it about this man that made her flush? True, he had exotic, movie star looks and a smooth line of patter, but Nik knew it was something more. He was probably used to making women swoon. Practiced at it. Any guy with a mirror would figure that out PDQ and use it to his advantage. She reminded herself that Dr. Lee was a stranger and a viable suspect in Shelby's murder. That doused the flames of passion in a hurry.

"Okay," she said. "Shall I meet you there?"

"No, no, no. I'll pick you up at home unless that's a problem. Any fiancés, husbands or potential suitors lurking about?"

"None. I'm not much of a party animal. You'll probably be bored out of your skull around me."

He chuckled, a deep masculine sound, more like a guffaw. "Somehow I doubt that, Ms. Nelson. See you soon."

She forgot she had a visitor. Jett sat facing her, arms crossed, his frown firmly affixed. Nik made a conscious effort to wipe the smile from her face.

"Which one of your admirers was that?" Jett groused. "Fuselli?"

"What are you, my keeper?" She took a deep breath. "We've already discussed this, Jett, several times."

He waved his arms in pseudo-surrender. "Sorry. Didn't mean to offend." He downed his coffee, holding out his cup for more. "Hey, I know Jarrod's on his way over here. Give me a refill, and I'll be out of your hair."

Nik's tender heart swam with guilt. "Forgive me. You're a good friend, and I know it. With Shelby gone you're my only real friend in Goodhaven." She patted his arm. "Thanks for staying last night. I felt much safer."

"Really?" Jett brightened. "Look, after I open the store I'll do some more research on this comic book stuff." He shrugged. "Might help you out."

"You're an angel." Nik blew him a chaste kiss and passed the coffee pot. "While you drink that I'll get dressed. Jarrod is the punctual type, and he already thinks he's slumming around me."

As she sped toward the bathroom she heard him sputter, "Creep!"

Jarrod Whitholm had dressed down that day. *Probably a concession to my humble abode,* Nik thought. Although his perfectly matched cords and flannel shirt were paired with a blazer that had to be cashmere, he'd abstained from wearing a tie, cufflinks or suspenders. A smart calfskin briefcase peaked from under his right arm.

"Sorry," he said. "Didn't know you had company." He glared at Jett, who was exiting through the back door.

Nicole counted to ten. Twice. These male mind games were getting her down. "I was antsy after that break-in, and Jett was kind enough to stay with me." She waved at Jett and ushered Jarrod through the door. "Watch your step. We probably didn't pick up everything."

He curled his lip as he surveyed the devastation. "Wow, someone wanted something, I guess. Must have been important. Do we really need a locksmith out here? That's a big expense, you know, and it seems like the damage is already done."

"Easy for you to say. Whoever did this used a key. A *key*, Jarrod. I can take care of myself, but I'm no fool." Nicole folded her arms and turned her back on him. Anger was a raging stream coursing through her veins. How dare he!

His eyes widened. Obviously, he hadn't expected her metamorphosis from humble student to Valkyrie. He was more accustomed to being in charge.

"No problem," he said. "It's probably a good idea anyway. Now what else did you want to discuss?" His eyes did a quick survey of Nicole's curves.

Planning was her strong suit. Last night she'd given some thought to the best way to help Fuselli solve the murder. He was smart enough but clueless about the close-knit community he policed. With Jarrod's help Nik could fill in the blanks. She had become an expert in all things Shelby over the past nine months, and the murder was tied to something specific. Why else had this woman, who most people considered a harmless crank, died so horrifically? The comic collection was the most likely motive, but Nik wasn't convinced. Not many people even knew about that. Shelby ruffled plenty of local feathers with her civic crusades and outright snooping. Had she hit someone's hot button and signed her death warrant in the process?

"Hello, did you hear me?" Jarrod tapped his fingers on the table like an impresario. "What's on your mind?"

She plunged right in. "We've got to get involved. Fuselli needs us. Otherwise, he'll never solve her murder. I made a list." She handed him a printout. "These are people who wanted Shelby dead or at least out of their way. I've deliberately excluded the two of us. I didn't know about this inheritance thing, and I doubt that you knew about the comic collection."

"Whoa, hold on here. I've got a career, you know. Demands. People count on me. I have no time to be running around playing super sleuth. That's what we pay people like Fuselli to do."

She suppressed a strong urge to slap his arrogant face. "I've got obligations, too. My dissertation, remember? You may not think it's important, but it's my livelihood." Nik deliberately kept her voice low, calm and unemotional. No sense in starting a war yet.

"You're willing to take your inheritance, I notice. That confers responsibility, too. Come on, Jarrod. You've got influence, connections. I'm not talking about rough stuff, just some digging. Sort of like investigative journalism."

He sighed—snorted, actually. "Okay. Let me see that list."

Jarrod stayed until noon, absorbing and debating Nicole's plan. Several of the names she'd listed surprised him.

"Morgan Haas, are you kidding? Why would he kill Shelby?"

"I'm not saying that he did. We have to investigate anyone Shelby was in conflict with. Face it. She gave Morgan a lot of shit. And remember, Shelby told me she had some kind of so-called neutron bomb that would keep him in line. She was a librarian and an amazing researcher. Shelby knew databases like Cousteau knew the ocean. She once told me that there were no secrets anymore, just databases yet to be breached."

Jarrod's red face signaled anger or alarmingly high blood pressure. "She was nosey. Too nosey. When she barged into my life, I told her to back off."

Nik didn't ask anything more. She didn't dare. But Jarrod's tirade triggered a thought. Maybe Shelby kept some kind of file on people. Blackmail. Well, not really blackmail, but information she could use to control things. Shelby loved to manipulate people. It made Nik feel disloyal to admit it, but it was true. Like the time Harris Goldman tried to close the animal shelter. Armed with a thick manila envelope, Shelby had paid him a visit. They never heard a peep out of the professor after that. In fact, he'd made a substantial donation to Lifelines and volunteered there.

"You're doing it again, Nicole. Shelby would have called it woolgathering, I guess. Come on. Tell me what you're thinking about."

She blushed. He'd think she was some kind of conspiracy buff. Those right-wing types like Jarrod were always making fun of people. Screw it! No matter what Jarrod Whitholm thought, he couldn't deny Shelby's murder. That was an established fact, cold and unrelenting.

"Okay, here it is. Your aunt … well, I think she might have kept files on people. You know, interesting tidbits. I know she subscribed to PrivateEye.com. She told me so."

For once in his privileged life Jarrod was speechless. He sputtered some really bad words before forming a coherent sentence. "What the hell is PrivateEye.com?"

Nicole reached into her bag and pulled out her laptop. Thank goodness the intruder hadn't destroyed that. Her whole life, her academic life anyway, was on that hard drive. "Here. Look at this. She accessed Google, found the site and typed in her own name and state. Information concerning her age, residence and relatives popped right up. For an additional fee, the system delivered information on criminal records, aliases, divorces, bankruptcies and credit reports.

"Good Lord." Jarrod pointed to the screen. "That damn thing lays out your whole life. You probably don't care, of course, Nicole, but someone like me with substantial holdings could be stripped bare by something like that."

She didn't correct him. Why bother? The economic gap between them was enormous. Nicole hoped that once she completed her education, all that would change.

"Anyhow," she said, "you see my point. Shelby subscribed to that service, the one with all the bells and whistles. I guess she discovered that stuff when she was a librarian."

"Too bad her computer was stolen. We'd get her search history." Jarrod yawned. "Fuselli can handle this. Probably has most of it at the police station anyway." He looked at his watch and suddenly leapt to his feet. "Whoa! Danny's going to be pissed. I forgot all about meeting her for lunch."

Nicole suppressed the grin lurking at the corners of her mouth. *How perfect! The mighty lawyer is just another whipped male.*

"That's too bad. One more thing, Jarrod. Do you know anything about Shelby's child?"

There was a full minute of stunned silence. When he responded, his fury was palpable. "Child! Are you insane? My aunt was a spinster." Jarrod noisily stuffed papers into his briefcase. "Where did you ever get that idea?"

"Fuselli mentioned it." Nicole gripped her coffee cup. "Look, I'm not trying to unearth a scandal. Far from it, but consider the possibilities. Shelby may have located, or been found by, her own flesh and blood. That throws a monkey wrench into the whole system, especially for you and me."

Jarrod was a large man, but the shock seemed to diminish him. "It can't be true. My dad would have said something. He talked about Shelby all the time, and believe me, they didn't always get along. I know he would have mentioned it even if only to prove she was some kind of slut."

The apple didn't bounce too far from that tree, Nicole thought. *How easy it is to blame the woman for everything.*

"Autopsies don't lie, and according to Fuselli the evidence is conclusive. Sometime in the past, Shelby had a child."

"Damn! Fuselli never mentioned it to me." That seemed to bother Jarrod as much as the information itself. "He'll hear about this, believe you me. In the meantime, I hope I can rely upon your discretion, Nicole."

Sometimes a demon surfaced within her normally placid soul. Jarrod's cherished belief in his own moral and social superiority chafed at her. What a lug. She couldn't wait to puncture his vanity.

"Are you so sure that I'm not Shelby's child? She was awfully fond of me, you know." Nik enjoyed the look of horror on his face as the possibility dawned on him. Pompous Jarrod Whitholm joined by blood with a non-Ivy Leaguer? Impossible.

"We might very well be cousins. That wouldn't be so bad, would it, Jarrod?"

He swallowed hard, regaining his composure. "Of course not. It's just … such a surprise. Aunt Shelby never once hinted about such a thing."

"Breathe easy. My parents definitely didn't adopt me. I heard the story of my birth many times, and trust me, Shelby was nowhere in sight."

To his credit Jarrod seemed embarrassed. He did the smart thing and zipped his lip.

Nicole relented, filling the conversational gap. "I agree we should keep that story under wraps. It was Shelby's business, not ours. We have no right to publicize it."

"It's something to consider, though. Might have been a grudge killing. Lots of violence involved." Jarrod shuddered. "I'll speak with my dad tonight and see what he thinks." One more glance at his watch made Jarrod jump. He gathered his things and strolled out the door without saying another word.

Nicole was used to dating. It was no big deal. Men had always pursued her, even though she refused most invitations and focused on her studies. Why, oh why, did a casual meal with a stranger, an acquaintance at best, cause her such angst? It was a business meeting, not a date. Dr. Lee had no real interest in her, she was sure of it. A man like that—gorgeous, exotic and full of himself—had all kinds of women. Maybe that was the problem. Nicole dated boys, and Alex was most certainly a man. Just thinking of him made her lower extremities tingle.

Her wardrobe was limited. If she'd had some of Danielle's clothes, it would have been easy. Nik settled for a slim black cashmere dress she'd bought on sale last winter. It looked elegant, especially when she put her hair in a French twist. She hoped Dr. Lee didn't get the wrong idea. This was a discussion, not a seduction. He knew a lot more about Shelby and the comic book collection than he'd admitted. For a split second his eyes had betrayed him when Fuselli broached the topic. Who could say how much Shelby had confided in him? Nik knew that any woman, even a crusty librarian, could be charmed by a lithe body, almond eyes and wavy, black hair. Despite appearances, Shelby had a streak of romance in her soul. Nik found that out when she'd caught her one night hunched over a novel with a lurid cover.

"Not a bodice ripper, young lady. That's a pejorative term." Shelby winked as she'd said that. "The romance genre is no different from other literature. Who's to say? These days D.H. Lawrence would be at home on the erotica shelf, you know, right there with Henry Fielding and Terry Southern."

That was the last time they'd discussed the subject. Now Nik wondered if she'd missed something important, an insight into the soul of a woman who had been disappointed by love but still yearned for it. Alex looked like he was in his mid-thirties. That made him a candidate for Shelby's love child. Maybe with a subtle nudge or two, he'd reminisce about his childhood tonight.

Confucius announced her visitor by flinging himself at her front door. Nik took a deep breath and approached, using slow, measured steps. "Who is it?" Caution was her watchword no matter how foolish she sounded. The break-in still had her spooked.

"Alex Lee. May I come in?"

Seven

Cliff House was Goodhaven's premier restaurant. During the season both locals and visitors vied for reservations. Prime tables, coveted by the burgeoning tourist crowd that swelled the town's coffers, usually went to strangers. Even now in winter's throes, most tables were occupied.

Alex eased warily into the dining room, scoping out the crowd of locals. Jarrod Whitholm was at the bar wrapped around the svelte shoulders of his fiancée. Danielle Stevens, what a piece of work. Alex understood women like her, knew that despite the luscious facade, she was nothing but trouble. Danny ignored Nik but bathed Alex in the luminous glow of her smile. She was the type of female who considered all members of her sex as competitors. He tightened his grip around Nicole, feigned indifference and nodded pleasantly to Danielle.

The hostess led them past mayor Haas's table to a black leather booth overlooking the water. Nicole and Alex sat opposite each other, awash in candlelight and a whiff of distrust. They made a handsome couple. Anyone could see that. Women eyed him as he glided toward the table and took his seat. He was used to that.

"They're staring at you," Nicole said. "Men with your looks don't appear on blustery wintery nights down here except in books or films."

He winked at her. "Is that so, Ms. Nelson? You got your share of attention, too, you know. Every woman in the room envies you."

"You're making fun of me."

"Not at all. In case you haven't noticed, you're one beautiful woman." Alex scanned the menu, carefully turning each page. "Hmm. Nice selection. Glad I brought my appetite and my credit cards." He shrugged. "This is probably old hat to you. I bet you could recite the menu from memory."

Nicole stiffened and pulled away. "I hate playing games. You know I'm not rich. Look at these prices, for God's sake. Not on a grad student's budget, at least this grad student's. I told you I'm incredibly boring. I spend most nights at home, working on my dissertation."

Alex leaned forward, touching her cheek. "Someone as lovely as you sitting home? Impossible."

"There's a local place, Crazy Eights, where we sometimes hang out. Good food, plain but tasty, with prices anyone can afford. What it lacks in ambiance it makes up in warmth."

"Hmm. Maybe you'll take me there with you some night. You know, introduce me around." He trained amber eyes on her. "Traveling as much as I do has its downside. I get lonely."

"You plan on staying here awhile?"

"Is that a personal question?" He gave her his mocking smile. "Right now I can think of many reasons to stay in Goodhaven, even some business ones."

Nik giggled. She couldn't help herself.

Alex peered at her over his menu. "What's so funny?"

"Nothing. It's just that for all I know you could be a killer. How crazy is that?"

Alex sat, hands folded, calmly studying her. "I haven't finalized my plans yet, but as long as my client wants that collection, I'll hang around. Goodhaven seems like a friendly enough place."

Nicole snapped at him. "I guess it's friendly if you don't count Shelby's murder. Everyone tiptoes around that, and it makes me mad." She took a big sip of wine to calm herself. "Forgive me, Alex. I'm usually not rude."

"Don't apologize for caring. After all, she was your friend." He took her hand. "Loyalty. That's an important quality, Nicole. Plus, I like women who are direct. Let's start over, get to know each other better. Come on. You first."

"Okay." She took a breath. "You spend a lot of time in California, don't you? Has that always been home?"

"Most of my life. My dad was a journalist, a real globetrotter. Maybe you've heard of him, Sylvester Lee?"

She shook her head. "My focus is awfully narrow, I'm afraid. Did you and your mom travel with him? That must have been fun."

Alex felt his mood darken, eclipsed by a touch of sadness. He sipped his martini and said nothing.

"Forgive me," Nik stammered. "I didn't mean to pry. I'm just interested in other people's lives. Occupational hazard."

He put her hand in his again and squeezed it, feeling a warm sensation spread slowly through his body. It was as if he'd known her forever. Something about Nicole made him want to curl up with her by the fireplace and erase the taint of evil that permeated her life. It was new to him, this urge to protect a woman he barely knew. New, but not unpleasant.

"Don't worry," he said. "It's just that I never knew my mom. She was British. I was raised by my Nai-Nai, Grandma to you. My dad died during the Bosnian conflict." He sighed. "Always after that last big story, no matter what it cost him or me."

Tears pooled in Nicole's eyes. "I lost my parents five years ago. Accident. I still feel like an orphan even though I'm an adult." She toyed with her butter knife. "I guess that's why Shelby was so special to me, more aunt than landlady."

He nodded. "Ah, yes, Shelby Whitholm. Quite a character, wasn't she? We connected right away the first time we met."

Nicole's eyes narrowed as if he'd grown horns or cloven hooves.

"Something wrong? You look funny." Alex tilted his head, giving her a quizzical look.

They locked eyes, each unwilling to yield.

"You changed your story," Nik said, "about meeting Shelby. You told Fuselli you'd never met her."

Alex chuckled. "Is that all? Surely you've heard of Skype. Shelby used it enough."

"I feel like a country bumpkin," she said. "Naturally I've heard of Skype."

"You're pretty sharp, Ms. Nelson, catching my evasion. I gave Fuselli a lawyer's answer, and he never pursued it. In the literal sense, I *met* Shelby at Comic-Con, but she was a complex woman. As I said, I never *knew* her." Alex tilted his head. "From all I've heard it sounds like you really didn't either."

Nicole charged ahead, dipping a toe into the conversational waters. "What can you tell me about this comic book collection of hers? It's a total surprise to everyone."

Alex felt his muscles tighten. "Has Fuselli deputized you? Law enforcement is upgrading its image, I see."

The timely intervention of their waiter saved the moment. After they ordered famous Goodhaven oysters with fresh scallops, Nik tried again.

"Don't blame the sheriff. It's just … I think he needs help. Maybe if I understood things, I could do something. No one knew Shelby better than I did, even though I've only been here a year."

"Hmm. That's strange. You lived with her, yet you knew nothing about her obsession with comics. What else about her life was a mystery? Can't that nephew of hers help you?"

"He's helping, but, you see, it's also a matter of self-protection. Someone broke into my home last night. I might be next."

All six-plus feet of him tensed up. "I'm so sorry. I had no idea. Forgive me." They ate their appetizers in silence. Finally, Alex said, "Look. Investment-grade comics are rare and very expensive. Collectors are coming out of the woodwork, trying to track them down. They hire guys like me to verify and acquire them at a competitive price. I know it sounds weird, but these men — most comic collectors are guys — will often stop at nothing if they're on the trail of a mint collection. And from everything I could see, Shelby's lot was absolutely choice."

Nicole savored her oysters and returned to business. "How did Shelby find you? There must be dozens like you." She gasped. "What I meant was, there must be plenty of specialists."

He shrugged, showing her a prime set of dimples. "Don't know. She emailed me some photos last May and suggested we meet at Comic-Con. She was very thorough, I can tell you. Almost intrusive. Virtually climbed my family tree before she'd agree to talk." Alex waved his hand in front of Nik. "Hello! Are you dreaming?"

"I'm making a mess of things. I'm so sorry. I didn't sleep well last night after the break-in. Please continue. I've got Overstreet's reference works, but I've only skimmed them. Here's what I just don't get: Why would anyone want comic books they can't even touch or read? Aside from the money, of course."

She was lying. Alex could see that. Sleep deprivation had nothing to do with the look in those velvet eyes. He felt it, too. Desire was cascading through every pore in his body, telling him in that most primitive of ways how much he wanted her.

He reached across the table and took her hand. "Look. Any kind of collector is a breed apart. Whether it's snuffboxes, trading cards or comics, they lust, actually lust, for acquisitions. Read the material. Classic comics are considered an art form."

"I know all about lust." Nicole's mouth dropped open and her eyes widened. "I can't believe I said that. Chalk it up to exhaustion."

Alejandro Lee had a hearty masculine laugh that made heads turn. That didn't trouble him one bit. He was charmed by the innocence of this lovely young woman.

"You're really something, Ms. Nelson. I know when someone's teasing me. Anyhow, money's a big issue among comic collectors. Auction prices for the most valuable pieces, golden age in mint condition, are off the charts. Two of them went for over a million dollars just last year, and they weren't mint, just near mint.

"Forgive me if I fantasize," Nicole said. "No more grubbing for tuition, room and board. Good Lord, I'd even have a car with a working heater. It sounds petty, but Shelby would understand."

He stayed silent, thinking of the things a woman like Nik could get from a man if she tried. Any man with a pulse and a wallet would be hers for the taking.

"What's this golden age thing?" she asked. "I haven't done much research yet."

Alex Lee flexed long, elegant fingers and stretched. Years of martial arts training had given him an almost feline grace. For years he'd used that skill to disarm and captivate women. Suddenly it felt like a cheap trick, unworthy of Nicole. She deserved better.

"Okay," he said. "I'll play professor, but don't blame me if you get bored. Golden age comics were published from the thirties up to right after World War II. You can imagine how tough it is to find any at all, let alone ones in mint condition. I mean storage, deterioration—it's a real crapshoot." Alex shook his head at the absurdity of his quest. "That's why when Shelby called, when she dangled a few choice tidbits in front of me, I couldn't resist. The Whitholm collection could be the greatest find in the history of comic culture, the Holy Grail for enthusiasts."

He hated to break the spell, but time was critical. It was do-or-die, now-or-never time. *Close the deal,* he told himself. *Forget about lustrous skin and eyes like mountain lakes. Do what you do best. Seduce the client; get the comics.*

Nik leaned closer to him, almost whispering. "How much would her comics have been worth, assuming they were in good condition? I checked that grading guide, so I have a vague idea what we're talking about."

He stared at his plate, feeling dazed. "Hard to say. Priceless." Alex crushed a baguette, pulverizing it into a mass of crumbs. "If you know … if you have any idea at all, give me first crack at it. You won't be sorry. I guarantee it."

Keep your eye on the prize he told himself. *You want those comics. Nothing more. Only a fool would risk getting involved. She's a needless complication. A distraction.*

Out of the corner of his eye, Alex saw trouble approaching. Harris Goldman, that damn sneak, had a bead on their table. He was hard to miss, impossible to ignore.

"Well, what have we here? Introduce me to your friend, Nicole." Harris Goldman, clad in tweedy blazer and slacks eyed them with owlish interest.

"Oh, yeah. Okay." Nicole stumbled through introductions.

Alex shook hands and turned on the charm machine. "Won't you join us? We were just getting to know each other."

"Too bad about that break-in," Harris said, accepting a chair. "You probably need some protection, Nicole. More than that worthless dog of Shelby's." A glance at Alex rounded out his sentence.

Nik bristled. "I see that the Goodhaven gossip mill is alive and kicking. Spreading rumors is big business on the lower Cape."

Goldman shrugged. "Winters here are bleak and boring. Strangers are what pass for excitement, and like it or not, you fit the bill. You and your friend here."

"How'd you hear about that?" Nik gritted her teeth, eking out a smile that was half snarl.

"It's all over town, Ms. Nelson. Naturally, it didn't surprise me. Nothing would after teaching at Amherst for so long. I know what you young people are up to."

Nik's face flushed crimson.

"What's your theory on the murder, Dr. Goldman?" Alex edged smoothly into the conversation as if nothing were amiss. He gave the professor his full attention. "I'll bet you knew Shelby pretty well."

Goldman scrutinized him as if he were a lab rat. "Nobody really knew Shelby. She shared parts of her life with people, but she was pretty cagey. I admired that about her. People today have no respect for privacy."

"You sound like a wise man," Alex said. "What does your wife think about it?"

Harris Goldman shrank back in his chair. "I'm no longer married, as Danny probably told you."

"Danny?" Alex asked. "Who's he?"

Nik tugged at his sleeve. "Danielle Stevens. You know, Jarrod's fiancée."

He returned her smile, showcasing his dimples. It was a practiced move that reaped big dividends with most women. Those liaisons and the memories accompanying them receded into the distant past each time he saw Nicole. They were worthless, tawdry reminders of a life without purpose.

Nik kept her head down, eyes averted like a naughty child.

She's a hard case, Alex thought. *Not so easy to seduce Ms. Nicole Nelson.* He turned back to Harris Goldman. "Forgive me, professor," he said. "I saw your wedding ring and presumed … "

"No offense taken." Goldman's rigid jaw threatened to crack. "Excuse me." He pushed back his chair and hustled out the door without another word.

"I'm speechless," Alex said. "That doesn't happen very often to a lawyer." He signaled the waiter for another drink. "How about you, Nicole?"

She shook her head. "I'm not much of a drinker. After listening to Harris I feel fuzzy enough." A jazz quartet started up, playing a soft, sweet version of a Coltrane song. Nicole leaned her head back, crooning the lyrics. "Jazz, especially Coltrane, makes me feel mellow. Too bad I can't carry a tune. Couldn't even make the school choir."

"Don't sell yourself short. You have a very distinctive voice." Teasing her was fun, he decided. He hadn't had much fun lately. "Dance?" Alex asked. "I'll bet you move like a dream."

Nik looked around the room. "Nobody else is out there. Maybe we should wait."

"Nonsense." Alex Lee pulled out her chair and led her to the dance floor. "You seem like a leader, not a follower. Am I wrong?"

Nicole squared her shoulders. "I'm a strong person, but I feel shy around here, like everyone's watching."

Alex held her firmly as they moved to the music. "Can you blame them? You're beautiful, Nicole. So lovely." His lips grazed her forehead. "Don't worry. I won't pressure you until you're ready. Not yet, anyway."

Easier said than done. He could feel the soft swell of her breasts pressed against him, and the faint scent of lavender in her hair. She was so young, ripe as a summer peach. Feisty, yet curiously innocent. Destroying that innocence would be a felony, a crime against nature itself. Preserving it might be a life's work.

Alex moved sideways as they were joined by Jarrod Whitholm and Danielle Stevens.

Jarrod's frown rivaled Zeus on a tear. "I'm surprised to see you out, Nicole." He gave a curt nod to Alex. "Thought you'd be home resting after all the excitement last night."

"She took mercy on a poor stranger alone in the wilderness." Alex returned Jarrod's frown with a wintery smile.

Something activated Danielle Stevens' sales radar. The realtor raised one perfectly arched brow and said, "Maybe you should consider buying property here. We warm up quickly to new neighbors, and Goodhaven really isn't the wilderness, you know."

"Point taken." Alex twirled Nik around, executing several intricate dance steps that were his specialty. She gulped, took a deep breath and clutched his arm in a death grip.

"Just a minute, Nicole," Jarrod called. "When can we get together?"

Danielle's face was a blank, impenetrable mask.

She's jealous, Alex thought. *Very interesting. Couture clothes can't insulate her from that green-eyed monster. Even she can see the danger.*

"I have to go into Boston on Monday," Nik said. "Maybe later on in the week?"

"Monday's fine," Jarrod said. "I'll drive and check out some things about Aunt Shelby's estate while you conduct your business."

Nicole looked stunned. "But I ..."

"I'll phone you tomorrow to firm up our plans." The music ended and Jarrod, a surprisingly agile dancer, led Danielle away without another word.

Nik ignored the sly smile on Alex Lee's face. "What just happened?" she asked. "Jarrod Whitholm has snubbed me since day one. Now we're suddenly best buds?"

"Who can blame him? Besides, you now share a financial interest. A pretty powerful one, too. Money can bind you like glue."

"I've been wondering about something," she said. "If the murderer tried to sell or fence Shelby's collection, could you trace it? Do they have a registry for comics?"

They'd returned to their table and were sharing dessert. Nicole couldn't resist a wedge of Lemon Meringue Pie. Alex wolfed down a slice bigger than Cleveland.

Nothing mandatory. There are several societies and associations, of course. Mostly online. All voluntary."

"Would Shelby have listed her collection there?" Nik asked.

Alex rewarded her with another of his sizzling smiles. "Everyone uses a screen name for protection. You can understand that. Who knows about strangers these days."

She shivered. "Shelby was smart. She would have tried to shield herself, wouldn't use her real name or give strangers a way to trace her. Otherwise something bad might happen. Huh! That's a laugh."

"Are you still with me? You look a million miles away." Alex hesitated. "Maybe we should leave. Whitholm was right about one thing. You've had enough excitement in the past two days to last a lifetime. I'll do some checking for you. Don't worry."

"I have to admit I'm exhausted. I haven't really slept since Shelby's murder. Do you mind?"

He summoned the bland poker face that all lawyers acquire. "Of course not. I'll do a quick safety check of your house and leave. Promise."

True to his word, Alex surveyed the premises, planted a chaste kiss on her cheek and drove away. He didn't go far. Someone close at hand was more than willing to meet his needs.

Eight

Nicole peered at her alarm clock through bleary, sleep-shut eyes. She'd had a difficult night. Each time she'd dozed off, a sharp noise or banging shutter had jolted her from the arms of Morpheus into total panic. Shelby haunted what few dreams she'd had, wearing her trademark smirk, winking slyly. Nik reached out, begged her to name her murderer. Each time, Shelby laughed aloud. "You already know, Cookie. Use your noggin."

The noise just wouldn't stop. Some oaf was pounding on the carriage house, raising one hell of a racket. Nik raised the outer corner of her window shade. Jett Hall pummeled the front door, undeterred by the early hour or the biting chill. Nothing, even good manners or conventional wisdom, stopped a man on a mission. Despite menacing growls from Confucius, Jett stood firm while waving a crisp cloth napkin in surrender.

"Come on, Double N. Open up. This shit's burning my fingers!"

Nik stumbled down the stairs and flung open the door. Jett could just take her as she was: tangled hair, raccoon eyes and all.

"Nicole?" His eyes widened behind the granny glasses. "What happened to you?" He thrust a paper sack at her. "Here. I brought coffee and scones. Espresso. Your favorite."

A good hostess would have thanked him. After all, he came bearing gifts. Nicole really didn't care. She couldn't suppress the scowl that enveloped her face or the tart comment lingering on the tip of her tongue. Jett had a terminal case of perkiness that gave her a rash. No matter how hard she tried, she couldn't escape him. Now that he considered himself her knight errant, things were even more difficult.

"Why are you here?" she growled. "Doesn't anybody sleep in this town?"

Nothing bothered Jett; he had the hide of a bull elephant. Nik couldn't speak to any other similarities, and she didn't care to know.

"Touchy, touchy." He plopped the bag down and checked his watch. "Hey! It's time for you to be up anyway. Get a move on."

She inhaled espresso as if it were her salvation. After several big sips, the caffeine kicked in, making Nicole feel human and vaguely guilty.

"Thanks, Jett. Sorry to be so grumpy."

"Rough night? I heard all about it." His eyes behind the granny glasses were alight with mischief.

Jett had told Nik on numerous occasions that he was in love with her, despite hints, snubs or outright refusals. He called himself her love slave, but Nik considered him her scourge, a penance for some unimaginable offense.

When Confucius plopped his head in her lap, imploring her with big doggy eyes to attend to his needs, Jett bustled toward the kitchen door, anxious to help.

"Here. I'll let him out in the yard. Anything to please you, my liege."

Nicole bowed to the inevitable, feeding Atticus and Annabel before their soft meows became outraged yowls. Apparently her night out with Alejandro Lee was already on the public airways. What next? A raid by the Goodhaven morals squad?

Jett dragged in a dining room chair and made himself comfortable. "So. Tell me all about it." His freshly scrubbed face, bright red sweater and pressed khakis were standard preppie garb for Amherst students of his era. In Goodhaven his aggressive wholesomeness seemed odd, almost as if he were trying too hard.

Nik held her breath to a count of ten, telling herself that Jett was a good-hearted friend who only wanted to help. Normally that worked, but today something about him seemed more creepy than kind.

"We have anti-stalking laws in Massachusetts, Mr. Hall. I'd hate to call Fuselli on you." She summoned a smile to mitigate the sting of the words.

"You won't say that after you hear my big scoop," Jett said. "I did some cyber-snooping. Nothing illegal, just interesting. You wouldn't believe the number of chat rooms, threads and blogs about comics." He grabbed a scone and took a huge bite. "I chose the two biggest ones, American Comic Culture and Comic-Corner. That second one's kind of shady, I think, but, anyway, I signed in and did my thing."

Jett stopped, giving new meaning to the term pregnant pause. If he expected Nik to cheer him on or beg for more, he was disappointed. She sat silently, sipping espresso and staring into space.

"Ah, for Christ's sake, Nicole, what are you, some kind of stone?" Jett pushed away his espresso and folded his arms. "Aren't you the least bit curious?"

She had to give in. Only a monster would prolong the suspense. "Okay. What did you find?"

"Lots of chatter. Nobody mentioned Shelby's name, but lots of entries about a major collection, the Holy Grail, that's just surfaced. And get this. Now it may all be bullshit, but plenty of speculation about one specific comic. They called it the Ashcan edition, something like that. According to these freaks, it's worth five million bucks. Five million!"

Nik shivered. Suddenly, her cozy living space seemed barren and unwelcoming, full of shadows and ghosts. Had Shelby owned this Ashcan thing? Alex had hinted at something big, something that dwarfed the million-dollar comics sold last year. People would kill for a lot less than that. No wonder someone ransacked the carriage house. Fuselli said Shelby had been tortured. He didn't use that word though. He was being delicate, probably thought he was sparing Nicole more anguish. No matter. Shelby was tough. She may have held out despite the pain. That's when her murderer used the bat on her. That's why she died.

"Whoa, what's the matter, Double N? You aren't going to faint on me, are you? You look awfully pale." Jett pushed back his chair and clutched her arm as Nicole shuddered and leaned back on the cushions.

"Oh, my God! Where's the phone? 911!" Jett's hysterical yelps revived Nik better than smelling salts. She shook herself and struggled to sit upright.

"I'm fine. Actually, I'm embarrassed." Nicole was not the type of female who swooned or played the frail vessel. That honor was reserved for southern belles and pregnant women, and she was neither of those things.

Jett fluffed her pillows and stood poised to save her again.

"Any more of that espresso?" Nicole reached for her cup and slowly sipped. "You've done a great job of research, Jett. Now let's go tell the sheriff."

"Wait a minute. Fuselli's okay, but he'll probably go all cop on us and insist on getting a subpoena or something. That'll spoil everything." Jett got a terrier-with-a-bone look on his face. She'd seen it before and found it incredibly tedious.

"Look. I've got a lot to do today. I'm meeting with my academic advisor on Monday, and I'm way behind." She cringed at the pain in Jett's eyes. Nik was never cruel — hardly ever — but she knew how to set limits. He'd attach himself to her like a barnacle if she were not firm.

"You probably have a date anyway," Jett said, blowing on his coffee, "and I have a business to run. Harris is holding down the fort right now, but I can't take advantage of him. He's pretty old."

"Humph." Nicole never had bought Goldman's harmless old man act. The guy was mean. Mean and nosey. The type who passed judgment on others while feigning empathy.

She could see that Jett was stalling, working himself up to something big. Nik couldn't take another messy scene with him no matter how much it wounded his pride.

"Let me ask you something. What does he have that I don't? Alejandro Lee. Even his name sounds phony. He looks good, I admit that, but what do you really know about him? Mark my words, Nicole. He'll use you, break your heart and take off."

Whining men were irritants, especially when they begged. Nik acted quickly and decisively to forestall that.

"Back off, will you, Jett? I'm not interested in anything permanent with you, Alex or anyone else." Nik rose cautiously. "Until Shelby's estate gets settled and my dissertation is finished, I am definitely off the market." She batted her eyelashes at him in a bad Mae West imitation. "Even for a gorgeous hunk of man like you, big boy."

Jett seemed mollified, even though she was joking. Nik couldn't explain his obsession with her. He had options, even in Goodhaven. Some women actually found Jett attractive, or acted like they did. After all, he was intelligent, well educated and had his own business. None of those attributes mattered to Nicole. From the moment they'd met, she'd considered Jett a brother at most, a pal at best.

"Hey," he said, "I better get going. Don't worry. I'll keep poking around this comic thing. Who knows? I just might get lucky."

Nicole stood on tiptoe and patted his cheek. "Thanks, Jett. You're a really great guy. You know that?" She walked him to the door. "Talk to you later."

The phone rang just as she locked the door. Nik sped toward it, hoping that maybe, just maybe, it was Alejandro Lee. Some of Jett's warnings made sense. After all, she knew very little about Alex. Glib, gorgeous criminals often targeted vulnerable young women with financial prospects. All the newspapers said so. Something told her Alejandro Lee was no criminal. He might lie, cheat and mislead her to get Shelby's collection, but he wouldn't harm her. Not physically.

"Hello?" She tried to sound world-weary, disinterested in whoever called. Nik suspected that she'd failed miserably.

Fuselli's cheerful baritone rang out. "Hey, Nicole. I was wondering if you'd found anything. You know, something of Shelby's that might be a clue."

"Sorry. Not a thing."

A furious spate of barking erupted as Confucius launched himself against the back gate. She had difficulty hearing anything with him on the warpath. Nik padded over to the window to check out the yard.

"Nicole? Everything okay?" Fuselli's voice wasn't cheerful anymore. He sounded grim.

"Fine. Look, Sheriff, I'm late for an appointment. If you need me, I'll be at Lifelines all afternoon. Okay? I promise to call you if I find anything that might help."

"Make sure that you do. I don't have to tell you there's a killer out there somewhere."

Nik shivered as she hung up the phone.

Alejandro Lee had no interest in real estate. None whatsoever. He'd come to Stevens Realty, Inc., on a hunch but somehow found himself sitting in an elegant suede chair, staring at the equally elegant Danielle Stevens. She perched on an antique loveseat, tapping the toes of her mile-high heels on the polished oak floor. Alex knew her game. It was as old as sin and animal lust. His eyes were riveted on her smooth, shapely legs showcased by sheer black stockings. He caught his breath, knowing just what she could do, would do, to you with those legs. That was her game plan, of course. Alex knew that, too. She was as different from Nicole as day from night. Nicole was a lethal combination of intellect and innocence; Danny was street smart and wise beyond her years. Both could be deadly if a man lost control.

She was flirting, giving him a sales pitch, ostensibly about Goodhaven real estate but actually about the exquisite pleasures only she could confer. To illustrate, she glided toward her desk and grabbed some glossy brochures. As she bent over, a sheaf of papers littered the floor. To Alex's trained eye, they looked suspiciously like overdue bills.

"Need some help?" he asked. "I'm pretty handy with numbers."

She scooped up the bills and slowly handed Alex the brochures, making sure to brush his thigh with her fingertips.

"I bet you're handy with lots of things, Dr. Lee." Danny lit a Gitanes with a jeweled lighter and inhaled deeply.

"Hmm. Smoking is against the law in public spaces, and I'm an officer of the court."

"Arrest me." Her pose was as seductive as Eve's in the garden. "I won't resist."

Alex shook his head. "Nice talk from an engaged woman."

Danny cocked her head and looked at him. "From what I hear, you're practically engaged yourself. What's the matter? Little Miss Muffet rings your bells more than a real woman?"

"Forget about Nicole. Let's talk about you and Shelby Whitholm." As he flipped through the brochure, trying to keep himself grounded, an advertisement for 'round-the-world cruises flew out and fell at his feet.

"What's this, Ms. Stevens? Planning a vacation?" Alex masked surprise with a grin.

The seemingly unflappable Danielle sprang forward and snatched the circular from him. "My honeymoon. Unless you missed it, Jarrod and I are getting married."

Just then Jarrod Whitholm burst through the door with the downcast look of a supplicant.

"Sorry I'm late, hon." He walked over to Danny and kissed her cheek. "Forgive me?" Jarrod whirled around, spying Alejandro. "What the … ? Wasn't expecting to find you here."

Danielle made a moue of distaste. "Oh, for heaven's sake, Jarrod, grow up. Dr. Lee is a prospective client and my guest."

"Someone's grumpy today," Jarrod said. "Good thing Dr. Feelgood has some medicine with him." He dangled a turquoise box in front of her. "Check this out."

"Hmm. Tiffany, very nice." Danielle put it down without opening it. "You know I prefer Cartier."

Alex felt uncomfortable, ashamed to witness Jarrod's humiliation. No woman had ever done that to him. No woman would even try. For some reason he thought of Nicole and her kindness to Shelby's pets.

"Where were you anyway? Nosing around your new cousin?" Danielle's anger flamed into rage. "You men make me sick, falling for that sweet, sensitive act." She kicked the wastebasket with the toe of her stilettos. "For an innocent,

Little Miss Muffet wormed her way into Shelby's pocketbook pretty damned fast." Danielle's eyes spit fire. "After all you did for that old bag, she gave half of everything to a stranger."

Alex chuckled to himself. Now everything made sense. The seductive Ms. Stevens was all about cold, hard cash. Jarrod might as well be an ATM as a man. Women like Danny never had enough money. They blamed the recession and bad investments for their plight, but the truth was far simpler. Spending more than you earned was a sure source of debt. He'd bet that Stevens Realty hemorrhaged money like arterial spray.

"Hey, don't get upset. Come on. Let's grab some lunch. I'm starving." Jarrod wore the anxious look of a whipped pup.

She ducked when he reached for her, giving him a vicious frown. "Go without me. I'm not hungry."

"I have to get busy inventorying aunty's things," he said. "They need me back on my show by next week."

"That's right," Alex said. "I've caught your show before. Gets lively, doesn't it?"

Jarrod laughed. "That's what we try for. Let me ask you, Lee. You're an economist. What do you think of my deficit-reduction plan?"

"No one cares about that, Jarrod. Stop boring us to death." Danielle's temper was on overload. Alex could tell by the murderous gleam in her eyes and the grim set of her mouth. He couldn't imagine what their married life would be like. Lovely Danny would nag Jarrod to his death, or when she felt generous, treat him to a little taste of heaven. Not like Nicole.

"You're sure you're not hungry, Danny? How about you, Lee?" Jarrod patted her arm, turned around and ambled out the door, chatting with Alex.

"Ms. Stevens seems like a handful." Alex prided himself on his gift for understatement. "Guess she's having money problems."

Jarrod surprised him by laughing. "Always. She calls it keeping up appearances. I call it profligate spending." He shrugged. "I bail her out, and she rewards me in ways I can't begin to describe. Danny has talent. No intellectual, for sure, but get her in the bedroom, and she's a goddamn genius."

They strolled toward the restaurant with smiles on their faces.

Nine

Lifelines defied the stereotypes of animal shelters. Hardworking volunteers had created a warm, caring environment, very different from the grim death chambers so often found in big cities. For the orphaned pets it housed, that meant play time, plenty of hugs and long beach walks. For Nicole, who had always loved animals, her days at the shelter were closer to therapy than work. Communicating with animals was easy for her, much more satisfying than dealing with humans.

Each worker took her turn doing the less savory chores. Today was Nik's time to mop floors, clean bedding and wash food bowls. She greeted the other volunteers, opened her locker and dumped her stuff. Suddenly she realized that Shelby's locker hadn't been emptied. It was next to hers, secured with a stout combination lock that looked untouched.

Confident that no one could see her, Nik palmed the lock and punched in the combination. Shelby always used the same numbers for any password. She'd said it didn't matter because she had nothing worth stealing. If only that were true, Nik thought. Someone, a brutal murderer, had thought otherwise.

She swiftly opened the locker and peered inside. The contents were unexceptional: old clothes, worn shoes and one slightly soggy towel. Nik's throat closed as she touched Shelby's shapeless wool cardigan. That garment was synonymous with its owner: serviceable, battle-scarred and unglamorous. It was too motheaten to donate, but Atticus and Annabel would love cuddling up on it. Shelby, the doting pet mother, would like that, too. Nik slipped the sweater off the hanger and folded it over her arm. The shelter felt chilly today, probably an attempt to save a few dollars on heating. Nik's legacy would do some good here. She smiled at the thought and threw the cardigan over her shoulders. Shelby would have scolded her for daydreaming. "Come on, Cookie, get to work. Time's awasting."

Classical music and show tunes were played continuously to soothe the shelter's inmates. Happily, they had the same effect on humans as on their animal friends. Nik filled the bucket with hot, soapy water, found the mop and started her chores, singing aloud to one of her mom's old favorites, "Looking for Love." There was a lesson to be learned in those lyrics. Nicole had looked for love in the wrong places plenty of times and had often been hurt.

As she pondered her past escapades, a hand grasped her shoulder. Nik's scream filled the cavernous space, echoing off the walls. Every dog in the place answered the call by barking its fool head off.

"You again, Miss Nelson. Sorry if I frightened you." Harris Goldman stood in front of her, wearing his rictus grin.

The man was a cipher, trying to relive his glory days. Nik chided herself, knowing she should be charitable. After all, Harris Goldman was ancient and alone. The imp in her argued that he was alone for a reason. He had some admirers but no friends in Goodhaven other than Jett. Small wonder. The grim reaper was in for a tussle whenever he came to collect this guy. Goldman could give as good as he got, Nik was certain of that.

She wasn't frightened. Not in the middle of the day. Not by creepy Harris Goldman, an octogenarian who could be blown about by a strong ocean wind. Of course, Shelby had died at this time of day in the comfort of her own home, but Nik didn't dwell on that. She didn't dare.

"Looking for something, professor?" She forced herself to be civil.

"I heard a noise. Didn't know it was you." His eyes shifted toward Shelby's locker. "Hmm. I thought the police cleared that out. Fuselli probably forgot about it."

"It's almost empty," Nicole said. "Just a few personal items. I'll call the sheriff and ask about it. Excuse me."

His expression said that he didn't believe her, but Harris Goldman's generation had been raised not to make a scene. He leaned against the locker, openly eavesdropping on Nik's conversation.

"The sheriff likes you," he said when she hung up. "Most men probably do."

She flushed more with anger than emotion. How wrong is it to kick an old man's ass? It might be worth the punishment.

"Jett told me about Shelby's collection," he said. "Guess you'll be sitting pretty before long. Now you won't need that Ph.D., will you?"

"My professional plans are no concern of yours." Nik bit her tongue before she said something she'd really regret. Shelby had been right about him. Harris Goldman was a Grade A jerk.

"I saw him that day, you know."

"Who? I have no idea what you're talking about." Nik forced herself to power down before her voice became shrill.

Goldman smirked. "Your boyfriend, Jarrod Whitholm. He was at Shelby's house right after lunch." He checked his ancient Timex. "Right about the time she was murdered."

Nicole waged an internal battle between outrage and curiosity. Outrage won.

"Jarrod Whitholm happens to be engaged, and he is definitely not my boyfriend. If you know something about the murder, you should tell the sheriff." A wicked impulse overcame her. "Do it soon. If word gets around, the murderer might target you."

The old man gulped, blinked several times and looked around him. "Oh. I never thought about that. Maybe I will." He rabbited down the hallway at a speed that belied his age.

The moment he arrived, Sheriff Bob Fuselli launched his full-charm offensive. It didn't deceive Nik. It amused her.

"Stupid of me not to have thought about this place." He bagged and tagged Shelby's few pitiful relics with a sad little smile. "You know, sometimes I think I'm losing it." He grimaced. "Seeing their things is tough. Worse than viewing their corpses, somehow."

Nicole stared up at him. "I understand. You can steel yourself for the body, but the little everyday things creep up on you." Her eyes teared up as she saw him collect Shelby's glasses. Her spare pair. Predictably, they had the cheapest frames available. She'd even refused to have plastic coating or the lighter lenses. "Phooey," Shelby scoffed. "That's for fancy people."

It was a conceit, a deliberate repudiation of beauty. Shelby made a virtue out of plainness, questioning any woman who cared about her appearance. Except Nicole. Shelby hadn't held her appearance against her. In fact, she seemed to approve and bask in her protégée's glory.

"You're the real deal, Cookie. Not one of these plastic babes like Danielle Stevens or, God forbid, Amanda Haas."

"You okay?" Fuselli's face crinkled as he stared at her.

"Fine." Nicole moved away from the lockers and dabbed her eyes with a hankie. "What about the storage facilities? Any luck?"

Fuselli shrugged. "Not yet. We've only checked the ones on the Cape so far. Should be a piece of cake unless Shelby went farther afield."

Fuselli's big hand crushed an empty evidence bag into a plastic mass. "I'll solve this thing, Nicole. Count on it."

Nik understood and commiserated with him. After all, murder had been committed on his turf against one of his citizens. If the state guys or the FBI came trampling over everyone, they'd hog credit and dodge blame. Jarrod Whitholm was already making noises about that, as if anyone local, even a former big-time Fed, wasn't good enough for his aunt. Too bad he hadn't been that solicitous when Shelby was alive.

She was lonely before Nik moved there. She'd said so. Beneath her crusty facade, Shelby Whitholm had a soft heart and a thirst for love. Nik's eyes teared up every time she thought of it.

"I'll find him, Nicole. Don't worry. I'll find the bastard who murdered her, even if it's my last official act." She saw steel in Fuselli's eyes.

Nik stopped crying and smiled up at him. "I believe you. Shelby trusted you, too."

She mopped her tears with another pristine handkerchief from Fuselli's endless supply.

"Can I get you anything? A Coke or some water?"

"You're very nice, Sheriff. Thanks anyway." Nik put her cleaning supplies away and headed toward the pet kitchen. "I'd better get going, or the guests here are going to rebel." She hesitated before taking the plunge. "Have you ... did you find anything from the crime scene? Trace evidence, isn't that what you call it?"

His smile was kind, not patronizing. "They're not finished analyzing it yet, but so far it looks like half the citizens of Goodhaven tromped through Shelby's house rather recently."

Nik bit her lip. "I'm so dull-witted lately. Sorry, Sheriff, I forgot to mention it. Shelby hosted a meeting of the Lifelines board that night before she died. I can get you a list of people who attended."

Fuselli nodded without much enthusiasm. "That's the problem with this close-knit community. Everyone's in and out of each other's homes all the time. Even a semi-recluse like Shelby did her share of gallivanting. You'd never find that in Washington."

Gradually, Nik worked up the courage to ask her question. "Is it possible … I mean, could it be … that the murder wasn't about the comic collection? Maybe it was something local, a secret someone didn't want shared."

"Now why would you say that? Is there something I should know, Nicole?" Fuselli's eyes were shards of anthracite, dark and cold.

"No. No. Honest." Her tongue felt fuzzy. She wished she'd taken that water he'd offered her. "It's just … look, Sheriff. I wondered if Shelby found something out. You know, some secret someone might kill to protect."

Fuselli put his hands on his hips and frowned. "Why?"

After sputtering for a minute, Nik told him about Shelby's "neutron bomb" and her prior brush with Harris Goldman. "It's only supposition, but that might explain all the destruction and the theft of her computer. Maybe someone was searching for something incriminating. Blackmail." She hated thinking it, let alone saying it. Blackmail was an ugly word, and Shelby Whitholm was no criminal.

"Listen." Fuselli clasped her arms as if he intended to shake her. "Stop playing around. Do you hear me? This stuff is ugly. If you'd seen her body ... " He dropped his hands and stomped toward the exit, leaving her subdued and shaken.

Last week—had it only been a week ago?—Shelby Whitholm had been the *force majeure* of this small town, causing waves wherever she went. Someone had ended that threat in the most brutal way imaginable. Nik did a quick reality check. What could she possibly add to the investigation? Maybe Jarrod was right. Better to let Fuselli and other professionals handle it.

She snuggled into Shelby's old sweater, feeling the scratchy warmth of its wool. Suddenly her nose twitched, and before she could thwart it, Nik sneezed violently. Her fingers automatically sought the wad of tissues Shelby always stuffed into the worn pockets. No luck. There was something there, wedged in the lining of the right pocket, something stiff like cardboard. When she pulled it out Nik couldn't believe her eyes. It was both a business card and the answer to her prayers.

Jarrod was prompt. He pulled the Hummer up to the carriage house the next morning at six o'clock sharp and beeped the horn. Weather was no problem. The sky was a deep cerulean blue with high fluffy clouds.

He didn't have to honk twice. Nik bolted out the door, dragging her backpack with her. So what if Jarrod was a prig? She hadn't heard from Alejandro lately, and she was bursting to share her findings with someone. Like it or not, Jarrod fit the bill.

"Guess what? You won't believe it."

"It's too early for a pop quiz. Get in. Traffic's miserable this time of day." Jarrod's jaw locked tighter than a vault. For a moment Nik felt a pang of compassion for Danielle Stevens. Imagine facing Jarrod over the breakfast table for the rest of your life. Maybe he showed his sunnier side to her. For Nik, he barely mustered a smile.

The Hummer was a black, hulking vehicle with military swagger. Despite its mammoth proportions, the seats were comically small and uncomfortable, which was fine for Nik but awkward for most men, including the present owner. She leaned forward, brushing her hand against the sharp steel nameplate.

"Why call this thing an Alpha? Rather gratuitous with this kind of beast, wouldn't you say?"

Jarrod made a noise approximating a growl. "You wouldn't understand. Women never do."

"Try me."

He spoke through gritted teeth. "It's special. A one-year production model. They don't even make them anymore."

Boys and their toys. Nik didn't want to pick a fight with him. She needed Jarrod's help to find her legacy.

"I know where those comics are," she said. "Aren't you even curious?"

"Where? How did you find them?"

"Rampart. That's the name of the place. I found their card in her sweater and verified it last night. Shelby was a regular client."

Jarrod's bland expression fit him like a custom suit. "Give me the address, and I'll check it out. That way your school work won't be interrupted."

"No problem. I've already rescheduled. Whether you like it or not, we're partners in this enterprise. Equal partners." Nik tempered her words with a sunny smile.

His scowl eclipsed the sun shining off the Cape Cod Canal. Jarrod maintained a stony silence halfway to Boston until the Hummer sailed past Route 93. "Where is this damn place?" he asked. "I didn't bring the power-of-attorney, you know. We're wasting our time. They probably will tell us diddly. Fuselli will have our hides."

Ignoring Jarrod was fun. Nik knew that he wasn't used to that. Men like Jarrod never were. Most women hung on their every word as if it were Sacred Writ.

"Take exit sixteen," she said. "We're looking for Andover Street, 99 Andover Street. I've driven by it a million times. You can't miss that big lock and chain on the outside of the building. Looks like something out of the Macy's parade."

Jarrod grunted something rude as he swung the behemoth into the parking lot. That sparked a flame of anger in Nicole that quickly became a conflagration.

"You like to control everything, don't you? Tough. Get used to having a partner. An equal partner, remember."

"Equal partners, indeed!" Jarrod's fair British skin showed every emotion. "Just who do you think you are? I'm nationally known, a respected scholar, not an academic nobody from a second-rate university."

Nicole doused the flames of temper. They still had to work together, despite the fact that he was an arrogant snob. Use honey to catch flies, she reminded herself, like she really wanted a bunch of flies.

"Let me handle this," he said brusquely. "Did you get a contact point?"

Nik's smile was beatific. "Not a problem. The building manager is expecting me … us. By the way, did you really call me a minx on the make? That's almost poetic."

He sputtered helplessly. "I won't dignify that with a response."

"Hmm. Your fiancée was my source. Is she a liar?"

"Certainly not! You're making that up. Danielle is a very successful businesswoman, not some flake." Jarrod folded his arms, pushing out his lips in a decided pout. He scrambled out of the Hummer and hustled Nik up the cobbled walkway.

"You think you're so smart, don't you? The big Ph.D. candidate." Jarrod's eyes bugged out as he sputtered. "If you're so smart, how come you moon over Alejandro Lee? Huh? Tell me that, if you dare. You're no different than any other woman. Just mouthier."

"Ouch! What's wrong with you?" Nik jabbed a sharp elbow into his side. "Stop acting so juvenile. Come on. We're looking for the manager, a guy named Bob Rochford. I'll go tell the receptionist we're here."

The manager was prompt and professional, a middle-aged black man wearing a well-cut suit. Nik was impressed.

"Thanks for seeing us on short notice," she said after introducing Jarrod. "You probably read about Shelby's death." She didn't say the word murder. Couldn't. It reeked of blood and brutality.

"Shelby Whitholm was my aunt," Jarrod snorted. "Ms. Nelson and I are her heirs."

Bob Rochford nodded. "I contacted our attorneys after Ms. Nelson's call. Naturally, I can't grant you direct access to her collection, not with a crime involved. The police intend to seal everything." He motioned them to a seating area. "But I'd be glad to answer any of your questions and show you the display room. After all, you're both on the access list."

Nik tried not to gasp. "What access list?"

Rochford flashed a patient grin. "Security and safety are our watchwords. That's what people pay for. Rampart is HPR-rated. That means something in our industry."

"HPR?" Jarrod glared at him. "You'll have to explain that."

"Highly Protected Risk. That's the top rating, you know. Lloyd's of London underwrites us. We offer nine layers of protection for the items here." He folded his arms. "Nothing leaves without the client's okay."

Nik gave him the look that melted most men. "Terrific. You mentioned an access list?"

"Certainly." Rochford nodded. "I made a copy after you called. You're on it, Ms. Nelson. So is Mr. Whitholm."

Jarrod barked an expletive. "What? That's news to me. Are you sure, Rochford?"

"I don't suppose anyone accessed the collection recently?"

Rochford shifted from foot to foot, seemingly struggling with himself. "That's confidential information."

Nik knew a guilty man when she saw one. The nuns had taught her all about sins of omission. Rochford was avoiding something, and his evasiveness was almost comical. "I appreciate your predicament, but Ms. Whitholm was murdered." It hurt using that word, but she forced herself.

Bob Rochford's eyes searched the room. "I can't give you this list. Legal red tape and all. But I might be able to help." He thrust the document at her, waving it under her nose. An instant was all it took. Nik scrolled down the list staring at five familiar names: Shelby, Jarrod, Nicole, Morgan Haas, and Alejandro Lee. Three names had an X next to them.

"What do those marks mean?" she asked, as Jarrod loomed over her shoulder.

Rochford wrung his hands. "Those people accessed the collection. That's what surprised me, Mr. Whitholm. You've already been here."

Ten

"Are you daft, man? I've never been here in my life!" Jarrod's voice quickly scaled the upper ranges from baritone to soprano.

"Forgive me, sir, but our recordkeeping is meticulous." Rochford folded his arms, ready to defend his turf. "You and your aunt accessed the viewing room and the collection itself just five days ago."

Nik gulped. "There must be some mistake."

"It's all computerized," Rochford protested. "Check it out for yourself."

"You don't understand," she said. "Shelby Whitholm was murdered on April 8, the day *before* your records place her here."

Rochford staggered backwards, steadying himself by grasping the edge of the credenza. "This can't be right. Look." He pointed to a discreet sign at the reception desk. "All transactions here are taped and we keep a digitalized version for ten years. I'll have the technician access the information."

He led them to an enclosed area with plush seating and a large flat-screen mounted on the wall.

"Have a seat." Rochford signaled an attendant to start the show.

Nik hunched forward, focusing on the grainy images that filled the screen. One male and an older female slowly approached the viewing room with their backs to the camera. Despite the creepy, funereal sound of it, the viewing room was not unlike that of a high-end jeweler.

Jarrod did a fine imitation of a granite outcropping, the kind that jutted out of craggy mountain walls. He seized the arms of the upholstered chair in a death grip and said nothing. In her heart of hearts Nik enjoyed seeing the imperious Mr. Whitholm reduced to an ossified lump. *Serves him right!*

"They asked to see the collection," Rochford whispered. "Our agent brought it out for her. That's the only way it would ever leave the storage vault. Ms. Whitholm had total control."

The video continued for twenty minutes as the duo patiently examined the carefully wrapped comics.

"Mylar," Rochford babbled. His poise had vanished, a probable casualty of Jarrod's menacing frown. "We only use Mylar to store high-value art. It's inert, space-age plastic. The best." He dabbed his forehead with a crisp white handkerchief.

"Edifying," Jarrod said. "Here's the problem, Rochford. You haven't got one clean shot of these people. They could be anyone. With the rates you charge, I'd expect better results. Highschool kids could do a better job." He snatched the printout from the manager's hands. "Look at the first date. I was in Boston taping my show that day, and I can prove it."

"They had identification," Rochford dithered, "and only Ms. Whitholm knew all the codes. That's a special security feature here at Rampart."

Jarrod was a grumpy grizzly roused from his winter's nap. "Impressive. Now who the hell did you clowns let in? I wasn't here. We've established that. And you agree, I presume, that my aunt didn't rise from her shroud just to make an appearance. In fact, I'll bet you never actually met my aunt, did you?"

Jarrod's lips were locked tighter than the vaults surrounding them. Nik was surprised that any sounds could escape.

Before the beleaguered Rochford escaped, she stopped him. "Maybe you could show us the other tape." She patted his arm, flashing her friendliest smile.

They had no problem identifying the third visitor to the vault. Alejandro Lee was quite distinctive.

Sheriff Bob Fuselli appeared in record time, accompanied by a familiar face. Alejandro Lee, dressed in Ninja black, played the sidekick role. They'd saved themselves three hours by commandeering a police helicopter before it left for Boston.

No doubt about it. Alex had an unsettling effect on Nik. She caught her breath as sunlight illuminated the tendrils of his shiny black hair. His ponytail was perfect, just the right length. She spent a pleasant moment musing about perfection and the rest of the luscious Mr. Lee. Fortunately, Nik valued restraint. She'd never play the fool or give anything away. Men like him used their looks to manipulate susceptible females like Shelby Whitholm. After all, he was on her short list of murder suspects, very near the top.

The Rampart viewing room was a popular place. As soon as Fuselli entered, a grim legal duo from Rampart converged upon them and joined the party. Everyone sat, silent and unsmiling, in stiff Old Testament poses, as if awaiting the final judgment.

Fuselli seemed oblivious to stress. He strode into the room with an air of command and a touch of swagger that Nik found reassuring. Things were spiraling out of control, threatening to overwhelm her world. She'd planned this trip as an intellectual diversion, something to take the edge off her grief. The clash of fantasy with reality brought Shelby's murder home, making this chess match with Jarrod seem pointless and puerile.

"I've got a search warrant," Fuselli announced, "Just a precaution. I don't intend to remove anything. Not yet, anyway."

Rampart's legal eagles nodded approvingly.

"Good job, Fuselli," Jarrod said. "You're thinking like a lawyer now."

Nicole stared at him. Was he a patronizing prick or simply dense? Either way, the learned Jarrod Whitholm must have zoned out when Yale gave the diplomacy course. His emotional intelligence was nonexistent.

"I'll take that as a compliment, Counselor." Fuselli gave Jarrod a patient smile. "Turns out, I am an attorney. American University alum. Good to see I haven't lost my skills."

Jarrod sputtered something unintelligible, feigning indignation to cloak his embarrassment. "What's he doing here?" He stabbed an accusatory finger at Alex.

"As they say on *Masterpiece Theatre*, Dr. Lee is assisting the police with their inquiries." Fuselli kept that smooth grin firmly in place. "I asked him to come, Jarrod. We need all the help we can get, and Alejandro is an expert on premium comics." He shrugged. "Besides, one more lawyer can only help things. Right?"

"Get on with it, man." Jarrod said. "I, for one, have plenty of questions."

"Okay," Fuselli said. "Shoot." He folded his arms, playing the nice guy. "Too bad you didn't contact me first. You knew we were checking storage facilities, Mr. Whitholm."

Nik jumped in before Jarrod sputtered himself to death. "That's my fault, Sheriff. I wanted to surprise Jarrod." She hid her face behind a curtain of black hair. "I'm sorry. I just didn't think it through."

Fuselli grunted. "I'm tempted to charge both of you with obstruction of justice. You're educated, intelligent people, and you know better. Fortunately, Dr. Lee came forward." His grin became a grimace. "A bit late, but he did it. We're on the same side here, people, finding Shelby's murderer."

Jarrod mumbled something about being an officer of the court.

"Bottom line time," Fuselli said. "Dr. Lee showed up two days before Shelby's murder to verify her collection. Had the approval codes and written permission from her to examine the loot."

"You said you never met her," Jarrod bristled. "How do we know you didn't take something?"

Alex showed no contrition. "A white lie. I said I didn't know her, and that's the truth. Apparently, you people didn't really know Shelby either. She was a complex woman." He paused, allowing the truth of his statement to sink in. "She sent me the paperwork several weeks ago. We met at Comic-Con, just as Nicole suspected. Naturally, we spoke on Skype, although I'm not certain that meets the legal definition of a meeting."

His amber eyes never left her face. She ignored them and those dimples, too. Shelby was vulnerable, easily flattered by the attention of a gorgeous, younger man. Any woman would be. Nicole silently cursed Alex Lee and the stirrings in her own body every time she looked at him. Far easier to train her eyes on Jarrod or Fuselli. They were safe, stolid men who posed no danger at all to her. Unfortunately, dimples trumped dependable every time. She turned back toward Alejandro Lee.

"If you've finished gaping, Nicole, we'd like to start." Jarrod supersized his frown. "Dr. Lee was about to explain his actions."

Fuselli waved his hand, giving the okay sign.

Alejandro Lee undulated like a Black Mamba, long, lean and lethal. He transfixed Nik, making every other man in the room disappear.

"First, let me emphasize that I had Ms. Whitholm's written permission to examine her collection." He brandished a sheet of paper and continued. "I'm certified to grade and evaluate pedigreed comic collections and ... "

"Hold on there," Jarrod interrupted. "I have no idea what you're talking about. I've just inherited this stuff, so explain the jargon."

Perfect white teeth flashed in a fleeting grin. "Of course. Ms. Nelson must be interested, too, since she's the co-owner." Alex tapped his iPad and looked up. "Pedigreed collections are nirvana, for a number of reasons. Okay, there are four criteria that are generally applied to pedigree collections: origin, quality, completeness and market acceptance."

His audience was zoning out, so Alex immediately changed tactics.

"Look, folks, it boils down to money. Big bucks. A topflight pedigreed collection can rake in several million dollars. Why, last year a single copy of Detective No. 27, sold for well over a million dollars."

That got everyone's attention. Bob Rochford mopped his brow; the lawyers' eyes brightened; Fuselli took notes.

"Are you suggesting that my aunt has that kind of thing, Lee? I demand to know." Jarrod folded his arms and puffed out his cheeks, giving his best bulldog imitation.

Alejandro's shrug was full of insolence. "Shelby had a lot of interesting pieces, all right, but she might have something even better: an Ashcan."

Silence followed the announcement. No one, especially Jarrod Whitholm, got the joke. Only Nicole stirred.

"Good Lord," she gasped. Jett had been right on the money. "Isn't that ... didn't I hear something about that? The Holy Grail, they called it. Listed for five million dollars."

"This thing keeps getting weirder," Fuselli said. "What the hell was a retired librarian doing with that kind of loot?"

"*Quien sabe*? I can't say for sure that Shelby has or had it. All I know is she hinted about an Ashcan Flash comic graded at 9.6. That's as close to mint as you can get." The unflappable Mr. Lee paused as though he, too, was overwhelmed. "Someone listed that on eBay for just shy of five million last summer. The sale fell through, but the rumor mill went wild. That's all they could talk about at Comic-Con."

"You think my aunt listed that ... that Ashcan thing on eBay? That's pretty fanciful, Lee. She wasn't part of some exotic scheme." Jarrod pursed his lips. "Glamorous, she wasn't. She was pulling your leg, Lee. Shelby loved puncturing a person's vanity." He sighed. "She did it to me often enough."

Bob Rochford struggled for control. "What the hell is an Ashcan Flash comic? How would I even know it was here?"

Alex waited until the room was tomb silent. "Ashcans are the rarest of comics, almost a myth in the collector world. They're discussed by aficionados in whispered conversations late at night after too many drinks."

No one spoke or even dared to breathe. This time his audience was spellbound, entranced by a tale that might have led to murder.

"Ashcans weren't real comics," Alex said. "They were legal proofs, made to secure copyrights. Most of them didn't even have much text between the covers." He saw their blank looks and tried again. "Think of those rare stamps that were never issued because of a flaw. Most Ashcans went right into the trash after they served their purpose. Rarity trumps everything else in the collector's world. When something's unique, the only one in the world, a collector will do anything to acquire it."

"Even murder?" Fuselli asked.

Alex nodded. "Perhaps."

Rochford sent out for sandwiches and coffee, plenty of coffee, as everyone claimed a seat at the table. Nicole sat next to Fuselli, as far away from the addictive Alejandro Lee as space permitted. She was a firm believer in self-control, even if she didn't always practice it. Besides, Fuselli was old enough to be her elder brother at least. More like an uncle, a kindly uncle. Safe harbor when her hormones raged.

"Shelby Whitholm was quite a lady," Alex said. "Smart, tough and not too trusting. She acquired the Whitholm Collection stealthily over many years. She told me that she'd started collecting when she was a kid. Her dad started her off, gave her some golden agers he'd had for years. Her brother liked baseball cards, but Shelby loved comics. She never cared much for girly things, and her father approved."

Jarrod narrowed his eyes. "My dad had trading cards. That's true. He gave me a bunch of them when I graduated from Yale. Danny hit the roof, called them dust catchers. The joke's on her if they're worth something after all." He tugged his tie when he saw Nicole staring at him.

Alex continued. "From what I saw, Shelby had herself an exceptional pedigree collection, one of the best finds made in several decades since the Mile Highs first surfaced." When he saw hands raised, he laughed and explained about the various pedigreed collections. "She sent me a partial inventory. Just a teaser, but it was enough to make me pack my bag and head to Cape Cod. You see, comics are graded on a scale from one to ten. Shelby said she had lots of stock in the eight to nine range. That translates to a sizable sum."

Fuselli interrupted for the first time. "What did you find last week when you came to Rampart?"

"I did a quick inventory," Alex sighed. "Just one hundred or so. Her storage vault's full of them, and man, are they beautiful. White, white pages, crisp spines. Pristine condition."

"Give us a rough estimate," Jarrod said, "just to whet our appetites."

Alex cooled his ardor and acted like an attorney who'd been inoculated with caution at law school. He gave a neutral smile and shrugged. "Oh, a couple hundred thousand easy, but don't hold me to it, counselor. I didn't grade every one of them. No time for it then."

"What about this Ashcan thing?" Jarrod asked. "The rest is just chump change. How do we know what you really found on your little excursion?"

Alex's features resembled exquisitely carved marble. "You don't." He faced Jarrod head-on. "Believe what you will, but I saw no trace of it. At least, nothing that jumped right out at me. We made a date, Shelby and I, to discuss everything." Alex sighed. "That didn't happen, of course."

The Rampart attorneys shifted in their seats. Finally, Bob Rochford cleared his throat and voiced their concerns.

"Sheriff, we pride ourselves on precise, accurate inventories of our clients' possessions. I confess this is most disquieting. Ms. Whitholm, well, quite frankly, she misled me. The entire contents are insured for only one hundred thousand dollars. I have a listing for Dr. Lee to work with, if that'll help, but it's damn awkward."

Jarrod mumbled under his breath until his frustration boiled over. "We have no way of knowing if half of what this so-called expert says is true. He might have stolen this Ashcan himself."

Fuselli adjusted his glasses and scanned a text message. "Think for a minute. If he'd taken it, why would he stick around Goodhaven? Mayor Haas is Shelby's executor, as you know. He's commissioned Dr. Lee to catalogue your aunt's entire collection for estate purposes."

"What?" Jarrod yipped. "Talk about the fox and the hen house."

"Enough." Fuselli's frown quieted them all. "I assume you'll have someone work with Dr. Lee," he said looking at Rochford.

Jarrod Whitholm leapt to his feet. "Come on, Nicole. We're done here."

Eleven

Nicole felt uneasy as she trailed Jarrod out of the room. No one had mentioned the two strangers impersonating Shelby and Jarrod. Who were they, and what had they taken? They'd arrived the day after the murder with all the codes and authorizations. The film was grainy, and both impersonators wisely kept their backs to the camera. The only thing she knew was that one was male and the other female. Shelby would never have willingly surrendered those codes. That spelled a motive for murder.

"Why didn't you say something?" she asked Jarrod. "Aren't you curious? After all, they used your name. You might be implicated."

He ignored her, striding purposefully toward his Hummer, fists clenched, jaw locked.

"I'm speaking to you, Jarrod Whitholm."

"I'll soon be deaf if you keep bellowing like a fishwife. Wait 'til we get to the car." He opened the passenger door and helped Nicole in. "There. I didn't want to discuss things with that crowd milling around. Plenty of time to grill Fuselli tomorrow." He shot her an evil grin. "Unless you have private channels, of course."

"Don't be absurd. You're disgusting." She did five minutes of yoga breathing until the crisis passed.

"You okay?" Jarrod asked as he edged into traffic and dodged a car hauler. "You were panting like a dog. I thought for a minute you might keel over."

Limited exposure to Jarrod Whitholm was preferable. Small doses. Nicole conquered the urge to punch his patrician nose.

"Let's get something straight," she said. "I have nothing against money. In fact, I like it more than most. Certainly need it more than you do. Right now, I only care about one thing, finding Shelby's murderer. I owe it to her. *We* owe it to her." Nik fumbled for her handkerchief and mopped her eyes. "She suffered, Jarrod. Horribly. I can't forget that. I won't."

He set the cruise control for seventy and focused on surviving the homicidal impulses of Boston drivers. When they reached Route 3, Jarrod relaxed and cast a sideways glance at Nik.

"You don't know me. Not really. And you definitely don't know much about my relationship with my aunt." He gripped the steering wheel of the steel beast as if it might fly away. "My mom died when I was five. Shelby was the one constant in my life after that. Oh, my dad meant well, but his job was his life. Yale was his real child, not me. The summers I spent on the Cape with Shelby were … magical." Color suffused his face, and Nik figured this was as close to a revelation as she'd get with Jarrod. She nodded.

"We didn't always agree. Hell, we fought like cats and dogs about things. Especially politics. Shelby was a real bleeding heart, as you know. She didn't approve of Danny either, but you probably figured that one out, too."

His smile was rather attractive. Nicole hadn't noticed that before. Buried beneath that Yankee rectitude, Jarrod Whitholm had a sense of humor. Who knew?

"So you agree with me then?" she asked. "We need to help Fuselli."

Jarrod growled an expletive. "Wait a damn minute. You're just interested in hanging around that pretty boy, and I'm not talking about Fuselli."

Patience, Nik told herself. We don't need another Whitholm murdered. "I have a plan, if you're willing to listen."

He paused a full minute before replying as if he were considering his options. "Let's hear it."

Nicole spent the rest of the trip sketching out her proposal. Jarrod stayed relatively silent, interrupting occasionally with cogent, well-reasoned questions and observations.

"So," he said after she'd finished, "you think there might be a local component to this murder? Something unrelated to the whole comic book charade?"

Nicole squirmed. "I'm not sure but it's worth considering. You know what Shelby was like. Let's face it, she was nosey. Got under people's skin. Especially some of the locals."

Jarrod scratched his chin and nodded. "Okay. Give me some examples. I know most of the names, but that's about it."

Fortunately, he was absorbed with taking evasive action against two teenagers in a Jeep Wrangler, who drove as if they were immortal.

"Shit!" he roared. "Those homicidal little bastards should be arrested!"

Nicole Nelson knew how to soothe the savage breast of any man. She'd done it so many times, it came naturally. After a few comforting words, she started her narrative.

"We have to consider the political angle. Shelby never missed a town meeting, and she researched every proposal until it bled ink. Mayor Haas argued with her over taxes, and his wife threw a hissy fit when Shelby targeted her." Nik paused. "I actually think that Mandy hated her."

"Who's Mandy?" Jarrod asked.

"Mrs. Haas, Morgan's wife. For heaven's sake, man, keep up."

Jarrod shrugged. "Oh, that skinny woman, the one who looks like Olive Oyl? She wouldn't be strong enough to kill Shelby. She was one tough old bird."

"Not tough enough," Nik muttered under her breath, "and don't forget Harris Goldman. He's a despicable man."

Jarrod harrumphed. "That old guy, the professor? Get real. He has to be eighty if he's a day. Maybe you should accuse someone who's at least ambulatory. Besides, what motive would he have to kill Shelby? Tell me that."

His scorn was eroding her confidence, but Nicole was resilient. She'd had to be in order to survive.

"Harris Goldman is no pushover, believe you me. He's a survivor, a cockroach. Don't buy his learned professor shtick either. He and Shelby locked horns over Lifelines, and he backed down in a hurry. Shelby had something on him. I'm sure of it."

When they sailed past Hyannis, Yarmouthport and Dennis with no problem, Jarrod relaxed. "What about your other admirer? What's his name, Jett?"

"Jett! He and Shelby loved each other. She never missed their Monday chess games, and she brought him a bunch of customers. Nope, that's a dead end."

" Hmm. Interesting choice of words."

Nicole had to say it. "Ms. Stevens had plenty of motive."

"Danny?" Jarrod wrenched the steering wheel to the right. "What the hell has she got to do with this mess?"

His patience is at the breaking point, Nik thought. He was longing for the cushy life he'd had just a week ago. Intellectual stimulus at work and raw sex provided by Danielle Stevens. Most men would go for that. Not that he and Danny debated Keynesian economics or spent much time discussing anything substantive. Nik doubted that Danielle could even spell Keynes, let alone explain his theories. Woman like her didn't have to. They had more graphic ways of communicating. Nicole winced at her own cattiness. She had chosen to exploit her mind instead of her body. Why be jealous of a creature like Danielle who took advantage of her own assets?

They were in Goodhaven before she realized it, parked in front of Shelby's old Tudor. Fire damage had been minimal, mostly confined to the front eaves. Still, the house looked abandoned, almost sad.

Jarrod pointed at the mailbox. "Look at that stupid sign Shelby plopped in front of her flowers: Friends for Peace. Huh! Lots of good it did her. She was arrogant, my aunt. Thought nothing bad would ever touch her."

"I don't see it that way. Shelby had courage. She believed in doing the right thing." Nicole gathered her purse and eased onto the Hummer's running board. "I've got to work on my dissertation tonight, but call me if anything comes up." She hadn't deliberately used a double entendre, but if the quip fit …. "You'll be at Danielle's, I presume?"

"Wait a minute." Jarrod seemed chastened, as if he were responsible for her. "You're so reckless. Be careful. You can't just go poking around a murder scene without stirring up stuff. My aunt knew her murderer. Remember that. It was someone she trusted at least enough to open the door to. Goodhaven isn't the idyllic place tourists think it is."

"You're right. Thanks for the warning. I'll keep it in mind." Nik waved at him and ran into the carriage house just in time to catch the phone.

"I thought I'd missed you." Alex's voice was deep and sultry, the kind of sound that captivated most women. Nicole wasn't like the rest; he knew that with a certainty that stunned him. To Alex love was a fantasy, an illusion that had capsized men throughout history. It wouldn't happen to him. Never had, never would. Love was a luxury he couldn't afford. Until now.

"I just got in," she said. "Let me catch my breath."

He laughed. "Good. I was afraid I'd interrupted something. I'm using my cell."

"What? No!" Nicole stammered like an ingénue. "Very funny, Dr. Lee."

Alex swallowed a laugh and visualized her, flushing from embarrassment. She thought she was sophisticated, but Nicole was charmingly naïve. Way too charming.

"You mentioned a spot where the locals hang out. Crazy Eights, I think you called it."

"Yes. It's near the harbor, across from the water. Nothing fancy, though. You'd probably hate it."

Alex paused. "Not if you were with me. How about showing me this place in person tonight? I haven't had a decent meal all day."

"Sorry. I have to work on my dissertation."

"I might be able to help you. I'm a double threat, remember? Economist and lawyer. Great combo."

He could tell she was weakening. Her voice softened as the conversation progressed. Alex couldn't fool himself. He'd spent too much time thinking about her perfect skin, lustrous hair and tiny waist. And those breasts! World class by any standard, assuming they were real. He slipped into the timeless role of hunter, a legacy as primitive as man himself. When he'd conquered her, he could shed the obsession and concentrate on business. Unless the unthinkable happened. There was still a chance that Nicole Nelson would turn the tables and conquer him.

"Come on," Alex wheedled. "You have to eat. I promise to behave." The tone of his voice hinted otherwise. "If I speed, I can be at your doorstep in thirty minutes flat."

"Slow down, big boy," she said. "Make it an hour."

It took forty-five minutes. When Alex Lee knocked on her door, Nicole peered out the window and gasped. The man was perfect from his crisply pressed cords to his cashmere jacket. She groped blindly for a lipstick, anything to improve her appearance. Despite good intentions, a phone call from her thesis advisor had gobbled up almost all of her prep time. Still, she'd changed into her favorite sweater and paired it with her best black jeans. She'd been told that red was her color and Alejandro's dancing eyes corroborated that.

"Wow," he said, "you look great. I'll have to fight off every man in the place."

"Don't count on it. The weeknight crowd is fairly sedate." She hugged Foo Dog, doused the lights and followed Alex to his car. "How'd you guys get back so soon? Another helicopter ride?"

Alex shivered. "Worse. Some state trooper barely old enough to shave drove us back to Goodhaven with sirens blaring." He shook his head. "My ears are still buzzing. Maybe we should walk to this place."

"Whatever. I guess you'll be staying near Boston while you do the evaluation." Nik scrubbed emotion from her voice.

"We'll see," he shrugged. "I don't mind a long commute when it's worth it." There was no mistaking the look in those amber eyes. Alex took her hand and kissed it. Nothing improper about it at all, no sir, but Nicole felt a tingling in her nether parts anyway.

As they walked the five blocks to Crazy Eights, she peppered the conversation with comic book questions. By block four Alejandro stopped, put his hands over his ears and pleaded for mercy.

"Give me a break. I want to spend the night relaxing with a beautiful woman and eating Goodhaven oysters. Enough about the damn comics."

Social courtesy was important to Nicole. Her mother had emphasized handling every situation deftly, like the lady that she was. Not tonight. Not this time. Shelby's murder cried out for justice, no matter how much Alejandro Lee whined.

She planted herself in front of him, blocking his path. "I'll relax when my friend's murderer is behind bars. If that's old-fashioned, so be it. Now, will you help me or not?"

His response was quick and decisive. He kissed her, a long, lingering kiss that promised nothing and assumed too much. Instead of resisting, she found herself leaning forward, answering the heat of his lips with some of her own. It was dangerous, foolhardy and absolutely sublime.

"I thought the entertainment was inside," a harsh voice said. "My mistake." Harris Goldman wrinkled his nose. He'd been spying; Nik was certain of that. Distain spread across his wizened face like jam.

"Something wrong, Dr. Goldman?" She tried her wide-eyed waif routine as she peeled herself off Alex.

Alex loomed over the old man and grinned. "We have something in common, sir. My best friend teaches at Columbia." His tone suggested that the grin was only pretext. Goldman got the message loud and clear.

"I left Columbia long ago," he said, scuttling through the door without a backward glance. "See you inside."

"He's vermin," Nicole spat, "plague-carrying vermin."

"Cool it. Don't let the old grouch spoil our night." Alex winked and held the door open.

The joint was jumping that evening. Despite a discreet placard announcing that Crazy Eights was closed for a private party, half the town huddled around the stone fireplace in the main dining room. Their eyes swiveled toward the newcomer, giving Alex Lee a gender-based appraisal. Men checked out his size and calculated his professional status and bank balance; women eyed his lithe form, sensuous smile and flowing locks.

"You're here for the service," their waiter said, pointing to an inner room. "This way, please." The private space was aglow with candlelight and nothing else.

"Watch your step," Alex warned, grasping Nik's arm over the uneven wooden planks. They exchanged puzzled glances. Was this the private party?

"Uh-oh, incoming. There goes my quiet night of oysters." Alex pointed to the table in the center of the room that was filled with some very familiar faces. Morgan and Amanda Haas, plus Harris Goldman and Jett Hall had formed an unlikely alliance this evening, clinking glasses and breaking bread with Jarrod and Danielle.

Jarrod pushed back his chair and charged over to them. His clenched jaw and flushed face betrayed him, showing the telltale signs of Whitholm ire. He seemed stuck between rage and chagrin.

"You said you had to study," Jarrod hissed at Nicole. "What's he, your tutor?"

Alex nodded, giving Jarrod his nice guy grin. "Precisely. I'm tutoring her in economics. I must say that she's an excellent pupil. Straight A student."

"It's an impromptu memorial for my aunt," Jarrod told Nik. "I would have invited you otherwise."

"Come join us, Dr. Lee. There's plenty of space." Danielle Stevens slithered to their side, giving Alex a smile full of promise as she gestured toward the empty seats. She angled her body to block Nik's view. "We've been waiting for you."

"Sounds like fun," Alex said. "Shall we?" He herded Nicole toward the larger table.

"Well, well, well. I wondered where you were, Double N. Take a seat." Jett seemed delighted at the chance to edge out his rival. He made a show out of settling Nicole into a chair beside him. "Now you'll have to hold hands with me. It's part of the ceremony."

"Ceremony?"

Jarrod immediately bristled. "Oh, for God's sake! What is this? Kindergarten? I should never have come. We'll all look like fools."

For once, Jett stood toe to toe with him. "But you did, Whitholm. So come on. Be a good sport and play along."

Nicole was puzzled. This was weird even for Jett. "What's going on?"

"Nothing special," Jett grinned. "A few friends remembering Shelby. I thought you knew. Mandy suggested it. Seems she has psychic abilities we never knew about."

"You should like this, Dr. Lee. Very California, spirits and such." Jarrod looked ready to bolt at any moment. Danielle patted his arm with more menace than comfort.

"We Californians do like the *avant garde*." Alex shrugged. "Keeps things interesting."

A derisive snort, sounding suspiciously like Harris Goldman's split the air. Nicole couldn't be certain. At his age it might be a death rattle.

Minutes ticked by slowly, echoing the heartbeats of everyone in the room. Jett squeezed Nicole's hand as the room temperature changed from comfy to chilly. His fingers felt like icy claws stabbing her palms. Foolishness, Nik knew that. Nonsense, but compelling nevertheless. Shelby would have gotten a hoot out of the whole thing, especially Mandy's bid for center stage.

Amanda Haas shuddered. Had her husband not moved closer to her, she might have fainted. Something in the room had changed. Jett moved to the edge of his seat, nudging

Nik's shoulder with his in a display of naked angst. Some protector he'd be, she thought. Needs his own nanny.

"She's here," Mandy wailed in a thin reedy voice, closing her eyes and swaying back and forth. "Oh, Shelby, you're among friends. Tell us. Who murdered you?"

The silence in the room was crushing, affecting even skeptics like Jarrod. His rigid posture proved that.

"Oh, Shelby, you suffered so much." Mandy raised her skeletal arm and pointed toward the double wooden doors. "Tell us. Free your spirit."

The doors parted with a sudden whoosh of wind, and Mandy slumped toward the floor.

Twelve

Fuselli charged into the room, catching Mandy before she hit her head. "What the hell's going on here?" he yelled. "Don't any of you have any sense? Mayor Haas! I'm surprised that you'd allow this spectacle."

With the lights on, the terrors of the past half-hour receded. Morgan Haas straightened his jacket and pushed back his chair, grinning sheepishly. "You made quite an entrance, Fuselli. Caught us acting silly." He gestured toward Mandy. "My wife thought she could reach Shelby's spirit. Guess not."

"I felt her," Jett stammered. "Shelby. She was with us, I know it."

Jarrod curled his lip and snorted. "For fuck's sake, man, get a grip. You're embarrassing yourself. My aunt was murdered by some vagrant or druggie desperate for a fix. She never listened to warnings."

"You sound like a guilty man, Whitholm. Share your theories with all of us." Harris Goldman's smirk was wider than a fishing trawler. "After all, you came out on top. You and Ms. Nelson."

"You little worm. If you weren't already senile, I'd deck you." Jarrod's ears went tomato red.

"Calm down," Fuselli glowered at them. His eyes fixed on Alex's tranquil face. "Why so calm, Dr. Lee? Don't believe in the supernatural?"

Alex's smile was one inch short of insolence. "I'm a lawyer, Sheriff. I don't believe in anything."

Nicole didn't speak right away. She feared she might make a fool of herself, but Danielle had no such qualms.

"Something strange happened in here," she said. "Even the temperature changed. And when that dog barked .... it was so like Shelby. She loved animals more than her own flesh and blood."

Fuselli's eyes held a quiet fire that was more impressive than rage. "You don't get it, do you? None of you people do. I doubt very much that Shelby Whitholm visited you tonight." He paced the length of the table and stopped. "What you felt—what I believe happened—was something much more frightening. You felt the presence of evil tonight. I believe the murderer is in here now. Stop playing around with this, or one of you might join Shelby in heaven."

After Fuselli's pronouncement the room emptied in five minutes flat. No one wanted to linger. Alex kept a firm hand on Nicole's shoulder, shepherding her out of Crazy Eights into the crisp night air. For a time they walked in silence, each content to ponder the evening's events. When they spoke, it was in cautious, measured tones.

"What happened in there?" Nicole asked. "Was Fuselli serious?"

Alex sighed and shook his head. "Who knows? Screwing around with this stuff can be dangerous. I agree with him. Someone in that room murdered Shelby Whitholm. The light was too dim to watch faces, but someone was spewing fear big time. I felt it."

Nicole swiveled toward him. "What do you mean? Tell me. You know more than you admit, especially about this Ashcan thing."

"Stay out of this, Nicole. Please. You might get hurt, and I couldn't stand that. Let Fuselli handle everything. He's trained for it." Alex drew her close, hugging her until she yelped.

The growl of an engine made them step aside. Nicole recognized it without even turning around. It was the aggressive rumble of Jarrod Whitholm's Hummer.

"Hop in," he said. "We need to talk."

Danielle wound a cashmere muffler around her slender neck and pouted. Apparently her idea of a fun date did not include Nicole Nelson. A threesome involving Alex Lee was probably more her taste.

Alex opened the rear door and boosted Nicole in. "Riding in style, I see. Shelby mentioned something about this behemoth."

"Shelby was a mass of contradictions," Jarrod said. "An environmentalist who smoked like a chimney? A hermit who lived like a pauper when she was worth millions? At least I admit my vices. Hell, I embrace them."

He swung the Hummer to the right, prompting Danielle to wake up and join the conversation.

"Shelby was a joke. Why would anyone brag about buying T-shirts at K-mart and wearing them until they rotted? Disgusting." She rolled her eyes at the thought. "And she spied on people. Nosey. Always creeping around. Shelby was no better than Harris Goldman."

Nicole was torn between defending her friend and ignoring both of them. Friendship won out.

"Shelby was kind and generous," she said.

"Of course you'd say that," Danielle hissed. "You tricked her into leaving you millions. Who knows? Maybe you killed her."

"Me!" Nicole squeaked. Fortunately Alejandro intervened, averting a verbal smackdown.

"Cool it, ladies. After all, you have a mutual interest in solving this puzzle. We all do." He grinned. "Assuming, of course, that *you* didn't murder Shelby."

"Us? What about you, Lee? For all we know, you may have killed her for this Ashcan thing." Jarrod took a deep breath and powered down. He parked the beast in Shelby's driveway and extinguished the lights. "Come on. I have the makings of a nightcap in here if you're interested."

"Count me in," Alex said. "We need clarity of thought."

After wrestling open the front door, Jarrod waved them inside. "That new lock is stiff as hell," he said. "A small price to pay for peace of mind, I guess. Go on into the main room. Aunt Shelby's horsehair sofa is murder."

An uncomfortable silence descended. Murder, that cruel, harsh word, cast a pall on everyone. Used carelessly in the home of a victim, it shouted rather than whispered.

Jarrod tousled his hair, looking abashed. "Hey, I'm sorry. Tiptoeing around every little thing is tough." He disappeared into the kitchen, returning with a pitcher of martinis. "Hope this is okay. I couldn't find anything else."

Martinis. Nicole flashed back to Shelby Whitholm once more. How she loved martinis! Called them the only civilized cocktail. Nik pictured her standing there, holding the silver shaker aloft. Evenings at six were martini time in this household. Shelby loved the ritual, reveled in it. Nicole wasn't much of a drinker, but she'd dutifully joined in, sipping cautiously while Shelby reminisced.

Shelby seemed very much alive in that room, the chatelaine in residence, watching her guests imbibe. When Alex proposed a toast, some of the tension dissipated. He rose slowly, drinking in every ounce of drama. "To Shelby Whitholm, quite a lady."

Danielle downed her drink and shivered. "Mandy seemed way too calm tonight. She's usually a basket case even over normal things. I say she was either drugged or faking."

Nik hunkered down in her jacket, trying to get warm.

"Forget about that kook for a minute." Jarrod sprang up and started pacing. "Come clean with us, Lee. What's the bottom line on this Ashcan thing?"

Composure was Alejandro's middle name. He gave a superior smile and spread his hands. "I've told you everything so far. When I finish grading Shelby's collection, you'll be the first to know, after Nicole."

Alex turned toward Nicole, sending a searing glance her way that turned her into mush. She had mixed emotions about Alejandro Lee, but in this instance Nicole longed to leap into his arms and damn the consequences. She turned away, summoning her cool, analytical self. Alex was still a murder suspect, even though he was the hottest man she'd ever kissed.

"Maybe we should consider something else," she said. "Danielle was right. Shelby did a lot of snooping into other people's business. If she kept records, the police haven't found them yet — or mentioned it if they did."

Danielle fluffed her shiny bob. "That's your big plan, Nicole, digging up petty secrets on our neighbors? Count me out. I do business with these people."

They'd reached a stalemate. Both women staked their claim, forcing the men to take sides. Jarrod answered the challenge by punting.

"Let's table that for now," he said. "If Fuselli's right, someone in there killed my aunt. Anyone care to speculate?"

Alex's face was granite smooth. "You're a lawyer, too, Whitholm. Making accusations is a risky proposition, wouldn't you say?"

"Not really," Jarrod said. "We're among friends, friends of Shelby."

Nicole surprised herself by speaking up. "I agree. Why not evaluate each person by a standard: motive, means, opportunity. It's a cliché, but so what?"

She pulled her iPad from her bag and tapped. "Start with mayor Haas. He has a lot to lose, and Shelby said she had a poison pill to use on him. Her words, not mine."

Danielle uncoiled her long, lithe body from the chair and beckoned her fiancé. "Take me home, Jarrod. This is foolish. I'm not wasting any more of my time."

To Nik's surprise Jarrod showed some spunk. Maybe that taste of heaven Danielle bragged about was getting old. He waved her away and turned toward Nicole. "Okay. Let's start. Morgan Haas, former financial guru and mayor of our esteemed town. What's his motive? I hear he has major bucks."

"Might be an illusion," Alex said. "Plenty of those guys live in a house of cards. Maybe Shelby threatened to topple it."

Nicole wrinkled her brow. "She had something on him. Remember Shelby was an ace researcher. She prided herself on that. I don't think she would have exposed anyone's secrets, but she loved knowing them. Kind of a power thing, I guess."

Jarrod nodded. "Okay. You follow up. Research the financial press, anything that might tell us something. He was in Goodhaven that day, and Shelby would have let him in without thinking." He grimaced. "Those money guys are sharks. Haas might have the stones to handcuff an old lady and beat her to death."

"Huh! I'd put money on Amanda Haas before her husband." Danielle's tone was tinged with bitterness. "Social standing is everything to that woman, and she loathed Shelby. Made no secret about it."

"So what's her motive? Same as her husband's? Worth checking out, I suppose. That's your assignment, Danny, if you'll agree to it." He paused. "Status means a lot to people. Harris Goldman prances around spouting all that nonsense, trading on his professorship and Ph.D. Maybe he's a phony. Everyone in Goodhaven just accepted him, after all." Jarrod bit his lip. "Let me check him out. I've got some pull at Columbia. That's where he allegedly got his degrees."

"I guess that leaves me," Alejandro said. "Jett Hall said he's interested in comics, so that gives us a bond." Alex shrugged. "Personally, I think he's interested in Nicole, but together she and I might pry some information loose from him. It's worth a try."

They sipped their drinks in companionable silence, digesting assignments and planning strategies. Despite the warmth of the oak logs crackling in the fireplace, Nicole felt chilled. Until Shelby died Goodhaven had been her refuge, a place where neighbors cared about each other and their town. That illusion had been shattered, replaced by suspicion and a nagging sense of menace that lurked among the simple storefronts and familiar faces.

The antique tall case clock chimed the hour, startling her. Oh, my Lord! Midnight. Foo Dog would be frantic. The cats would be royally peeved, and they'd make her pay in the way that only felines can. Nicole leapt to her feet, narrowly avoiding a collision with Alex Lee.

"Steady, girl," he said softly, grabbing her arm. "Ready to go home?"

Jarrod Whitholm scowled. "Home? Don't tell you're my neighbor, too. Moved in, have you, Lee?"

They stood toe to toe, taking each other's measure, gladiators locked in a testosterone tunnel. Nicole wondered idly which one would prevail in a struggle. They were the same height, but Jarrod was bigger boned. On the other hand, Alejandro Lee had the quick, lithe movements of a jungle cat. Her money was on him.

"It's certainly tempting," Alex said smoothly, "with the beautiful scenery. But rest easy, Whitholm. I'm still staying at the Inn." He helped Nicole into her jacket, guiding her toward the door. "Let's report back in two days. That should give me time to finish cataloging the collection."

The carriage house was close, only yards from the main building. They walked slowly, prolonging the moment and the intimacy that they shared. When they reached her door, Nicole handed Alex the key. She suddenly felt weary, too bone-tired to move, let alone wrestle with the lock.

He swung the door open with one deft twist, as Confucius charged the door. "I'll check the house just to make sure everything's okay," Alex said, patting the dog, "although your guard dog probably has everything under control."

Nicole closed her eyes, savoring the faint woodsy scent of his cologne. It was Bond No. 9. She'd smelled that once while browsing at Louis, the most exclusive specialty store in Boston. It left her spellbound, so engrossed in pleasure that she zoned out, oblivious to everything. When he touched her hair with long, languid strokes, Nicole jumped back.

"Hey. What's wrong?" Alex asked. "I know it's been crazy tonight. I'll just leave."

She gazed at him, watching those amber eyes soften. "Don't go, Alex," she said. "I don't want to be alone. Stay with me tonight."

Thirteen

As she fired up the Bialetti the next morning, Nicole's hands shook with remembered shame or passion. She didn't know which. Maybe both. Reliving the touch of his hands sliding down her skin and the gentle firmness of his lips as they explored her body made her flush. *I'm no vestal virgin,* she thought. *Why is he so different from anyone I've ever known?*

Alejandro Lee was everything she had hoped for and feared, a consummate lover with eyes that bored into her soul, hands that knew every inch of her and lips that whispered endearments. It wasn't just his physical perfection, although God knows that would have been enough for most women. His tenderness overwhelmed her. He made Nicole feel cherished, protected from the chaos surrounding her. She hadn't felt safe in a very long time. Not since her parents died.

"You're up early," he said, suddenly appearing in the doorway. His smile melted her soul like sealing wax. She fought to regain control. After all, Alex was a stranger—a relative stranger, anyhow—and caution was required. She might lose her life as easily as her heart if he were involved in Shelby's murder.

"Espresso?" she asked holding a cup aloft. "I'm afraid I'm addicted to it."

He moved swiftly, imprisoning her in his arms, softly brushing his lips up and down her neck. "There are worse addictions, my love, although I could use that caffeine buzz."

Nicole clutched her coffee cup as if her sanity was at stake. She feared that it might be.

"You have a long drive ahead of you. Let me fill the thermos." Rituals were useful. Comforting. They let her avoid those amber eyes and make a stab at normalcy.

He must have read her mind. Alex tilted her chin upward, forcing her to face him. "Don't do this, Nicole. Don't pull away from me now. Okay?"

She nodded and spun out of his grasp. "I've got an appointment at town hall this morning. Mayor Haas promised me copies of the minutes so that I can analyze them. It's a big part of my dissertation."

His frown was a thing of beauty, rather like a thundercloud straight from Mt. Olympus. "Can't you wait until I'm back? Haas might be dangerous, you know."

Nicole knew how easy it would be to give in. Everything she'd fought for—independence, confidence and strength—could be sapped by yielding to this magnificent male. Such sweet surrender was tempting but ill advised. It came with a huge price tag.

"Thanks. Don't worry about me. I'll be on guard. Morgan has been very helpful so far. Besides, he'd be suspicious if I suddenly started avoiding him."

Alex silently sipped his espresso. "You're not sure about me, are you? That was very brave of you, Nicole. Spending the night with someone you considered a potential murderer."

She buried her face in Annabel's soft fur, comforted by the cat's steady purr. "Thanks for the compliment, but I don't deserve it. Courage is a virtue I'm still working on. Anyhow, my pet brigade was here to defend me." Nicole handed him the thermos. "You were a big hit with Danielle, by the way. She told me so."

"Hmm. That woman is a man-eater from way back. Jarrod must sleep with one eye open around her." Alex thrust a vellum business card at her. "Here's my number. Keep it handy in case you need it. And listen to me for a change. Be careful with Morgan Haas." With a sharp nod of his head, Alejandro Lee gathered his things and stomped out the door.

Alex didn't like Fuselli, but he respected him. His sources in D.C. described the sheriff as a top-notch lawyer and investigator. Smart and honest, a good combination in Alex's book. Before driving to Boston, he popped into the police station for a quick chat with the lawman. Nicole would be livid if she knew, but that was a risk Alex was willing to take. Something wasn't right. He could feel it. Goodhaven looked like a postcard-perfect town, but that was pure illusion. Currier and Ives. A murderer with Nicole in his sights hid among those smiling faces and homey storefronts. Alex shook his head. Can't assume that the killer's a man. Lots of women today were strong and motivated. Strong enough to subdue an old woman, mean enough to wield a club. He shivered as he pictured Nicole with her lofty ideals and head full of nonsense doing battle with a killer. That wouldn't happen. Couldn't happen. He'd make sure of it.

Maybe Fuselli was right. Alex suspected that Shelby's comic collection had tempted someone beyond reason. Maybe she'd told someone, let it slip that she had a fortune sitting somewhere. He hoped it wasn't Jarrod, but as her nephew he had to be suspect number one. Blood: thicker than water and twice as messy.

Times were tough for a lot of people, and Shelby was often cocky, even cruel, in her dealings with others. Alex had seen that himself. He'd also seen her corpse. The stark brutality had sickened him. It seemed so personal that he doubted the murderer was a stranger. He or she was probably an acquaintance or even a friend, someone Nicole might know and trust.

Nicole. It always came down to her. Alex yearned to protect her, shield her from harm. Maybe he was getting soft. Maybe he was in love. Neither possibility thrilled him.

"Dr. Lee. What a surprise." Fuselli's face suggested that the surprise wasn't a pleasant one. Although the sheriff was neatly pressed and polished, he wore worry like an ill-fitting suit.

"Sorry to interrupt. You seem busy." Alex stared at Fuselli's empty desk and soiled coffee cup to make his point.

"Let me think. I've burned half my overtime budget and all my shoe leather, and I'm no closer to finding Shelby Whitholm's murderer than I was last week. Her nephew is thumping his chest and name-dropping about calling in more competent help, and damn it to hell, I can't even blame him." Fuselli patted his pocket. "God, I wish I still smoked. Right about now I could use a cigarette."

Alex raised his eyebrows. "Jarrod's not so bad, if you know the type."

That made Fuselli grin. "Oh, I know the type. Do I ever. Washington, D.C., is full of self-important men with fancy girlfriends, itching for a fight." He took a deep breath and clenched his fist. "It's been five days, and the trail's colder than Aunt Maude's freezer. I know, I'm positive, that this thing is local, probably related to that damn comic collection." Fuselli put his head in his hands and massaged his temples. "Not that Shelby was beloved. More people feared her than loved her."

"Why commit murder, if not for a big payoff?" Alex was genuinely curious.

"You jest, counselor. Folks find all kinds of things to kill for. Greed, money, love, hate, pick anything. Even lowlifes grappling in an alley have some kind of motive, something that makes sense to them."

"What did you make of that memorial service last night?"

Fuselli grabbed his pencil and snapped it in two. "Of all the stupid, foolhardy stunts ... oops. You caught me before my caffeine kicked in." He got up and poured more coffee. "Want some?"

"No, thanks. Nicole packed me a thermos." Alex saw Fuselli's face darken.

"Nicole. Got her playing housewife already, have you, Dr. Lee? Good for you."

Alex tried to salvage a bit of good will. "Is there anything I can do to help? Anything at all?"

"Probably not," Fuselli snapped. "Make sure you call me this time if you find out anything. I'm missing something, but I'll be damned if I can figure it out.

Nik slipped silently into Goodhaven Town Hall carrying the tools of her academic trade. Things were never busy there, but today the seat of government resembled a grade B horror flick. Desks were empty with just the occasional potted plant or abandoned cardigan to give proof of life. Office doors were locked down good and tight, like puny fortresses against the horror of murder.

Is this what violence does? Destroys the heart and soul of a community? Nicole bit her lip to keep from weeping. *Shelby would be heartbroken.*

"Looking for something?" a deep voice asked.

Nik leaped back, banging her knee against an aged metal desk. She hadn't seen Morgan Haas standing in the shadows. His smile was there, etched on his perpetually tanned face. His tailored sport coat, razor cut and grey flannels were the same, too. But something was different. Missing. Something had robbed Morgan Haas of his vitality and the sheen of political innocence he'd worn like a talisman.

"Did you forget?" Nik asked. She waved a tape recorder in front of him. "We can reschedule, if you'd prefer. I understand, really, I do."

His smile was letter perfect, a reasonable facsimile of his former self. "Nah. Come on. I'm still reeling from that spectacle last night." He gestured toward the empty desks. "As you can tell, things are pretty quiet around here today."

Haas led her to the conference room that adjoined his office. It had a solid, homey feel complemented by the judicious use of antiques from Goodhaven's past. Nicole had always felt comfortable there before Shelby's murder. Now the long walnut table seemed ponderous. The imposing size of the Chippendale highboy had sinister overtones. *Big enough to hide a body,* she thought. *Mine.*

Stop this nonsense. Nicole reined in her imagination and forced herself to focus. Shelby would understand. She knew how critical the dissertation was. *Find your own way, Cookie. Never wait for a man to pay the freight. Look what it got me.* Nicole had heard that from her a hundred times. Just thinking of it brought a smile to her face.

"Care to share the joke?" Morgan asked. "I could use a good laugh."

"Sorry. It's just something Shelby said." She slipped a silver barrette around her hair and uncapped her pen. "You know how she was, a quip for every occasion."

He grunted. "She could be charming, that's for sure. Unfortunately, some of her other habits were less endearing. I won't miss them at all." Morgan flipped open a folder, then closed it again. "Just tell me this. Was Fuselli serious last night? I mean, a murderer in our midst. Sounds like a substandard movie plot."

Nicole studied his square, capable-looking hands with neatly trimmed nails that suggested a manicure. Could those same hands have manacled Shelby and wielded a club? Morgan was familiar with ropes. He kept a sailboat in the Harbor, or as Mandy always stressed, a *sailing yacht*. Nicole knew nothing about boats, but she was a student of semantics. Yacht implied big bucks, and even she could tell that Morgan's craft was expensive, not the humble sailboat most people envisioned.

"Still with me?" he asked. "Seemed like you were a million miles away."

"Sorry. I was thinking about boats. Stupid at this time of year, I guess."

His eyes lit up immediately. "No kidding. As soon as the weather clears, I'll be on the Alger all the time."

"I don't know anything about boats, but yours is beautiful." She pointed at the painting over his desk. "Odd name, though."

"Hey, it's perfect! Horatio Alger is the American dream writ large. I got that boat for a song from a guy who got caught short on his margin calls."

She switched on her recorder after giving Mayor Haas a copy of her questions. "Forgive me for not asking sooner. How is Mandy ... Mrs. Haas ... holding up?"

He gave her a look so opaque it chilled her. "Fine. Why do you ask?"

"No reason. I just wondered." She tried to regroup. "The last time we discussed the building fund. I plan to study the community's reaction to the proposed head tax, show how citizen participation can coalesce support or opposition to an expenditure."

Morgan Haas sighed. "Is anyone really interested in that? Not that I'm denigrating your project or anything."

Nik grew animated. "Are you kidding? Think how timely it is. Tax increases, budget deficits, everyone's wrestling with them. If I show the impact of direct democracy, it might have some real impact." She leaned back, flushed with passion and conviction. "I have just a few questions. According to your prior budget reports, you had enough in the rainy day fund for repairs to the community center." She gave the mayor her killer smile. "So what happened?"

His reaction puzzled her. Morgan Haas shed his cool demeanor and imploded.

"She told you, didn't she?" he barked. "That old biddy thought she knew everything. Well, she didn't know shit about business, Missy. Rainy day funds target routine maintenance and repairs, not catastrophic events like last spring's blizzard." His hands shook as he fumbled through a thick file. "Here!" He thrust an envelope at Nicole. "Check out this estimate, and compare it with our treasurer's report. Then we'll discuss your paper, Ms. Nelson."

Nicole gripped the edge of the table but held her ground. "I'll do that, Mayor. But Shelby told me she had a poison pill that would stop you in your tracks. Any idea what she meant?"

His eyes weren't twinkling now. They bulged like those of a manic forest toad. "I don't have a clue what you're talking about, and Shelby's dead. Guess we'll never know, will we?"

A fine mess you made of that! Nicole scolded herself for lacking finesse. Had she chosen the right words, Morgan Haas might have opened up to her. Instead, she'd alienated him and risked losing her best source. The Mayor went ballistic each time she mentioned the building fund. Maybe that required more scrutiny. After all, dipping into a pool of money was child's play to a Wall Street guru.

She searched her pockets for spare change, hoping she had enough for a cup of tea and *The New York Times*. Hot tea, just the ticket to ward off the seaside chill. A crumpled five-dollar bill gave Nik hope. By prudent money management, she could wait until tomorrow to cash a check. Shelby's legacy still seemed unreal, more illusion than truth. Another of Grandma Duffy's bromides sprang to mind. Something about counting un-hatched chickens. She'd watch her spending until a check, not just the promise of one, had fattened her bank account.

"Yo! Watch yourself, Double N." Jett Hall swung her out of harm's way just in time to avoid a swerving delivery truck. "What would I do without my chess partner?"

"Oh, God! Thanks, Jett. I think I'm losing my mind. All I could think of was having a cup of tea."

"Come on. We'll open Mindbender early and have that tea." Jett reached into his backpack and handed her a newspaper. "Here. I know how you love the *Times*. Be my guest."

Nicole wanted solitude, needed it desperately. She met Jett's puppy dog eyes and weakened. After all, spending a little time with him wouldn't kill her. She shivered at her choice of words. Did even common expressions portend death these days? Jett was her closest friend, and he might know something important. How great would it be if she found the answer? Alejandro Lee would croak; Fuselli would eat his gun. "You're very persuasive. Let's do it."

Jett's eyes sparked with hope, as if Nicole's words promised what he'd longed for since the day they met. He swung open the door to Mindbenders with exaggerated cheer, avoiding any sudden moves. Nicole shook her head and ducked under his arm. How many times had she told Jett that she trusted him, valued his friendship? Friendship, just that and nothing more.

He usually played it cool, coloring just within the lines. Cautious, always so cautious. Today the slender thread of restraint seemed to have frayed. *It was like watching an oncoming train wreck,* Nik thought. *Disastrous but unavoidable.*

"What do you see when you look at me, Nik? A small-town bookseller with no future? I know I'm not rich like Jarrod or some big stud like this other guy."

Nicole put her finger across his lips. "Hush, now. When I look at you I see a wise, kind man, my best friend." She patted his cheek and took a seat at one of the small round tables. *Don't do it, Jett,* she prayed, sending an urgent mental message his way. *Leave it alone.*

Jett hesitated but he just couldn't let it go. He sat across from her and took her hand. "I could have gotten a Ph.D., too, you know. Amherst is one of the best colleges in the country."

"I know."

"I got accepted at Yale just like Jarrod. I could have been a hotshot lawyer if I'd wanted to." Jett stopped one inch short of whining.

"Why didn't you?" Nicole had often wondered about that.

He got up and retrieved the tea service. "Earl Grey, okay for you?"

She nodded. He spent some time pouring water from the kettle, carefully measuring the tea into the strainer, arranging cups and saucers. The ritual lulled them both into tranquility. After placing the tea tray on the table, Jett folded his arms and stared at her.

"What's wrong, Jett?"

"Ah, no big deal. It's just … why is it wrong to like simple things and small-town life? People act like it's some disease, almost a character flaw."

Nik's eyes widened. "Wow, I'm sorry. Did I do something?"

"You think I'm lazy, don't you? No ambition?"

Her mouthed gaped in protest. "I never said that."

"Yeah, but you thought it. Ambition isn't the same for everyone, you know. Some things are important to me."

Nicole stirred her tea. "Okay. Put-up-or-shut-up time, Mr. Hall. What's your ambition? You already know mine."

"I want to write books, serious works about important things that make people think." Jett turned away for a second as if to summon his courage. "It may not be trendy, but I like being my own boss. Kind of like those old-time movies, you know. Settling down in a small town doesn't make your life small."

Nicole looked at him as if she'd never seen him before. Maybe she hadn't. This wasn't jovial Jett, the court jester. No sir.

He stroked the rim of her teacup. "There's more. I want a family. Lots of kids."

"That's wonderful, Jett. Nothing wrong with that. You'd be a great father."

He smiled, shaking his head. "Just have to find the right girl, I guess. Who knows? Maybe she's closer than you'd think."

Nicole pinched his cheeks. "You shouldn't be too hard on yourself. You're quite a catch, you know."

He took off his glasses, polishing them on his napkin. "Feel like a snack? How about a crumpet or two?"

"Heavenly! Oh, Jett, you know how to tempt a girl." Nicole sat down at one of the small tables, opened the *Times* and started browsing." What did you make of last night? Weird, even for Mandy, wasn't it?"

"Saying weird and Mandy in the same sentence is redundant. You know how strange she can be." He took a gulp of Earl Grey and wiped his lips. "Although I must admit, the woman surpassed herself last night. And Fuselli! Wasn't he the drama queen?"

Nicole coughed as she swallowed her tea. "You mean you don't believe him?"

"Nope. I think he was baiting us." Jett leaned back, tipping his chair on two legs. "Why? You did?"

She thought it over. Except when it came to her and other men, Jett was a good sounding board. "I don't know what to think. Ever since Shelby died … since her murder … I suspect everyone and no one." She bit back the tears that threatened to swamp her. "I just want it to be over, Jett. All this stuff about comic books, abandoned babies … "

"Babies?" The round spectacles gave him a learned air, rather like a quizzical owl. "What the hell are you talking about?"

Nik tried to backtrack, but Jett wouldn't let it go.

"I repeat," he said. "Abandoned babies? It's so Victorian. Even has a touch of Agatha Christie. Remember how illicit spawn were always showing up in her books to claim their inheritance?"

"I should have kept my big mouth shut," Nik said. "The medical examiner found that Shelby had given birth. No other information." She touched his hand. "Please don't tell anyone else. Shelby was such a private person. I don't want people snickering over it. It's no one's business anyhow."

After another cup of tea, Nik finally calmed down. "What can you tell me about this comic book stuff? Did Shelby ever mention anything about Ashcans? It's been driving me crazy."

Jett stroked his chin before replying. "Shelby came in here twice a week to play chess and gossip. Sure, we discussed comics. We spoke about almost everything. When the Batman and Superman sales went through the roof, Shelby kind of hinted around. I mean they both went for over a million bucks. We did the usual, you know. What would I do with a million dollars? That kind of stuff."

Nicole leaned forward, brushing back the wings of her silky hair. "That Ashcan thing was advertised for five million dollars? Do you believe it? It's not in the carriage house. I searched everywhere. Of course, Alejandro may find it in the collections he's working on at Rampart."

"Yeah, I bet he will, and he'll turn it right over to you." Jett thrust his jaw out bulldog fashion. "Be realistic, Double N. Once that guy finds what he's looking for, he'll be out of here like a shot. Back to California."

Her back stiffened. "You're probably right."

"Did he really move in with you? I know it's none of my business, but I care about you. After all, what do we actually know about this guy? Maybe he's the murderer."

Nicole gathered her things and slipped on her coat. "Thanks for the tea, Jett. I'd better go."

He touched her muffler, winding it lovingly around her neck and tucking it into her coat. "Hold on. I didn't mean to upset you or pry. Still friends?"

"Always. Don't worry. It's no big deal." She exited the bookstore and headed home to the comfort of her pets.

Fourteen

Alex grinned every time he thought about it: he and Jarrod locked in a partnership tinged with enmity, grudging admiration and outright suspicion. Despite their differences, the twin tasks of finding Shelby's murderer and resolving her estate bound the lawyers with hoops of steel. Like it or not, they were stuck with each other.

Since Shelby's murder, Alex had felt achy and out of sorts. He assumed it was a cold, probably a touch of the flu. This Goodhaven venture was full of distractions that sapped his energy. The sooner he resolved things and returned home, the better. He was in control on his home turf. He never felt ill in California.

"What's wrong, Lee? Not up to this New England climate?" Jarrod smirked at his own joke. "Better watch out, or someone might think you're lovesick."

Alex nodded, returning the jab. "How's your fiancée doing? She was on the warpath last night."

"Don't remind me." Jarrod ruffled his fair hair. "I'm late with my blog entry, and to top it off I had to cancel my television spot. You know, the *Great Thinkers Panel*?"

"I have to admit that show's terrific. I'm a fan."

"Really?" Jarrod slapped Alex on the back. "You're okay, Lee. I love that show. Going at it with sharp guys is such a rush. Even Shelby watched. Nicole, too. They loathed every stand I took, of course. Typical liberal nonsense. Danny thinks it's boring. Too highbrow for her."

Nicole. Alex didn't react to her name. Not in front of Jarrod. He refused to admit that his condition, his bizarre ailment, might be connected to her. Falling in love was out of the question. He had big plans for his future that didn't include a wife or family. The old ball and chain, as his buddies often described their wives. Hard to picture Nicole that way.

"Know what?" Jarrod spoke through gritted teeth. "I actually miss the old trout. Shelby, I mean. Kind of like a nagging toothache. My mom died so long ago, I hardly remember her, and with my dad globe-trotting to every backwater in Asia, I kind of feel like an orphan now." He brushed an imaginary speck of lint off his trousers. "Stupid, huh?" Jarrod shed self-pity like Shelby's dog shed his coat. "I'll go call my contact at Columbia and check on Harris Goldman. Surprising how those academics love gossip. You never know who might be a fraud."

"I agree. Stanford's the same way." They exchanged looks, and each grabbed a phone.

Nicole spent the afternoon cocooned in the coach house with the cats and her computer. Foo Dog stayed outside, prowling the yard as if to ward off any malefactors. A week had gone by. Just seven days since Shelby Whitholm met her maker. Nicole still felt her presence every time she stirred her tea or thought of some wry slant on *The Divine Comedy*.

Nicole was a realist, but she firmly believed that Shelby's spirit would hover until her killer was found and punished. Lots of old New England homes had resident ghosts. Most were amiable sorts who just couldn't let go. They caused no harm and often became a tourist attraction that enriched the property owners. Shelby didn't fit that mold at all. She was definitely the vengeful type who would throttle the life out of any intruder.

A spate of ferocious barking brought Nik back to earth. Confucius was enraged, flinging himself at the wooden fence posts like Orestes on a tear. She peeped out the window and saw visitors. Ugh! Danielle Stevens and Amanda Haas. A more unlovely duo was unimaginable. Before opening the door, Nicole slipped into the kitchen to free Foo Dog from the yard. No sense in taking chances like Shelby had. Too bad if either one of them had a problem with dogs. She finger-combed her hair and donned her company manners.

Danielle's face was an impeccable mask, groomed with just the right touch of cosmetics. *Too bad she's such a bitch*, Nik thought. *I'd love to ask about her eye shadow.* One look at Danielle confirmed that this was no social call. She nodded to Nik and gripped Amanda's arm firmly, as if the poor woman might try to flee.

"Hi, Nicole. Sorry to bother you. We need to chat." Danielle slid through the door like a wraith, pulling Amanda Haas through the opening right behind her.

Every guard hair on Confucius's back stood at attention. Both women stepped back as the dog issued a low, menacing growl. Nicole spoke softly to him as she grasped his collar.

"Can't you put him outside?" Amanda asked, shrinking from the dog. "He looks vicious."

"Sorry," Nik said. "This is his home, too. He's still out of sorts, missing Shelby." She waved her guests into the kitchen. "Coffee or tea? I have both."

"No, thanks," Amanda said. "We won't disturb you for long." Her eyes were bloodshot, and to Nicole's surprise, Amanda's hair looked unkempt, as if it hadn't been styled or colored in many moons. Stripped of makeup, her face had the ghoulish pallor of the undead.

Danielle hovered over the computer, boldly reading the text document. "Hmm. You've been busy, haven't you, Nicole?"

"As you know, I'm writing my dissertation. Now what can I do for you ladies?"

"You and Shelby were close, weren't you?" Amanda's voice was barely audible. "I'm glad she had a friend."

"Shelby had many friends," Nicole said. "I thought you were among them." Her words had more bite than she'd intended, but she was weary of playing games.

Danielle slithered into the conversation. "Enough fencing. We want it, Nicole. Give it back. Now, before it's too late." Her body language alarmed Foo Dog, who planted himself firmly in front of Nicole.

"What are you talking about? Comic books?"

Amanda shifted in her chair. "This was a mistake. Let's go." She twisted her wedding band until it spun like a top on her shrunken finger. "I'm sorry we disturbed you. Please forgive us."

Nicole was both annoyed and intrigued. She wasn't frightened. Foo Dog's presence bolstered her courage.

"You're not leaving before you explain yourselves. I have no idea what you're talking about."

Danielle's gaze mixed cynicism with surprise. "You really don't know, do you? Well, listen to this, Ms. Holier-Than-Thou Nelson. Your dear friend and benefactor was a blackmailer. She bled half the town dry for years, and it's got to stop."

"Blackmail? Shelby?" Nicole caught her breath. "Shelby lived very frugally. Those comics were the only valuable things she owned."

"Blackmail is just another name for control," Mandy said. "Shelby didn't want our money. She bludgeoned her victims into doing good works."

"Yeah," Danielle spat, "like that dreadful animal shelter. We all had to volunteer there. Ugh!"

"Morgan gave them sizable donations," Mandy said faintly. "He wouldn't tell me why."

Now things made sense to Nicole. No wonder Harris Goldman showed his face at Lifelines. That man was no animal lover. Shelby probably enjoyed torturing him.

"Look, I don't know what to say. Maybe if I knew what Shelby had on you," Nik said, holding out her hands in supplication.

"Not likely," Danielle grinned. "I haven't told anyone else, and I'm not about to spill it now. If you don't know, so be it."

Amanda Haas had a greenish tinge to her skin. She clutched her throat and croaked a plea. "Don't mention this to Morgan. Please. He'd … well, he wouldn't be happy with me." She leapt up and ran out the door with Danielle close on her heels.

"Don't tell Jarrod either, or you'll be sorry." Danielle gave a three-fingered wave and disappeared.

"What the hell!" Nicole veered between anger and fear. Everything had gone haywire. Maybe she should abandon Goodhaven, return to Boston and find a new topic for her dissertation. Her thoughts were disrupted by a nudge from Foo Dog's cold, moist nose. His soft, cocoa eyes radiated intelligence and a silent plea. What would become of him and the cats if she left? Jarrod Whitholm was the last person she'd entrust them to.

Think Nicole. No sense in resisting it any more. She should contact Fuselli. Maybe he'd found some clue. Either way, she'd have to tell him about this blackmail charge. She had no choice. Did she?

The sharp ring of the telephone triggered Foo Dog's warning bark. He'd acted as a type of hearing aid for Shelby, alerting her to every errant sound. She'd denied any impairment but had never complained when her pet helped her out.

"Hope I didn't disturb you." Alejandro's voice was as deep and mysterious as he was. Nicole closed her eyes and immersed herself in the sound, feeling that sense of contentment once again.

"Nope. Just working on my paper." She crossed fingers and toes to negate the lie.

He hesitated, sounding almost shy. "How would you feel about having dinner at Cliff House tonight? With me."

"Oh. I'd like that." She tried to sound nonchalant, even though flames scorched every inch of her soul. *Go slow*, she cautioned herself. *Take it easy.*

"I have news," he said, "but it'll keep 'til tonight. Eight o'clock okay with you?"

"Fine," Nik took small breaths, forcing herself to relax. "Shall I meet you there?"

"No way. I'm your escort. I'll call for you."

When he hung up, Nicole heaved a big sigh. Something about that man made every nerve ending tingle. Even his language was different. Courtly, that's what it was, almost quaint. Jett was probably right about him. The moment he found the Ashcan, Alex would be gone, fading into the ether like the fine, faint scent of his cologne. A wise woman would send him packing. Despite her impressive IQ, Nicole wasn't wise when it came to love. She'd hunker down and enjoy the ride while it lasted. To hell with caution.

The hours crawled by like a tortoise parade. Nicole was awash with emotion incapable of even reading her manuscript. She'd spent the balance of the afternoon vacillating between abject fear and total euphoria. She'd also spent more time debating wardrobe choices than a serious scholar should ever admit. Nicole was no clotheshorse—her situation didn't permit it—but she was a savvy shopper who could smell a bargain at a hundred paces. Go for quality, her mom had taught her, and that's what she did. Tonight she paired a pink cashmere twin set with a grey pencil skirt and soft leather boots. Her opera-length pearls were a cherished legacy from Grandma Duffy, a perfect complement to her ensemble. Classy not ostentatious. She pirouetted in front of Atticus and Annabel, seeking their approval. Both summoned that neutral feline nod that gave no quarter and kept her guessing.

In the midst of the preparations, a niggling doubt assailed her. Their team had divvied up assignments last night without facing one key issue: Who would validate them? Alejandro, Danielle, Jarrod, even Nicole, were all viable suspects in Shelby's murder. Maybe it was Fuselli's job to do that, but maybe not.

Nik hadn't contacted the sheriff, even though she knew she should have. It was disquieting to think of Shelby, her friend and mentor, as a blackmailer. If thinking it seemed disloyal, telling Fuselli would be treasonous. Nicole examined the issue as dispassionately as possible, considering that Mandy might have fabricated the blackmail charge. Not possible. Although she was spiteful, Amanda Haas didn't have an imaginative bone in her desiccated body. She'd been frantic this morning, close to hysteria. Had her secret driven her to murder? And what had compelled Morgan to succumb to blackmail? Nicole wracked her brain for some idea of where Shelby's hiding place might be. Surely she'd kept something tangible, some proof of her victims' crimes. Unfortunately, Nik's normally agile brain was too obsessed with Alex to function properly. It remained stalled until the door chime rang.

He stood silently, clutching a spray of orchids, his solemn face framed by the weathered door. Alejandro was seldom awestruck. After all, words are an attorney's stock in trade, and he was skilled at his craft. Why did he feel like an awkward adolescent whenever Nicole appeared? It made absolutely no sense. Women liked him—they always had, too much sometimes. He'd used charm, finesse and occasional deception to manipulate them, stopping just short of anything unethical.

Even a hard case like Shelby had a soft spot for him, although she'd shown no interest in any type of physical relationship. That would have jeopardized a very lucrative arrangement and cost him a bundle. He'd had a few narrow escapes in the past, mostly with wealthy suburban types looking for diversion. Alejandro Lee was no one's afternoon delight. He'd bet the same was true for Nicole.

"You're lovely," he whispered as she opened the door. "Irresistible."

Nicole flushed as her eyes scanned him head to toe.

"Problem?" he asked.

"No ... please forgive me. It's just that you're dressed in black again."

He folded his arms, saying nothing.

"You see, most men look sinister without a dash of color, funereal at the very least."

"Aha. I remind you of an undertaker. Not very romantic."

Nicole's cheeks turned bubblegum pink. "Not at all. Forgive me. I read too much. Truth is, you remind me of every Byronic hero I've ever read about: Heathcliff, Mr. Rochester, even Mr. Darcy a little bit. It sounds stupid, I know."

Alex gave her the orchids. "Not at all. I'm flattered to be in such august company."

Their fingers touched, and he took her hand, gently kissing each finger.

"I love flowers," Nik said, shying away like a nervous filly. "Let me find a vase. Shall we leave, or do we have time for a drink?"

His eyes never left hers. "We have all the time in the world. We don't even have to eat dinner." He forced himself to focus on his task. After all, he was no pimply adolescent begging for favors. He wanted more than a casual affair from Nicole. Much more.

"That's okay. I'm starving." Nicole grabbed one of Shelby's crystal vases and hastily filled it. She fingered the velvety petals as she arranged the orchids and placed them on a table.

He knew she was stalling, trying to forestall the inevitable. Alex reined in an impulse to scoop her up and head upstairs. She'd probably scream her head off and sic Fuselli on him if he tried that. The good sheriff would love charging him with a felony.

Alex helped Nicole into her coat, carefully guiding her arm through the sleeves, fastening each button deliberately to prolong the contact. Touching her was exquisite, the sort of agony he'd never experienced before. He felt adrift, unsure if Nicole was penance or pleasure.

"Ready?" he asked. "I have a lot to tell you."

"Me, too. I mean, I found something out today. Something important." She seemed uneasy too as if she, too, was wrestling to control her emotions. That comforted him.

Alex patted her hair and led her to his car. "Ladies first." He reached over, adjusting her seatbelt with one deft tug. How in the world could the simplest touch be so infused with sweetness? Was he going mad?

Nicole took a deep breath and described the morning's scene with Danielle and Amanda.

"It was so odd, Alex. Something about Amanda really frightened me. I swear she could have clobbered me without turning a hair."

"Hmm. Obey your instincts. Stay away from her unless you really are Wonder Woman and have those magic bracelets."

"I'd settle for the Lasso of Truth," Nik said. "Then I'd really find out who murdered Shelby. Maybe I could loan it to Fuselli. He needs all the help he can get."

"Too much truth can be harmful," Alex said. "The world runs on illusion, you know." He parked in front of Cliff House, threw his keys to the valet and guided Nicole through the restaurant's heavy doors.

Fifteen

"Tell me everything," Nicole said as she took her seat.

"Everything? That's a pretty tall order." He arched thick black brows. "How about confining it to my work today? Time enough later for my life story."

They ordered wine, Goodhaven oysters and a cup of chowder.

Alex clinked glasses with Nicole and nodded toward the panoramic view of the ocean. "Natural beauty. I'm used to the Pacific Ocean. You know, calm and tranquil. But I've come to love the Atlantic. It's wild, unpredictable and beautiful. Pretty hard to compete with most of the time, unless I'm looking at you."

She turned away. "You're joking, making fun of me."

His fingers lightly raked her arm. "Never. I'm just confused. You must feel it, too, ever since we met." He shook his head. "I'm not used to it. Guess I'm kind of a control freak."

Nicole sipped her wine, fortified by the strength of the cold crystal flute and the liquid warmth within. "Let's stick to business. Tell me about it, Shelby's collection."

"I haven't finished cataloguing and grading everything, but I made a lot of headway." He paused. "No Ashcan so far. Sorry to disappoint you. But Shelby amassed an impressive collection, really impressive. Believe it or not, unless I've lost my marbles, the Whitholm comics qualify as a pedigree collection. That's incredible. It'll shake up the comic cosmos big time."

"I don't understand a thing you said. What in the hell is a pedigree collection?"

Alex laughed. She'd never heard him really laugh before. His voice had a rich, mellow timbre, like the sensuous song of a baritone sax.

"Okay, I'll play professor. Stop me if you get bored." He spread out his hands. "Some collections—a very few—are of such importance they're classified as pedigrees. They're usually vast and have very few defects. I think the Whitholm collection qualifies. Somehow Shelby amassed almost five thousand near-mint golden age comics. That's amazing. Of course, we'll need a second opinion, someone from the CGC ..."

"CGC? Speak English, for heaven's sake."

He patted her cheek. "Sorry. I get carried away. CGC is the Certified Guarantee Company, a professional grading service. They have very strict ethical guidelines, the industry standard. I was on the grading team at one time."

Nicole leaned forward, forgetting everything but the issue at hand. "So why can't you just certify Shelby's stuff and be done with it? Then we can dispose of the damn thing." She stopped and stared him down. "You didn't get kicked off this CGC team or anything, did you?"

Now it was his turn to flush. "No, nothing like that. It's just that they prohibit employees from buying or selling comics, and I saw a business opportunity I couldn't pass up."

Nicole considered that for a moment. "So, you can find a buyer for us and arrange the entire transaction, right?"

Alex shook his head again. "Not so fast. No reputable collector would touch it unless we had formal CGC certification. There's too much money involved. Anyhow, the estate has to go through probate first."

She took a deep cleansing breath. "Any idea how much money we're talking about? I hate to sound mercenary, but … Oh, God, I sound like Jarrod, or worse, Danielle."

"Slow down. Stop being so hard on yourself." Alex speared an oyster with his fork, rubbed it on her lips and fed it to her as if she were a nestling and he the papa bird. "I know what it's like to worry about bills and pay tuition. Don't sell yourself short. In comic book terms you, Ms. Nelson, are a solid nine-point-six.

"I don't get it."

He dabbed the corners of her mouth with the soft linen napkin. "That means near mint. Almost perfect with no wear, a tight flat spine, no stress lines, high gloss and supple, fresh white color."

His language was staid, but those eyes telegraphed a very different message. A tremor swept across her like an ocean current. She shivered, wearing her vulnerability like a shroud.

"What? I'm not perfect? I'm crushed."

She wanted him to beg, anything to get her to abandon dinner and head straight home. Instead, he winked. "We can work on those minor imperfections, but it'll take time. A very long time. Restoration must be done very gently by an expert."

They faced each other, silent prisoners of the candlelight and their own unspoken needs. In the distance a vocalist crooned a sultry jazz song.

Every seat in the restaurant was filled, but to Nik the room held only them. Her sensible self urged caution. Men like Alex—sexy, impossibly handsome men—were nothing but trouble. Women were expendable commodities to them, something to be used and carelessly discarded. She knew it, but she didn't care. There were worse things than being used by a gorgeous man. Shelby's words reverberated in her skull.

Life's a wild ride, Cookie. Go at it full throttle while you can. Nicole realized with a sudden, throbbing pang just how lonely she'd been, existing, not living, shackled to a computer and her distant dreams.

He patted her arm, sending electric current through her yet again. "Back to money. Right now, based on recent sales of similar items, I think you're looking at close to two million dollars minus expenses, taxes and the like. That's the per-issue price, and you might get substantially more if one buyer nabs the collection intact."

The thought of all those zeros made Nik's jaw drop. She could actually feel the hinges creak. Money meant freedom and the chance to spread her wings a bit. It didn't consume her, but it raised lots of possibilities. Before she could answer, someone approached their table and pulled up a chair.

"Oh, here you are. Thank God." Fuselli's face was stretched into a weary mask.

"What's going on, Sheriff?" Alex's voice was dangerously close to a growl.

"We've had another incident. Someone vandalized Mindbenders tonight."

"Is Jett hurt?" Nicole found it hard to form the words. "He's not dead, is he?"

Nicole's face was pale, and she felt close to fainting. In contrast Alejandro seemed glacier cool. If the news upset him, it wasn't evident.

"What happened?" he asked Fuselli.

The cop leaned back and closed his eyes as if he were reliving the crime scene. "When Jett closed his shop at six, he went into the alley to dump rubbish. That's when someone knocked him on the head, stole his keys and tore up the store."

Alex nudged Nicole's foot with his. "We may know something that can help you. Tell him, Nicole."

"Okay, but it probably doesn't mean anything." Nicole described her encounter with Danielle and Amanda, downplaying Shelby's role as blackmailer.

"Hold on. Are you telling me that my murder victim blackmailed people, and you didn't think that was significant, Nicole?" Fuselli slammed his fist on the table, causing silverware to clatter and diners to stare.

"Maybe it isn't true. She didn't take money or anything. I mean, I'm not even sure it counts as blackmail." Nik was losing, and she knew it. Gone was the affable town sheriff. An angry, snorting Minotaur had taken his place.

"What do they teach you at B.C. these days? Ever heard of coercion, extortion … you know the drill. Check your Massachusetts criminal code, Ms. Nelson. Forcing someone to do something against his will is a crime. Period."

Alex locked eyes with Fuselli and glared. "Whoa. Hold on, Sheriff. No need to upset her. She's trying to help."

Nicole didn't flinch. She raised her chin, forcing herself to meet Fuselli's eyes. "Okay, I was wrong. Now you know everything I do." She felt the comforting presence of Alejandro's arm around her.

"Looks like you've got some suspects now, Sheriff. Shelby may have been too good a researcher for her own safety." Alex chuckled. "Personally, I say follow the money. That comic collection is a much more satisfying motive than hurt feelings over an animal shelter."

Fuselli narrowed his eyes and rose, hands on hips. "I can tell you've had a long career in law enforcement, both of you. Now if you can't or won't help, at least get the hell out of my way." He stomped out of the Cliff House without another word.

"What happened to him? He's usually not that way." Nicole peeled a chip of nail polish from her thumb and studied it.

Alex retrieved his iPhone and tapped in a number. "We need to meet," he said when a voice answered, "now."

He signaled the waiter, handed him some bills and held out Nicole's coat. "Let's get out of here. We're expecting a visitor."

Jarrod Whitholm looked like a pufferfish, swollen with rage and twice as lethal. He'd parked his Hummer outside the carriage house with the engine on, aggressively spewing noxious fumes. *A fitting metaphor for Jarrod himself,* Nik mused.

"You have a hell of a nerve, Lee. How dare you summon me like I'm some sort of serf? Who do you think you are?" Jarrod's complexion passed fuchsia and went straight to magenta as he charged toward them.

"Hey man, slow down. No harm, no foul." Alex held out his hands, palms up. "Fuselli just read us the riot act, and I thought we'd better compare notes. That's all."

Nicole played peacemaker by linking arms with both men and urging them toward the door. "Did you hear about Jett?"

"Of course I did. That guy is broadcasting it like he's auditioning for town crier." Jarrod heaved a sigh, making a concerted effort to power down. "I'm not sure I believe him. He'd do anything just to get sympathy, especially from you."

After ushering them inside Nicole took center stage. "You may not know about my little encounter with Amanda today. I've told Alex and Fuselli, so you might as well hear it, too." She pointed to the Scotch that Alejandro had brought the other night. "Is that okay for both of you?"

Jarrod brightened. "Johnny Walker Blue. That's more than okay. Must be your handiwork, Lee. I can't see our impoverished grad student here springing for it."

He really is a clod, Nik thought. *I'm not ashamed of being poor. It's only temporary.* She poured them each two fingers of Scotch and motioned toward the wing chairs flanking the fireplace. Then she replayed her conversation. "You should know that Danielle was with her and warned me not to tell you."

"I don't believe it!" Jarrod coughed as he swallowed his drink. "My aunt was many things, but a blackmailer? Never."

They gave him a moment to process the information.

"Fuselli said it was coercion, maybe extortion, even though no goods and services changed hands." Alex shrugged. "Of course, that's just legal gobbledygook. Your aunt was playing head games with these people, very dangerous games. It's one of the reasons I found her so enchanting."

Nicole twisted the hem of her sweater into a ball, wondering how she could have been so wrong. She hated everything about the conversation. Shelby, the woman who'd seemed so transparent, was anything but. Feisty librarian was just one facet of this complex woman's character, no more definitive than shrewd comic collector, scrappy politico or generous friend. Foo Dog's furious barking plummeted her back to earth.

"Can't you stop that racket?" Jarrod snarled. "You can hear that mutt halfway up the block."

"Interesting, isn't it," Alejandro said, "like in Sherlock Holmes. Somehow that dog kept quiet while his mistress was being slaughtered. There had to be noise. Shelby was no pushover. She'd scream her head off. He only barked afterward."

"Unless someone doped her or took her by surprise." Jarrod shivered as he considered the possibilities. "Fuselli didn't mention anything about drugs in her system. God knows he didn't miss anything else."

Nicole thought about Shelby's child, another secret she'd concealed from everyone.

"By the way, as soon as my dad gets in from Asia, I'll quiz him about that kid thing. Hard enough to tell him she died but that ... Why a man of his age had to run off to Tibet to study Buddhism is beyond me." Jarrod ignored the grin stealing over Alex's face.

After pouring them a refill, Nicole asked. "Did you find out anything? About Goldman, I mean."

"Actually, I did. His Ph.D. is genuine enough. My friend at Columbia confirmed that." Jarrod was stalling, enhancing the drama of his announcement. "Here's the kicker. Harris was asked to leave. It was one of those informal requests with real bite. You know the type."

Alex inched forward, his muscles tense. "Don't torture us, Whitholm. Why did they dump him? Tenured professors usually stick like glue."

"Apparently, he has quite a temper, not to mention a rather nasty habit of badgering students. Throwing things, shouting. Complaints were filed. Nothing ever came of them, but the university didn't fight it when Harris found a slot at Amherst. Probably encouraged it."

That punctured Nicole's heady sense of drama. Big deal. She already knew Harris was a mean old man. Everyone said that's why his long-suffering wife finally left him. "Jett seemed to know him pretty well. Should I ask him if anything happened at Amherst?"

Both men shot her looks of such disgust that Nik knew their answers. Jett was a good friend. She trusted him to tell her the truth about Harris as he always had about everything else.

"I spoke to a friend at Stanford today." Jarrod flashed a deceptively genial smile at Alex.

"Really? Wonderful place, Stanford. First-rate education."

"Funny thing. My pal's been at the law school ten years, but he doesn't recall you."

"Lee's a pretty common name out there. Half the students are Asian, you know."

Jarrod lowered his voice to a deep growl. "Listen here, Mr. Alejandro Lee or whatever your name is. You're a phony, and when I prove it, I'm going to run you out of the state. Don't think I can't do it either."

Alex looked bemused, not angry. "I'm sure you can. After all, you're a big television star and all. Maybe you should consider your motive. Big fish, small pond. Can't stand any competition. You're jealous, plain and simple."

"Why you … " Jarrod Whitholm sputtered. "How dare you!"

"How dare he what?" Nicole asked, shifting noiselessly in her seat. "What's wrong with you guys? Remember, we're a team."

"Right," Alex smirked. "The A-team."

"Cut it out. I forgot to mention my dustup with the mayor this morning." Nik shook her head. "It's been quite a day."

Sixteen

"What next, Lee?" Jarrod asked. "You called this meeting."

Alex flashed a bland, nice guy grin that fooled no one. "So I did. I've concluded my review, and as I told Nicole, both of you should get a sizable sum."

"After your generous commission," Jarrod sneered.

"I don't work for free, Mr. Whitholm. Do you?" They exchanged glares that elevated the room's temperature by ten degrees.

Nicole jumped in. "Hey, you guys, cool it. There's more than enough for everyone." She ignored their grumbling and grabbed her laptop. "Okay. First, consider Mayor Haas. I researched his old company, very cursory, nothing definitive, and found the usual litany of investor complaints and grousing by competitors. No SEC filings or rumors of impropriety, though." She scanned a file, frowning. "There was a major upheaval that led to the firm's dissolution, but he'd already left. I couldn't tell if it was infighting or something unethical. What if Shelby got wind of something compromising?"

Jarrod yawned, making no secret of his boredom. "I might be able to help you there. Some of my old classmates work on The Street."

"Great. Now, Harris Goldman." Nicole paused. "We haven't discovered any motive for him yet. Terminal meanness doesn't make him a murderer. Neither does being a brute."

Alex watched her cross and uncross her long, elegant legs, mesmerized by every move she made. A thrill flamed through his body like a blowtorch. Seeing this intellectual side of Nicole excited him as much as her soft lips did.

"What's wrong with you, Lee?" Jarrod asked. "Your face is contorted. Don't get sick on us now, for heaven's sake."

Alex snapped back to attention, forcing himself to focus on the task. This obsession with Nicole was puerile. He was off his game, acting like a fool. A romp in the hay was all he needed.

Nicole kept her head down and tapped the return key. "Any suggestions on next steps?"

"Maybe," Alex said. "Your friend Jett seems awfully chummy with Goldman. Ask him about his Amherst days."

"No wonder Mrs. G. decamped," Nik said. "How humiliating is that, having some old coot acting like the campus Grinch?" She swiveled her chair around to face them. "Harris told me something else, something I forgot to tell you guys." She hesitated.

"Oh, for Christ's sake, Nicole, spit it out." Jarrod curled his lip.

"Okay. Harris said he saw you at Shelby's the afternoon she was murdered."

"Me? That's a damn lie! You're making that up."

Nik stood her ground. Alex leaned back, arms crossed, as he watched Jarrod squirm.

"About one-thirty, Jarrod. That's when he saw your Hummer."

"Sorry, but you'll have to do better than that. I was in Boston when Shelby died. All day." He shrugged. "Hell, I didn't even have my car. Danny had to give me a ride."

A chill swept through Alex. "Wait a minute. Are you telling us that Ms. Stevens had the Hummer that day?"

Jarrod was a lawyer, trained by the best to avoid direct answers. "I said that I didn't have the Hummer. Danny picked me up in her Jag, if you must know. I dropped her off and went to a taping in Hyannis." He heaved a gigantic sigh. "Now, can we stop this nonsense and get back to work?"

Their meeting ended after midnight. Jarrod, fueled by copious amounts of Johnny Walker Blue, lumbered up the driveway to the main house while Alejandro headed for the inn.

"I'll be in Boston tomorrow," he said, raining gentle kisses on her forehead. "Better leave so I can get an early start." He tilted her chin toward him. "If I stay, I may never go."

"Would that be so bad?" Nicole patted Foo Dog as a distraction.

He shot her a look of such tenderness that she felt light-headed. Something—alcohol, anxiety or emotion—made her heart a quivering, captive bird. Yielding this way was crazy. Nik knew better, but she just didn't care. She watched, transfixed, as Alex loped gracefully out the door.

Sleep. She needed sweet oblivion to gain control and stop mooning over Dr. Lee. After all, Nicole Elisabeth Nelson was a serious scholar with a plan. Her well-ordered life had no place for distraction.

She'd quiz Jett about his good buddy Harris tomorrow. Scratch that. It was already tomorrow. If necessary, she would confront the old coot and pretend to know his big, bad secret. Maybe she'd bake cookies. Nik grimaced. On second thought, better to stop by the bakery. Homemade was no guarantee of anything. It depended on whose home things were made in. The last time she'd taken the culinary plunge, her cream puffs had the heft of bowling balls. Poor Jett had manfully swallowed one and begged for seconds. That's when she'd finally realized how he felt about her. Only a love-struck man would risk permanent injury by eating those cream puffs.

After making a security sweep Nik gathered her pets, turned down the bed and swaddled herself in down. The Louisville Slugger stayed next to her, just within reach.

Jett Hall brightened the minute Nicole entered Mindbenders. He rushed to the door and gave her a ferocious hug.

"Double N, I thought you were mad at me. C'mon in and have some tea."

His smile was tentative, reminding Nik of an errant schoolboy unsure of his welcome.

"Thanks. I could use some Earl Grey. Not enough sleep, I'm afraid." She sighed. "You'd think after two cups of espresso I'd feel a caffeine buzz." She stood on tiptoe and gently touched his head. "Are you okay? I was worried when I heard."

"No big deal," Jett said, "although it took me forever to clean up the place. Nothing much was taken. Probably neighborhood brats on a tear. Anyway, I'm glad you came in." Jett hesitated. "Has anything else happened? Anything bad, I mean."

He'd given her an opening, and Nik leapt once more into the breach. Not exactly Shakespeare but close enough. She'd always favored the direct approach.

"Harris Goldman. Tell me everything you know about him."

"What?" Jett's gaping mouth bore a marked resemblance to a gaffed fish. "I don't get it. What's Harris have to do with anything?"

"Maybe nothing. That's why I'm asking." She did a quick check of the room, lowering her voice to a whisper. "I think Shelby was blackmailing him, and I need to know why."

"Blackmail! What the fuck, Nicole? You're joking, right?"

She pointed to the cash register where a customer stood, impatiently fingering several bills. Jett leapt up and did the honors. When he returned his face had lost its bruise of color.

"Harris is a good guy. He doesn't have much to do since his wife left him. Gardening, he loves that. And books, all kinds of books. That guy has more bookshelves in his house than most libraries."

Subtlety was called for. Nicole knew that. Otherwise Jett would clam up and tell her nothing.

"What was he like at Amherst? Was he popular with the students?"

Jett squirmed in his seat. "Popular? I wouldn't say that. He wasn't weird or anything, but some people avoided him. He's kind of a curmudgeon, I guess."

"Mostly women?" Nicole pinned him with her fiercest look.

"There was talk but not about Harris. His wife was … flirtatious, you might say. Gave Harris lots of grief."

Nicole reeled back, stunned. Not what she expected. "I never met Mrs. Goldman. She left before I got here."

Jett shrugged. "Nancy was fun, lots younger than Harris and still attractive. Men liked her. No one was surprised when she took off."

"Any money worries? Something that Shelby might latch on to." Nicole flashed the beguiling smile that usually pulverized him. This time Jett seemed quite immune.

"Does Fuselli know you're doing this? I bet he'd hit the roof if I told him." His hands covered hers for a second. "Okay, Double N. Come clean if you want my help."

Nik shared the blackmail theory, excluding the information Jarrod had found at Columbia. As she spoke, Jett polished his glasses so carefully that she almost screamed.

"Wow, that's a shocker. Shelby was like a black widow spider, ensnaring people in her web. Way cool!" He waved his spoon in a faux salute.

"Knock it off." Frustration overwhelmed her. What made her think she was some kind of detective? No wonder Fuselli boiled over. All she'd done was muddle along and compromise the reputation of a woman she'd cared for. Big whoop. If she had any sense, she'd stop snooping right now.

Jett pushed out his chair and grabbed his jacket. "Come on. I can spare an hour for lunch. Might as well tackle Harris."

"Really? Thanks, Jett, you're a pal."

They linked arms and strode toward the car with Nik matching him stride for stride.

Harris Goldman was tidy. One glance at his meticulously groomed lawn and pristine shutters confirmed that. Despite her vow to detest everything Goldman, Nik was charmed by the trim yellow Cape at the end of a *cul-de-sac*. She followed Jett as he unlatched the gate in the picket fence and headed toward the back yard.

"Maybe we should knock first," she said. "He might be napping."

"Phooey. It's early spring. He'll be back in his garden, pruning."

Garden! Nik considered that an understatement. Harris had created a thing of beauty, a natural paradise that embraced the generous patio like a warm hug.

She knew zip about gardening, couldn't identify even one of the luscious greens covering the ground. That didn't stop her from coveting the fruits of someone else's labor. After all, she would soon be a property owner.

"Yo, Harris! Company." Jett hopped over a small mower and tapped Goldman on the shoulder. "I told Nicole you'd be out here. Looking good, my man."

Goldman's smile morphed into a scowl when he saw Nicole. He rose, brushed dirt off his pants and motioned toward the patio. "Have a seat, unless it's too cold for you, Miss Nelson."

Jett seemed oblivious to the tension. He plopped down on a rough-hewn bench and sighed. "Lots of excitement in Goodhaven lately, Doc. Guess you heard about my brush with death."

Harris shot him the look he'd once saved for obtuse students. "Whatever are you talking about?"

After Jett's unexpurgated account, the old man pursed his lips in a look of savage joy. "I hadn't heard, but frankly it's not surprising. Parents around here never discipline their children."

Nik steeled herself for confrontation. Despite her best efforts, she and Goldman had been antagonists from the start. Shelby found the situation amusing. "Don't let the bastard get away with anything, Cookie. That type feeds on weakness." Nik sent a silent entreaty Shelby's way and soldiered on.

"Sorry to barge in, Dr. G. Your garden's spectacular. Whatever you've planted here, it's wonderful."

He gave her a quizzical, almost hostile, look.

"Forgive her, Harris. Nicole's just like me, doesn't know holly from weeds." Jett could be charming when he applied the social saddle soap. Harris Goldman's manner gradually thawed to room temperature.

"If you're interested, I can show you." He pointed to the thick green shrubs hugging the ground. "That's evergreen.

Covers winter and summer. It gets frigid out here, you know, so I plant hardy varieties. The rest are boxwood and rhododendrons."

"You know a lot about gardening. Have you always been an enthusiast?"

Goldman's eyes clouded with pain. "I didn't really have the time until last year." He turned away. "I'm alone now, so I can do as I like."

"Looks like they're about to bloom," Nik observed, hoping she hadn't made another *faux pas*. Ingratiating herself with Goldman was hard work. She took a deep breath, pretending he was one of the many academic fuddy-duddies she'd had to face.

"Wrong, Miss Nelson. You won't see those purple beauties for another six weeks." His little eyes were pincer sharp. "But I doubt you came here for gardening tips. What do you really want?"

Jett cringed at the harsh tone, but Nicole welcomed it, even reveled in it. She leaned forward and locked eyes with her host.

"I came for your help, Dr. Goldman, and your candor. Why was Shelby blackmailing you?"

Seventeen

Goldman blanched. He staggered back, gripping the sturdy arm of an Adirondack chair for support.

"Hey! Everything okay, Harris?" Jett's eyes looked enormous behind his round spectacles. "Let me get you some water."

The old man waved him off and gulped a lungful of air. "You're most direct, Miss Nelson. Are you accusing me of murder?"

Nik's courage ebbed. What if the little creep stroked out or had a heart attack? They'd blame her; she knew they would. Academics stick together. Boston College would ban her from getting her doctorate, rescind her scholarship, have her arrested.

"I'm speaking to you, young lady." Goldman sounded fully recovered and in charge. "Explain yourself."

She glimpsed Jett's stunned expression. He really was a wuss. Alejandro—hell, even Jarrod Whitholm—wouldn't fold that fast. She'd bet Goldman intimidated plenty of students, especially young women. *Not this time, professor.*

"I'm asking for an explanation, not accusing. I've learned some things about Shelby that trouble me. Coercion, extortion, blackmail, call it what you will. She had something on you, and I know it."

"Ridiculous! She had nothing." Goldman's face was way too calm. "Besides, I have no money. Shelby knew that."

Now it was Nik's turn to laugh. "Let me explain. Shelby never wanted money. She wanted good deeds, expiation.

That's why you volunteered at the animal shelter and withdrew your petition."

"Leave it, Double N. Harris answered your question." Jett's attempt to man up was pathetic. Nik angled away from him. This was between her and Harris Goldman.

"I suppose Sheriff Fuselli knows your absurd theory?" Goldman's fierce little eyes were razors trimming away excess words.

"Yes."

Goldman's mouth formed a thin, straight line. "Why not? You have no proof of anything. Neither did she, for that matter. Shelby found out about an academic dispute at Columbia. Plagiarism. A rival brought me up on charges. Poppycock, of course. Everything was dismissed, but my reputation suffered, and I left." He rubbed his hands together like a magician. "That's your big mystery. It was common knowledge in my world. Hardly worth killing for, wouldn't you agree?"

Nicole was genuinely curious. "Why did you give in? Why not tell Shelby to publish and be damned?"

Suddenly, Goldman looked diminished. "I'm tired. Old. People in Goodhaven respect me. I couldn't risk losing that respect." He gave a wintery smile. "You're what, twenty-four? When you're my age, you'll understand."

He turned away, gathered his gardening tools and walked slowly into his house.

"I really blew that," Nicole said. "I even forgot to ask him about Jarrod's car."

"Well, don't go back now," Jett said. "For Christ's sake, Nicole, that was painful. He's old, feeble. Let him keep his dignity, at least."

They took the scenic route to Mindbenders, pausing to watch the sailboats skimming the velvet waves. Goodhaven's fishing fleet was a shadow of its former self, handcuffed by depleted stock, falling prices and federal meddling.

"Fisherman, they've got the life," Jett said. "Out on the ocean all day, battling the elements. Free."

Nicole spun around and punched his arm. "Are you insane or just overdosed on Hemingway? Listen to those guys sometime. They've got one of the most dangerous jobs around and barely eke out a living. If that's freedom, forget it."

"You'll have plenty of options soon, thanks to Shelby. I guess that's the real freedom, huh? Big bucks." Jett's face got that soft, filmy look that Nik had come to dread. "Could you ever … ?" He saw Nicole stiffen. "I guess not. Forget it."

"You'd better get back, or you'll lose customers," Nik said. "Thanks for playing sidekick today, good buddy."

Jett curled his lip. "That's me, every schoolgirl's friend." He hit the gas, guiding his sensible sedan down the narrow roads to Goodhaven.

As Alex sat in Fuselli's office, cooling his heels, he fumed. He'd gotten a slew of emails from angry clients wondering where the hell he was. Bunch of rich pissants with too much cash and nothing to do. They needed a nanny, not a lawyer. Now Fuselli was badgering him, summoning him as if he were the prime suspect. He thought about the break-in at Mindbenders. Fortunately, that paunchy bookseller had a hard head, not that it was filled with brains. Alex swore that Jett Hall knew something. He absently finger-combed his thick, black hair with no touch of grey. Good hair, courtesy of his Japanese father. If only the rest of life were so easy. Instead of wasting time waiting for Fuselli, he should hop the next jet to L.A. and forget about everything, including Nicole Nelson. Especially Nicole.

"Sorry to bother you, Dr. Lee. This won't take long." Fuselli gave him a cold, hard stare. "I've been checking up on you."

Alex raised his eyebrows. "And …?"

Something about him got under Fuselli's skin. That had been obvious from the beginning. It had happened before, too many times to mention. Alex knew his only option was to stay cool and tell the truth.

"Look, Dr. Lee. I always try to be honest, especially with myself." Fuselli shook his head. "You annoy me, plain and simple, and it's clouded my mind. I see the way Nicole moons over you, and Danielle, too, but I just don't get it. Who can figure women?"

Alex laughed. "Let me get this straight. You're harassing me because women like me. That's crazy."

"Not really," Fuselli said. "This power over women, it even worked on Shelby, the least gullible woman in the known world. She trusted you. Maybe more." He narrowed his eyes. "She was lonely and at that vulnerable age. Maybe a handsome guy like you made her feel young again." He leaned forward. "She gave you those codes. Who knows what you did with them? We only have your word. If she found out and threatened to tell, you'd have to shut her up."

Anger swept over Alex with gale-force winds. *Control yourself. Don't react.*

"You spin quite a tale, Fuselli. Too bad it's fantasy. Prove it, if you can."

The two men spent a full minute trading glares. Fuselli mangled his pencil as he sat there.

"Okay. Forget about that for now. This whole comic collection angle mystifies me. I admit it. After spending the last three nights reading everything I could find about collectible comics, my head's spinning."

"Anything I can help you with?"

Fuselli shook his head. "Naw. You know I used to work tax cases. Now I ask you, what's more boring for a jury than that? Know what I did? I outlined the case the way a juror was likely to think, logically and simply. Forget all the folderol, and reduce it to motive. Jurors understand greed, arrogance and stupidity. They convict on it. The same principles apply here. Some sociopath thinks his needs outweigh someone else's life. When I find the motive, when I pin it down, I'll have my killer. It may mean poking under rocks, annoying a lot of the locals, but I'll get there."

"Good to know."

Alex glanced out the office window and saw trouble on four feet. Morgan Haas, trailed by his dyspeptic wife, was heading their way. Morgan's face was granite-hewn, probably a trick he'd learned in the financial mosh pits. Amanda Haas was far easier to read as she stomped along, ridiculous in three-inch heels, with her spindly arms pumping away. She was furious and making no attempt to hide it.

"You've got company, Sheriff. Look out the window."

Fuselli swiveled around and cursed. "Shit. Just what I need. I told her to come alone. Fuck. The mayor will blow his top. Just when I was starting to love the Cape."

"Are we done here?" Alex asked.

"For now. Remember what I said, Dr. Lee. Greed and arrogance."

Alex opened the door as Goodhaven's mayor stormed in. He exchanged brisk nods with Morgan Haas and made his escape. As he left he heard Fuselli ladling on the charm.

"Mr. Mayor, Mandy, come on in. "Thanks for being so prompt."

Eighteen

Time stood still that day. At least it seemed that way to Nik. She spent the afternoon glued to her computer, stealing an occasional glance at her watch as the hours inched by. Who knew when he would be back? After all, Boston traffic was horrendous, and Route 6 was no bargain. Even a minor accident caused chaos, transforming the only highway to Cape Cod into a parking lot.

She knew how destructive obsession could be. Hell, she'd lived it before. Something told her Alex Lee might just be worth the risk. After all, Shelby had liked and trusted him. That meant something, didn't it? He was no murderer. She would swear to that. Wishful thinking or sound judgment? Who could say?

When the phone rang, Nik leapt up, nearly crushing Atticus in a mad rush to grab the receiver. Her behavior was puerile and ridiculous, but she just didn't care.

"I'm on my way," he said, sending chills down her spine. "Just passed Plymouth. I've got a lot to tell you."

"Me, too. You should be here by seven-thirty. Back in Goodhaven, I mean."

Alex chuckled, that rich deep sound that she treasured. "You got it right the first time. I plan to park right on your doorstep unless you sic Fuselli on me. I'm not his favorite person right now."

Instead of sputtering, Nicole remained silent.

"Silence is consent under English common law, so I'll take that as a yes. See you soon."

Nik hugged Foo Dog and dashed for the shower. She had just enough time to transform herself from plain Jane to femme fatale.

At times like these Nik yearned for a joint or maybe a Valium. Not that she used drugs; she couldn't afford anything that slowed her progress, even if it calmed her shattered nerves. Alejandro Lee ravaged her psyche like a cotton gin. No other man had ever done that. Certainly not Mark Murray, her faithless fiancé. He was a callow youth; Alejandro was a man.

She tried to dress down. No sense in looking like she had expectations. Still, she wore her best denim skirt with a flame-colored cashmere sweater. He'd be used to that, coming from California.

When he arrived, Nicole waited for the second ring of the chimes, much more civilized than charging the door. Fortunately, Alex abandoned caution and used his own playbook. He swept her into his arms while dangling a bright red bag over her head like mistletoe.

"What's that?" Was there a woman alive who couldn't recognize Cartier's exquisite logo? Nik feigned ignorance.

"Just a token, my lady. I had business in Copley Plaza this afternoon, and I couldn't resist. Come on. Open it."

Blood suffused her face from cheeks to the roots of her hair. "I ... I can't accept this."

He ruffled her hair. "Ah, come on. Don't be silly. Open it first. You might be disappointed."

She recognized it the moment she opened the little red pouch. A gold, bean-shaped pendant suspended from a delicate chain. It was lovely and priced within the bounds of propriety. In sum, the perfect gift.

"Well?" His eyes were bright with expectation.

"I love it," Nicole said, fastening the chain around her neck. "Thank you, Alex."

They sat at opposite ends of the sofa with Atticus and Annabel as chaperones and Foo Dog dozing in the corner.

"You said you had news." Alex said. "Well, come on. Don't make me beg." He gave her a dimpled smile. "Have I mentioned how well I beg?"

"It's an admirable trait in a man." Nik matched his smile and upped the voltage.

She centered herself and gave him a concise summary of her contretemps with Harris Goldman. "I still think he's a mean little man, but he's not the murderer. Academic rivalries aside, it's not worth killing for."

Alex's brow knotted as he digested the information.

There goes that Byronic thing again, Nik thought. *How many men look sexy when they frown?*

"I guess you're right about Goldman," Alex said, "but I'm not giving him a hall pass just yet. Age doesn't preclude violence. Let's keep him on the list."

Nik had to say it. "You're still on that list, too, you know."

He found her hand and gently brushed his lips over her knuckles. "Are you frightened, Nicole? Just say the word, and I'll leave."

"Not before you tell me your big news. Fair is fair."

"Brave talk," he said. "Okay. Here it is. I've finished the appraisal of Shelby's collection. It's still preliminary, mind you—needs an independent review—but the stuff is high grade. Primo. Definitely heirloom material. No Ashcan but …"

Nik leaned forward in her seat. "But what? Come on, Alex."

His body tensed. Nik had to admit that it was a pleasant sight. So many muscles, so little time.

"Hello, still with me?"

"Absolutely." Nik pinched herself to restore her sanity.

His grin acknowledged her lie. "As I was saying, there was no Ashcan in the group, but I found something very interesting."

Nik felt like jumping out of her skin. "Stop dicking around, or I swear Atticus will claw your eyes out."

"Okay, okay," he laughed. "Wow! You're like one of the Furies! Anyway, what I found was correspondence, evidence that Shelby placed that ad on eBay. You know, the one for a five million dollar Ashcan."

Her throat felt parched, as if she'd been stranded in the Gobi for a week. "So where is it? Oh, God, I knew it!"

"Rampart has an excellent login system," Alex said. "I found no record of an Ashcan or even some mysterious unnamed comic going out, but there was an ambiguous reference on the incoming list. That indicates one of two things. Either Shelby stashed the Ashcan elsewhere to deliberately mislead me, or someone nabbed it."

Nik gave him a cool, level glance. "I can think of other possibilities. Maybe it was a chimera. You know, another one of Shelby's games. Did she ever mention it to you?"

Alex hesitated before answering. "No, but she threw out hints. 'I've got something special to show you,' or 'you'd be surprised what an old lady can accumulate.' Stuff like that." He stroked his chin as if he were revisiting the conversation. "She liked playing games, Shelby did."

"You're right. She adored chess. Played it with Jett all the time." Nicole took a deep breath and summoned her courage. "Something else. Maybe someone close to Shelby stole the Ashcan."

Alex gave Nicole an opaque look and helped her with her coat, making a sweeping gesture. "We'd better get going. By the way, I called Jarrod. He'll bring Danielle over for drinks later on. Oh, and there's one other thing you should know. Fuselli has me in his sights as the prime suspect."

"What? That's absurd." Nicole started to object but caught herself. Dr. Alejandro Lee was mighty pushy for a hired hand. Did he want to find the murderer, or was it just the Ashcan he coveted? She pushed aside the niggling doubts. Alex was perfectly positioned to find it, even if it meant murdering an old woman who trusted him. His buyer with the deep pockets could sequester it from any public scrutiny. Private collectors did that all the time. If that were true, why was he still in Goodhaven?

"Something wrong, Nicole?"

His gaze seemed untroubled. Was that a look of innocence or the cold indifference of a sociopath? Nicole pinched herself again before things got crazy. Too many detective novels clogging her brain.

"Everything's fine. Let's go."

The Cliff House restaurant had barely opened its doors. They found an isolated table overlooking the ocean with only the hint of pulsating waves and the toss of whitecaps. Alex automatically ordered for both of them without even a qualm of guilt. Nicole observed him as he recited their choices to the waiter. He seemed pleased, as if the act conferred some sort of propriety rights.

Watch it, she told herself. *This guy has more moves than Mayflower. He'll break your heart and make you bleed.*

They spent the evening sipping wine, grazing on salad, and wolfing down Goodhaven oysters while revisiting the list of suspects in Shelby's murder. Shelby. It always came down to her. In some twisted way Nik thought Shelby would be pleased by the attention. She'd enjoyed manipulating others, even though her motives were usually pure. Murder was the ultimate puzzler, the mode of death most likely to wound the innocent and worry the guilty.

"You're pensive, Ms. Nelson," Alex said. "Want to share?"

She glanced down at the napkin crumpled in her lap. "I forgot to ask you. What about those imposters? You know, the ones on the videotape."

He shook his head. "No clue. That's Fuselli's territory and he wasn't in the mood to confide in me. According to the Rampart logs, they didn't take anything, but I wouldn't bet the ranch on it. They obviously knew something about Shelby's collection, including her passwords." Alex reached across the table for Nicole's hand. "Come to think of it, I've changed my mind. Unless we believe that another elderly woman masqueraded as Shelby, I don't have much faith in the security at Rampart. Pretty hard to impersonate that chin of Jarrod's, too."

"What's that? I heard you taking my name in vain." Jarrod Whitholm, accompanied by Danielle, stepped up to their table. "Mind if we join you?"

Danielle gave Nicole a scalpel-sharp stare designed to wound. *Not much of a challenge,* Nik thought. An exquisitely groomed woman could easily lacerate an impoverished student. Nik felt uncomfortably aware that she was wearing denim, while Danielle was garbed in a sensuous silk dress slit high enough to draw every man's eyes.

"Have a seat," Alex said, moving closer to Nicole. "We were just discussing our favorite topic."

He summarized Nik's encounter with Harris Goldman and his own tussle with Fuselli.

Taking charge again, Nik noted. *This guy never quits.*

Jarrod said little, although his pale blue eyes followed every word. Danielle had another agenda. She spent her time ignoring Nik and throwing come-hither looks at Alex. Nicole was wise to those tricks: rapt attention, fluttering eyelashes and flashes of thigh. They were stock pieces in every woman's playbook. She couldn't compete with Danielle's feminine wiles, but when it came to intellect, Nicole took a back seat to no one. Cold comfort under the circumstances.

"I thought your pal at Columbia was thorough," she said to Jarrod. "How come he never mentioned this plagiarism thing?"

"Who knows?" he snapped. "He wasn't under oath. Maybe they hushed it up. Universities abhor anything to do with plagiarism. It's worse than a sex scandal."

"Maybe Goldman was lying," Danielle purred, her voice sugar-sweet. "Men hate admitting things like that. Sexual kinks. Makes them feel inadequate." She glanced sideways at Jarrod, causing him to flush.

Nicole felt a surge of compassion for Jarrod. He was so obviously whipped by his fiancée that it was downright pitiful. Why stick with a bitch like Danielle? Jarrod wasn't in Alex's league, but he wasn't repulsive either. Some woman would appreciate him.

"Back to this Ashcan issue," Jarrod said. He was himself again, strident and a touch arrogant. "Has anyone checked in with Fuselli? Instead of poking around everyone's business, he should pursue the money angle. My aunt died because of it."

Nik recalled Jett had mentioned something about Danielle and debt troubles. "Fuselli's looking into finances," she said, "everyone's. Someone with money worries would have a motive." She gave Danielle a smile of pure innocence. "With the recession and all, I'll bet a lot of people are hurting."

"What about you, Danielle? Found out anything?" Alex kept his voice neutral and his arm around Nicole.

"Remember, I work for a living." Danielle bristled. "I did see Amanda Haas stumble out of Fuselli's office today. She looked distraught, as if he'd really worked her over." She shrugged. "I'm having lunch with her tomorrow. Maybe she'll know something."

"Good. I'll join you, if it's okay." Nicole felt Alex squeeze her arm. "After all, two heads are better than one."

"You girls work it out," Jarrod said dismissively. "I doubt that flake knows anything of value, but you never know. My Wall Street pal is supposed to call me tomorrow. Maybe he knows something about Haas."

Alex reached into his briefcase and produced a folder. "Here, Whitholm. This is my preliminary evaluation of Shelby's collection along with my recommendations on how best to dispose of it." He lowered his voice. "Remember, my client is still interested in it, with or without the Ashcan."

Danielle stiffened as if she were in the throes of rigor mortis. "What's the value of it? The collection, I mean."

"Ask your fiancé," Alex said. "He and Nicole won that lottery."

Jarrod ignored the daggers Danielle shot his way. He seemed lost in thought, oblivious to her or anyone else. "Shelby didn't have a safety deposit box," he said. "Too cheap to rent one, I guess."

Nik laughed out loud. "That sounds just like her. Shelby never was a big spender."

"What do you call those comic books," Danielle hissed, "chicken feed? Face it. Shelby was a selfish old bag who enjoyed taunting everyone. I'm surprised she lasted this long."

There was silence, dead silence. Nicole turned away, gritting her teeth. Might as well keep everything civilized. For two cents she'd kick Danielle's elegant behind out the door. Hell, she'd do it for free.

"Let's go, Danielle." Jarrod's face was carved in grim, unyielding lines. "Call you tomorrow, Lee." He nodded to Nicole and hustled his fiancée out the door.

"Don't forget lunch tomorrow," Nik trilled. "Noon at Crazy Eights."

Nineteen

Nicole poked her head into Fuselli's office the next morning, armed with two espressos and a big smile. "Got a second, Sheriff?" she asked.

He leaned back in his desk chair, shaking his head. "What I've got is a complaint about you, missy. Harassing senior citizens. Very naughty."

"That little creep. I did not harass him. Ask Jett. He's my witness." She handed Fuselli a cup and sat down in the guest chair facing his desk. "Harris Goldman has a nerve. Plus, I think he lied to us." She could feel the heat rising in her face.

"You like law enforcement?" Fuselli deadpanned. "You must, 'cause you're trying to do my job." He wagged his finger. "Times are tough when a college kid does my job."

"I'm helping you." Nicole gave him her earnest scholar look. "Come on, we have the same goal here: finding Shelby's killer. I'm surprised at you."

Fuselli closed his eyes and sighed. "This isn't Agatha Christie. Get that through your head." He winked at Nik when he saw her reaction. "Joking. Not about you snooping, though. This murderer overpowered an old woman and brutally beat her. What about that don't you understand?"

Nicole batted her eyelashes, giving him the biggest smile her lips could manage. "Okay, I'll keep my information to myself then." She tossed her cup in the trash and rose.

"Hold on. Tell me." Fuselli threw his hands up in the air.

She was proud of her analytical skills. In five minutes Nik gave Fuselli every scrap of information her group had gathered.

"Wow! Remind me to deputize you guys. Let me see if I've got this straight. Harris Goldman is a cheat or maybe a bully. Mrs. Haas was being blackmailed for unknown reasons. Mayor Haas might be an embezzler, and two unidentified people may have stolen a five million dollar comic. Frankly, it doesn't sound like much. Lots of mights and maybes"

That deflated her like a child's balloon. Nicole's pride in their work fizzled fast as she considered the evidence. Unfortunately, Fuselli was right.

He gave her a scowl that must have terrified tax cheats. "Funny thing. You didn't mention the money motive both you and Jarrod have. Dr. Lee is another issue. Oh, yeah, and then there's Ms. Stevens. She has several judgments against her already and just about lost that fancy car of hers. Maybe she wants her fiancé to inherit and bail her out."

Nik's mouth dropped open. "Really?"

"Really. Judgments are public record. I'm not divulging anything confidential. I just want you to realize that this thing isn't cut and dried. You keep poking around, and you may get more than you bargained for. Not every case has a happy ending."

Nicole left the sheriff's office consumed with doubt. Was Fuselli right? Was she wasting everyone's time? She'd thought—hoped, actually—that he'd use her as an unofficial partner like in the mystery novels she loved. Today's lecture made clear that it would never happen. Maybe she should step back, fire up her computer and stop playing sleuth. Shelby had been the ultimate pragmatist. She'd understand.

"Yo, Double N, what's up? Don't tell me you're under arrest." Jett's wide grin told her he was glad to see her.

"I'm free, no thanks to that creepy friend of yours. Can you believe he complained to Fuselli about me?"

Jett kept quiet, but his amusement was evident. "Ah, so what? Harris is kind of crotchety, but he's old and lonely. I'm about his only visitor since his wife left."

"Oh, boo hoo. If he'd been nicer, she wouldn't have left. Ever think of that?"

He put his arm around her, steering Nicole toward Mindbenders. "Forget about that. Come into the shop for a minute. I have big news."

She checked her watch. "Okay, but I can't stay long. I'm meeting Amanda and Danielle for lunch."

They claimed a corner table isolated from other book seekers. Nicole could barely hide her impatience. She needed quiet time to plan her luncheon strategy, not a gabfest with Jett.

"Okay," she said, "let's hear it. What's so damn hot?"

Jett rubbed his hands together like a third-rate magician. "I'm leaving Goodhaven. Moving to a big city like New York or Boston, maybe Paris." His face had a fanatical glow that Nicole found unsettling. Behind his carefully polished glasses, Jett's eyes radiated mania.

"Are you crazy?" she asked. "Not two days ago you spent an hour telling me about your life plan. Remember the drill? Small town doesn't equal small life. What about writing and family values, not to mention money, filthy lucre? All that idealism takes money, you know."

"That was before I won the lottery."

"What?"

"Oh, not the real lottery. It's just an expression. A couple of years ago I invested in an obscure e-business. A start-up, online shoes. I never thought it would amount to that much, but I knew the founder from Amherst. Yesterday a foreign conglomerate snapped it up." Jett chucked her under the chin. "I'm going to be rich, baby. Well, maybe not rich, but comfortable, very comfortable, and you can share it with me."

Nicole spoke without thinking. "You're delusional. I'm not going anywhere, at least until I finish my dissertation. Even then I've got another year of study ahead of me."

His body sagged as if she'd poleaxed him. For a moment Nicole feared he might cry.

"I see. Would you say that if Alejandro Lee made the offer?"

He caught her off guard. Nik tried to backpedal, but it was too late. How would she feel if Alex offered her the world? Even a little piece of it would do.

"Don't bother, Nicole. I get the message loud and clear. Just do me one favor."

"Anything."

"Don't let the others know yet. I've got to make arrangements with the store and get my things in order."

She got up and kissed his cheek. "Of course. And Jett, congratulations. I'm so happy for you."

The others were already there when Nik arrived at Crazy Eights. The restaurant buzzed with conversations among the usual crowd of locals, tourists and a sprinkling of fisherman. As soon as Nik appeared, Amanda Haas sprang up, waving her arms.

Great, Nik thought, *subtlety*. She'd already had two shocks that day and girded herself for another. She hoped the sight of Danielle's poisonous smirk wouldn't be the final straw.

"Nicole, so glad you made it." Danielle had managed the impossible, looking incredibly chic while wearing a simple black sweater and leggings.

"Have you already ordered?" she asked.

"No, we waited," Danielle said. "I know how much you enjoy a hearty meal." She patted her own taut abs.

"I'm famished," Mandy said. "Can't wait to dig into some clam bellies. Yum!"

Normally Nicole would have joined her, but under the gimlet eye of Danielle Stevens, she'd lost her appetite. "Maybe I'll just have chowder today. It's so tasty here."

Nik studied Mandy's face, noticing the dark circles under her eyes. "How are you feeling?" she asked her.

Amanda gave a robotic smile that said nothing. "Fine. Never better."

Time to make a move. Nicole leaned toward her and patted her arm. "You need to trust us. What did Shelby have on you? Your life may depend on telling the truth."

"She's right," Danielle snarled. "Cut the crap, Mandy. For once in your life, face facts."

Tears dripped slowly down Mandy's rouged cheeks. She seemed diminished, as if they'd robbed her of her innocence.

"I didn't mean it," she sobbed.

Danielle angled her chair to shield them from prying eyes.

"What? Let us help you." Nicole wasn't sure how far to push. Amanda had vaulted past normal years ago. Anything too harsh might throw her into the abyss.

"It's … sometimes I drink too much. I hardly ever drive anymore. You know that, Danielle. One night two summers ago, I hit someone."

Danielle gasped. "Oh, Lord!"

"He wasn't killed or anything," Mandy said. Her rheumy eyes pleaded for understanding. "He darted out in front of me. You know how those foreigners are on bicycles."

Nik could relate. Summer visitors to the Cape seemed to harbor a death wish.

"What happened?" she asked, dreading the answer.

"Just a broken arm." Amanda took a deep breath, as if steeling herself for more.

"You're hiding something," Danielle said. "Come on. Spill."

Mandy's face grew ashen. "I didn't stop. I should have, but I didn't." She clutched Nicole's sleeve in supplication. "Fuselli would have arrested me. It would have killed Morgan." She laid her head on the table and howled.

The stream of conversation slowed to a trickle as other patrons tuned into their drama. Their waitress scuttled over, pad in one hand, water pitcher in the other.

"What's wrong, hon?" she asked. "Need something?"

"She's fine," Danielle said. "Some water might help. We've recently lost a dear friend, and Mrs. Haas is very sentimental."

"I hated her," Mandy swore under her breath. "I'm glad she's dead."

Nicole couldn't process everything. "How would Shelby know about that? I assume there was no proof."

Mandy held a Kleenex to her nose, making noise a rampaging elephant would envy. "She was there, right behind me on that old Schwinn. Took a picture with her camera phone, too."

Things were now crystal clear. Shelby had meted out her own kind of justice by mandating community service for Amanda. Rather fitting when you think of it, unless it had cost Shelby her life.

Mandy grasped Nik's arm with surprising strength. "What should I do? Help me." Mascara trails inched down her tear-streaked face, giving her the look of a ravaged Kewpie doll.

"You have to tell Fuselli," Nik said, "before someone else does. With any luck he'll leave the matter as it is, probably make you surrender your driver's license or something."

Danielle rolled her eyes and pushed back her chair. "Come on. I'll go with you to find Morgan. He'll be too busy leering at me to give you a hard time."

Nicole stayed at the table, greedily sampling their newly arrived entrees. *After all,* she thought, *I need my strength.*

"I've been looking for you." Fuselli turned off the flashers on his cruiser and loomed over Alex Lee.

"Really? Couldn't you find a less dramatic way to contact me? I gave you my cell number yesterday when you grilled me." Alex kept his hands on the steering wheel in plain sight of the sheriff. No sense antagonizing a man with a gun.

"Come over to my office," Fuselli said. "I want to speak with you alone. Without Nicole."

"No problem."

Alex drove the five miles to Goodhaven, trailing in Fuselli's wake. He wasn't surprised. The sheriff had given him the fish eye from the start, and yesterday he'd practically accused him of murder. After all, conventional wisdom dictated that he who found the corpse was usually the murderer. Strangers were always suspects in small towns, especially when they hooked up with ripe local beauties fancied by other men.

Fuselli waved him inside and pulled out a chair. "Okay, Dr. Lee, let's talk turkey."

Alex burst out laughing. "Is that how you trapped tax cheats in Washington, Fuselli? The homey approach? Frankly, I'm disappointed."

"Tough." Fuselli glowered, his eyes more granite than grey. "What are your intentions toward Nicole? I know how you guys operate."

Alex knew how he should play it: respectful, low key. But something inside his sensible lawyer's mind rebelled. Fuselli had nothing on him, not really, and he'd be damned if he'd play tour guide on the lawman's fishing expedition.

"That's our business. We're both consenting adults. My intentions are my own business."

Fuselli was a big man, taller than Alex's six-foot-two by several inches. Alex was sure he'd had plenty of practice using that size to intimidate his prey.

"I'm concerned about Nicole. She's naïve, easily hurt." Fuselli spoke through gritted teeth. "Even worse, she's an innocent."

"What are you, her father? Sorry, older brother, unless you hoped for something closer. Nicole and I are friends. Good friends. I'm … very fond of her."

Alex looked down for a moment. Nicole. He was more than fond of her. Might even be in love with her. He should pull away, head for the hills. He knew that, but every time he saw her, something drew him closer. Soon he'd be unable to leave. If she gave him any encouragement, he'd stay forever.

The sheriff pulled a report from his top desk drawer, thrusting it at Alex. "I know your kind, mister. You're a pretty boy who victimizes women. This came in today from San Diego. Seems the police had a complaint filed against you."

Alex flushed, remembering the incident. "Had is the operative word. That was the act of a petty, spiteful woman who wanted more than I could give, nothing more."

"Hmm. According to this you defrauded her of her late husband's comic collection. It seems you became her very good friend, too, Dr. Lee, until she sold you that collection."

"I was cleared of any wrongdoing," Alex said, clenching his fists. "Check the facts, Fuselli. The California bar absolved me of everything. I paid that woman fair market value for those comics." He shrugged. "Can I help it if she thought she was in love with me?"

Fuselli leaned over until they were eye to eye. "Is that what Nicole can expect? You get her half of Shelby's collection and drop her like a hot rock? Maybe Shelby was the one in love with you this time. What's the matter? Did she threaten you when you wouldn't play ball?"

Alex hadn't had a knock down, drag out fight since high school. He'd trained in wushu to defend himself, not kick the ass of a love-struck cop. Still, it was tempting.

"Back off, man. You're an attorney, too. You understand how unpleasant a lawsuit would be. About Nicole, stay out of our lives."

Fuselli eased back into his chair, breathing hard. "Okay. Fair enough. Tell me what you found at Rampart today. Go slow so I can take notes."

Alex summarized his findings without giving a dollar figure. Things were volatile, and if Fuselli heard that millions were at stake, he'd go berserk.

"One more thing before I go." He scanned Fuselli's face without blinking. "What about those imposters, the ones who went to Rampart after me?"

"I've got no idea who they are, probably the same creeps who ransacked the main house and Nicole's place. They were looking for something important, that's for sure."

Alex pushed back his chair. "Are we done here?"

Fuselli's grin reminded him of a gator he'd once seen lurking in the shallows of the Everglades.

"Not quite. You discovered Shelby's body. Your prints are all over her house, and we have only your word that this

Ashcan is missing." Fuselli snapped his pencil in two. "Makes a man think."

Twenty

Nicole spent the afternoon writing. For better or worse, her research was done. Now the hard part started: finishing the dissertation. She'd promised her advisor to have everything ready in two months. That required focus and total concentration on her part. No more snooping. She'd leave the detective work to Fuselli and his minions. Probably.

Mandy's confession troubled Nik. Clearly the woman was unstable, childlike, actually. Had she lashed out at Shelby in a fit of rage? Drunk driving was no laughing matter, but it was all too common on the Cape. Hardly worth murdering an old woman over. Shelby's killer had been intelligent, methodical and highly organized. That didn't sound like the Mandy she knew, but it fit her husband perfectly. If Morgan decided to protect his wife, he'd have no problem planning a murder. Method and order were his watchwords.

Danielle had the icy blood of a cobra. Could she have subdued and tortured a woman who taunted her about her finances? In a New York minute. The theory was appealing but unlikely, unless Shelby just pushed Danny too hard.

How much did Jarrod really know about his bride-to-be? Maybe it was worth finding out. Nicole slipped a lead on Confucius and headed toward the main house. She wasn't meddling. After all, the poor dog deserved a walk.

Jarrod was home, if that snarling gas-guzzler he drove was any indicator. The Hummer was a steel sentinel sprawled across the driveway, daring intruders to come closer. Okay. She'd play it cool. Have a friendly chat. Trade information.

Nik left Confucius in a shady spot, chewing his bone. Jarrod, the dog-hater, would explode if Foo came anywhere near his precious house. Stealth and a delicate touch were called for. Right now she needed information and a bit of advice. Jarrod was many things, some of them dreadful, but no one could deny his intelligence. Alejandro was equally smart, but whenever Nik looked at him, it wasn't his mind that she considered. Not with those smoldering eyes, incredible hair and lithe body standing before her. She was a realist who knew that when his business concluded, Dr. Alejandro Lee would be in the wind, on to the next adoring female with something to trade. Reality stung, but it couldn't quench her dreams.

She rang the buzzer for what seemed like an eternity before Jarrod stumbled to the front door. His hair was plastered to his skull like that of the victim in a bad horror movie; his usually immaculate shirt was as wrinkled as a Shar-Pei pup's coat.

"What do you want, Nicole?" His manner was surly, his gaze unfriendly.

"I … I'm sorry to disturb you. I saw your car and thought … "

Suddenly Danielle glided past them and sped out the door without saying one word. Now everything made sense. Nicole pivoted, seeking an escape route. Jarrod was the last person she'd expect to find having an afternoon delight. So undignified. So human.

"Hold on," he growled. "Come sit down. Sorry if I was rude." He gestured toward Shelby's horsehair sofa. "Wait there for a minute while I clean up."

"I'll come back later," Nicole said.

He pointed to the sofa. "Sit. You just caught me at a bad time, that's all."

When he returned, Jarrod looked more like himself with neatly combed hair, pristine shirt and pressed trousers. Neither one of them mentioned Danielle.

"So," he said, "what can I do for you?"

Nicole pulled out a chart she'd made. "I need a sounding board, someone sensible who can give me an opinion."

"What's wrong with Dr. Lee?"

"Absolutely nothing." She spoke dreamily without thinking.

Jarrod rolled his eyes. "I get it. Okay, let's talk. I'm sure Fuselli warned you about interfering, right?"

She nodded. "Here's my list of suspects, motives and alibis. I included you, Alex and me for the sake of fairness."

He scanned the list, showing no emotion. "I see you've included Danielle, too."

"Did you know about her financial problems? Excuse me for getting personal, but it's important."

Jarrod's reaction was surprisingly good humored. "Yeah, I knew. Who do you think co-signed for most of her stuff? Danny's high maintenance. I've known that all along, but she was worth it, *was* being the operative word." He reached for his pen and crossed her name off the list. "We've ended our engagement. Still, Danny had no reason to kill my aunt. No financial motive, at least."

If the break-up bothered him, Jarrod concealed it well. He scanned the rest of the information and shrugged his shoulders. "What's this about Jett? Another of your boyfriends on the loose, huh?"

Nik repeated Jett's tale about some online shoe bonanza. "It sounded very suspicious to me," she said, "so sudden."

"Guess you don't read the business section. Yesterday, that e-business was bought for five hundred million bucks by a Swiss firm. His story rings true."

Guilt swamped her soul. She'd maligned Jett, her only confidant in Goodhaven, without giving him the benefit of the doubt. Some friend she was.

"Did your Wall Street pal come up with anything?"

Jarrod shrugged. "Nothing concrete. Haas did plenty of things that bordered on shady, but he left with a clean slate from his firm. According to my friend, Mandy is the head case, not Morgan. Our mayor's only crime is being obscenely rich."

"What's obscene?"

The corners of his mouth turned up in a grin. "Anyone richer than me."

Nik spent a long, lonely evening waiting for Alex. She didn't own him; she had no right to wonder where Alex was or with whom. Her mind agreed, but her headstrong heart agonized. Maybe Danielle, newly freed from Jarrod, had lassoed Alex. She'd licked her chops every time she saw him. This time she might have made a meal of him.

Work. That was the panacea for all that ailed her. It had always been reliable, far better than a pain pill. So why did footnotes and apt quotations seem so deadly dull tonight? She plodded onward, crafting meaningless phrases until her eyes burned and her stomach ached.

Foo Dog barked sharply just before midnight, causing Nik to leap up in panic. She'd fallen asleep with the lights still on and her computer humming. Terror consumed her as Confucius flung himself at the front door, snarling.

"It's okay, Foo, just the wind. Nobody's there." Her voice shook so much even Nicole heard the lies. She tied her robe snugly around her waist and took a deep breath. No need to overreact. Foo probably heard a raccoon, maybe a coyote. Oddly enough, they lived on Cape Cod, too, terrorizing domestic pets and small children.

Nicole turned off her computer, prepared to brew some tea and head off to bed. That's when she heard it. Someone was rattling her doorknob, trying to get in. Neither raccoons nor the wiliest coyote did that. Her heart started a series of Olympic quality pole vaults. She was young for a heart attack, but anything was possible. Visions of Shelby's grisly death quickened Nik's pulse.

Oh, God, had the murderer returned? She fled to her bedroom, desperate for a weapon. The bat, Shelby's Louisville slugger. It was peeking out from under a pile of clothing. Nik gripped it until her thumbs ached. *I can do this. Anyone who breaks in is toast!*

A steady diet of mysteries had taught Nik what not to do. No peeping out the door or heroics. She'd get her cell and immediately call Fuselli. Trouble was, she couldn't find it. To save money, she'd forsaken a landline, a sound business decision that might now prove deadly. That svelte little cell phone had a homing instinct for narrow crevices and hidey-holes. In her panic Nicole had zero chance of finding it.

She crept down the stairs, clutched the bat and hunkered behind the kitchen door, vowing to clobber anyone who opened it. For half an hour she strained to hear every ache and groan the old house made. Foo kept his hackles up, staying on high alert as he patrolled the perimeter of the house. Nicole forced herself to make the rounds, checking each window and door latch twice. It was almost two a.m. before she collapsed on the sofa, praying for the dawn. Things would be better in the daylight. Nothing would scare her then. Too late, she recalled that Shelby had been murdered on a sunny afternoon in broad daylight not fifty yards away.

Two firm knocks on the front door roused Nik from a dreamless sleep. Sunshine streamed through the woven drapes, ushering in the promise of a new day. Oh, God! Nine o'clock. Her head was a balloon poised to puncture at a moment's notice.

"Come on, Foo. Go get him." She clutched her bat and peered through the drapes, ready to do battle. Oh, joy! A matched set, Jarrod and Alejandro, stood shoulder to shoulder at her door. For once Nik ignored her appearance. After last night she'd earned her ravaged looks.

She flung open the door and faced them.

"What the hell happened to you," Jarrod gasped, "and what is this?"

He brandished a length of tri-colored rope braided into a noose.

Nicole awakened, stretched out on her sofa, ringed by the anxious faces of Jarrod Whitholm and Alejandro Lee. The troika of sleep deprivation, anxiety and shock had finally done their job. Weakness embarrassed Nik, especially her own. Now they'd brand her a fainter, some sort of frail vessel. Nothing could be further from the truth.

Alex squeezed her hand and spoke softly. "Stop worrying. You're safe now. Let us help you."

Nik balanced on her elbows and pointed at the noose. "So it's true. The murderer really was here last night." Despite the warmth of Gran's coverlet, Nik felt cold. Once the trembling started, it came in seismic waves that she was powerless to stop.

"Here, drink this. Do you good." Jarrod pressed a tumbler of copper-colored liquid to her lips." Don't shy away, girl. It's cognac, for God's sake, not poison."

Nik took a sip. "Fuselli ... "

"On his way," Alex said. "Relax. Wait 'til he gets here."

She closed her eyes, hoping it was a dream, a bizarre, particularly nasty fantasy. When Foo barked, Nik pulled herself upright, prepared to face the sheriff.

It comforted her, watching Fuselli's stolid form join the others. He was gentle, inveigling her to tell everything without using pressure. When she'd finished, he turned to Alex and frowned. "What's your story, Dr. Lee? I suppose you have an alibi for last night."

"The best there is. Truth." Alex locked eyes with Fuselli. "I drove in from Boston around midnight and went straight to bed. Alone."

"You live close by, Mr. Whitholm. An intruder would pass the main house."

Jarrod's jaw jutted out like a rocky shoal. "What's your point, Fuselli? If you're asking did I terrorize Ms. Nelson, the answer is no."

Fuselli used gloves to examine the noose. "I'll send it to Barnstable, but I doubt it'll do much good. Too many hands have touched it."

Somehow Nik found her voice. "Does it ... is it the same rope that hurt Shelby?"

He shrugged. "Hard to tell. It certainly looks similar, but that rope's very common around here." Fuselli tapped his foot as he sharpened his gaze. "Funny thing, though. I only told you and my deputy about the rope's color." He eyed the other men. "The murderer would know, of course. That's why I kept it quiet."

Nik hung her head, unable to meet Fuselli's eyes. "I'm the leak, sheriff. I mentioned it to Jett, and he told Harris. I was there when they discussed it."

"Great!" Jarrod barked. "Another clue wasted. It's time to throw in the towel, Fuselli. Call the state police or the FBI, someone who can handle this."

Bob Fuselli drew up to his full height and faced Jarrod. "That's not your call, Mr. Whitholm. Use your influence; do whatever you think is right. But I'll tell you this: Shelby Whitholm's murderer is here in Goodhaven. I'll find him—or her—no matter who takes over this case. That's a promise."

"What about Nicole?" Jarrod asked. "This maniac could murder her, just like my aunt."

Nik gasped. Being brave was tougher than she thought. Before she could speak, Alex put his arms around her.

"No one will hurt Nicole," he said turning those dreamy eyes her way. "I'm staying right here until this mess is over."

Twenty-One

She had never lived with a man before, just an occasional weekend with her faithless ex-fiancé. Nicole felt flustered, totally out of control. Being with Alejandro Lee twenty-four/seven would be impossible. She'd never finish her dissertation. Hell, she'd never get out of bed, if he were next to her.

"That's okay, Alex," she said. "I'm not frightened." It was a hollow lie that no one, including Nicole, believed.

Fuselli clasped Alex's shoulder. "Good idea. Word will get around that Nicole has a man staying here. It'll give the murderer something to consider."

"You really think the murderer left this rope?" Jarrod asked. "He's taking a big chance, sneaking around this property."

Nicole zoned out, imagining the scarlet letter some of the town biddies would brand her with. The rest of them, the ones who had actually seen Alex, would be absolutely bilious with envy. That didn't bother her. She worried more about the damage to her heart when he finally left her. Despite her tough exterior, the inner Nik was marshmallow soft, easily melted. She still believed in love no matter how unattainable it seemed.

"While we're at it," Alex said, "I've catalogued Shelby's collection. These estimates represent the price you might expect at auction." He fished an expandable folder from his briefcase as Jarrod loomed over him, reading the figures.

"Jesus! You weren't kidding. Aunt Shelby amassed a fortune here." He pointed at several items. "Are you telling me these Action comic things are worth over a million bucks each?"

Alex nodded. "Look at the dates, 1938. Not many DC comics still around, especially not in that condition. I'd be the first to say that Shelby knew her stuff and kept them pristine."

"I don't suppose you found that Ashcan thing?" Jarrod asked. His eyes had that glazed look common to small boys lusting after sweets and lottery winners.

"Nope. Remember, my client still wants these when the legal dust clears. Have my figures verified, though."

Jarrod smirked. "I intend to."

"I'm puzzled," Nik said. "Why murder Shelby if her treasure was safe and sound at Rampart?"

Fuselli shrugged. "Could be the murderer thought it would be easy to get at, which might explain those two impersonators on the tape. I know you favor the blackmail scenario, but it just doesn't wash. Nine out of ten times, murderers go for pure greed. Five million bucks buys a lot of greed."

"Why come after me," Nik asked, "especially after tearing this place apart once?"

Fuselli's voice was somber. "You've been poking around, asking lots of questions. Could be you made someone nervous."

"No more playing detective," Alex said, folding his arms. "That stuff stops now." He and Nicole locked eyes. Neither one of them gave an inch.

"I'm starved," Jarrod interrupted. "Got anything to eat around here?" He poked his head into the refrigerator, foraging for snacks.

"No time to shop," Nicole said. "Sorry. Don't you have anything at your place?"

"Of course not." Jarrod huffed like the big bad wolf. "That was Danny's job."

"Let's head over to Crazy Eights," Alex said. "Mmm. Oysters sound good to me."

After walking Foo and feeding her other pets, Nicole joined Alex and Jarrod. Her mind roiled with the impact of Shelby's legacy. Even after taxes, her share of the estate would be sizable. She had already vowed to donate ten percent to Lifelines in honor of Shelby. Maybe Jarrod would do the same.

Alex kept his arm firmly around her waist as they walked to the restaurant. It felt comforting, as if she were cherished and protected. Nik hated herself for yielding so completely to this stranger. After all, what kind of feminist allowed a man to waltz in and take over her life? The answer was simple: a woman in love.

She'd gone against every survival instinct, every rational impulse she possessed. At least she'd kept it to herself. No drama or cries of devotion. Alex had no idea how she felt, and she meant to keep it that way.

They'd just ordered lunch when his iPhone buzzed.

"Sorry, folks," he said, heading for the door. "I'll go take this."

Jarrod said little, but his eyes never left Nik.

"Okay," she said, "what's your story? You're acting weird even for you."

"You won't believe this, but I've grown to like you. Strictly platonic, naturally."

Ever the diplomat, Nik thought. "And ... ?"

He leaned forward, watching the door. "What do you really know about Lee? He's made some pretty fast moves."

Nicole was fed up with protective males. "What's your point, Jarrod?"

"Money, the root of all evil, the road to perdition. You know the drill. Maybe Dr. Lee really wants your comics instead of your body." He nodded sagely. "I've seen it happen. Not that you're undesirable."

"Oh, you're thinking of Danielle? Don't worry. I'm not that foolish."

Jarrod inflated like a puffer fish. He was still sputtering when their order arrived. Despite the provocation, five generations of Whitholm breeding kept him from causing a public scene.

When Alex returned, his face was a thundercloud. Zeus himself couldn't look more majestic, Nik mused, or more thoroughly hot. He said nothing, ignored the oysters and toyed with his drink.

"What's wrong?" Jarrod asked between forkfuls of fish. "You look like you swallowed a lemon."

Alex kept his voice steady. "Things are heating up. One of my colleagues just called to warn me. The Ashcan is in play again. Someone's offering it online for four million dollars. It was subtle," Alex said, "a very discreet inquiry addressed only to top-tier private collectors."

Nicole could barely speak. "How do we know it's Shelby's Ashcan? Aren't there a number of them?"

Alex stretched, showcasing impressive abs. "Very few. In fact, this 1939 Ashcan is unique, and so is the back-story. You see, two publishers, Fawcett and All American, were locked in a death struggle to establish ownership of Action No.1. The Ashcan was used as a legal proof of ownership. It's more of a shell, really, just enough for the courts."

"Big deal," Jarrod said. "You still haven't answered her question. What makes it so damn special?"

Alex leaned back as if he were in a trance. Was he praying or chanting? Nik couldn't decide which. When he finally opened his eyes, he seemed calm, almost tranquil.

"There's a reason they call this Ashcan the Holy Grail. Action Comics No.1 introduced Superman for the first time. Hell, it ushered in the whole concept of superheroes. Can you imagine? If Shelby had it, and that's a big if, it's priceless."

The whole Ashcan thing meant nothing to Nicole. Just a stupid hunk of seventy-three-year-old paper that could do a lot of good if it was sold. Alex, on the other hand, looked almost orgasmic. *I lack passion*, she concluded, *at least for comic books. I have plenty to spare for him.*

Jarrod was neither mystical nor passionate. He was a practical man who wanted action. Immediate action.

"What's the bottom line, Lee? Can you verify this, or are we back to square one with Fuselli?"

"You're an officer of the court. You know the drill. The sheriff has to handle this. After all, the seller may very well be the murderer." Alex gripped his drink as if his life hung in the balance. "There is something we could do to help."

"What?" Nicole and Jarrod spoke as one.

"Set a trap. Pretend to be an anonymous buyer. Draw out the seller. Lure him here."

"I'm in," Jarrod said.

"Me, too." Nicole surfed a tide of optimism. They were on their way. She knew it.

Alex glanced around. "Okay, boys and girls. Here's what we'll do."

The plan was simple but elegant. Alex would respond to the inquiry in his client's name, asking for details about the Ashcan's provenance and price. He'd set up a meet on the Cape, insist on some public space where Nik and Jarrod could observe everything. Then Fuselli could swoop in and arrest the culprit.

They spread out in Shelby's parlor, using the horsehair sofa as home base.

"I'm not sure it'll work," Jarrod groused. "How do we know the Ashcan's still in Goodhaven or on the Cape? It could be anywhere, for Christ's sake. This sounds too easy."

Alex shrugged. "What do we have to lose? Seems to me you have a couple of million reasons to do it. If the meet's beyond Fuselli's jurisdiction, he'll coordinate with the locals there."

Fuselli had plenty of objections. They started with entrapment and ended with jurisdictional issues. Nicole's head ached just hearing them argue. Three lawyers in one room were three too many.

"Stop!" she barked, holding up her hand. "You guys are overthinking this. First things first. Let Alex respond to the solicitation. He'll have to be cagey, but I'm sure he's up to the task."

"I'm not sure that's a compliment," Alex said with a lazy grin. "However, I accept the challenge. Everyone agree?"

Fuselli divided his time between scribbling things in his notepad and cracking his knuckles. He said very little, but Nik bet he was thinking plenty.

"Must you do that?" Jarrod snapped. "It's driving me crazy."

"Keeps me calm," Fuselli said. "Doesn't do much for my knuckles, though." He chuckled at his own joke and rose. "I agree with Nicole. Let's go for it."

Alejandro Lee slouched down in the Hummer, wondering how it all went wrong. He'd done it, actually agreed to Nicole's half-baked scheme for catching a criminal. *If* the seller really was a criminal, and the whole thing wasn't a hoax, that is. Sound judgment. He had always prided himself on his ability to use reason, not emotion. In the past he'd avoided lots of scrapes by being analytical. Since meeting Nicole, he was a mess. Anything she said, suggested or even hinted at became his command. The new Alex Lee was an impotent pawn, not in the physical sense, thank goodness, but in every rational aspect of his life. Each time she touched him, misery was mixed with pure ecstasy. It hurt so bad to feel so good.

"Are you in some kind of trance?" Jarrod asked as he swung into the driver's seat of his car. "You were talking to yourself again, Lee. Keep that up, and someone's going to drop a net over you."

Alex grinned. "Too late, I'm afraid. Someone already did."

"Oh, God, don't tell me." Jarrod shook his head in disgust. "You see what love did for me. Danielle took me for a bundle, then dumped me. Flat out cut off my nuts."

"You'll live. By the way, I responded to that solicitation using my corporate name, Eja Enterprises. Kept it low-key but trolled for information."

Jarrod fired up the Hummer. "Now what?"

"Now we wait."

Two days later Nicole got the call. Fortified by too much espresso and too little time, she had hunkered down with her pets and done some serious writing. Alex was away. He'd spent the day in Boston finalizing Shelby's arrangements with Rampart and waiting for something, anything, to happen. When he called, his voice vibrated with excitement.

"The fish took the bait," he said. "Let's assemble our team. Could be a long night."

"Okay. Anything special you want me to do?" She could hear the lust seeping through the cell phone.

"Oh, Ms. Nelson, you can't even imagine what I want you to do. But for now, just rustle up some snacks and contact Jarrod and Fuselli. The game's afoot, Watson."

"Hurrah," Nik said. "I got promoted from girl Friday."

Alex sighed. "Play your cards right, and I've got another big promotion for you tonight."

"I can hardly wait."

At eight o'clock they assembled at Nik's coach house, garbed in what they hoped was camouflage. Nik chose the universal student uniform, jeans and a black T-shirt. Jarrod bungled the concept of casual attire, but Fuselli got it just right. His disguise was perfect, indistinguishable from any Cape fisherman after a hard day's work. Jarrod's costume reminded Nik of a preppy gone bad or a frat boy on a scavenger hunt.

When Alex breezed through the door, her heart began tap dancing. She'd rarely seen him in business attire, but the wait was worth it. Dark navy suit, pristine white shirt with French cuffs and a red Hermes tie. Save us! She acknowledged him with a slight nod and said nothing.

"Ready?" he asked Fuselli. "Here's what I set up." He gave each of them a copy of his proffer to the seller. The second page contained a description of the article.

Nik scanned the sheet, looking for something, anything, that might identify the Ashcan as Shelby's. Although it was couched in colorless legalese, she found the basics. A 1938 Ashcan, Action Comics No. 1, CGC graded 8.5 (very fine).

"You really think this is Shelby's?" she asked. "What if we can't prove it?"

Alex shrugged. "Establishing provenance is always tricky, but that cuts both ways. The seller has to validate ownership, too. No one's going to pay huge sums for something that might be fraudulent or stolen."

"You didn't offer the full amount," Fuselli said. "Why not?"

A look of grudging admiration flashed in Jarrod's eyes. "I get it," he said. "Reel him in slowly. No need to spook the big fish by seeming too eager." He gave a mock salute. "Good job, Lee. Not your first rodeo, as they say."

Who the hell says that, Nik wondered, *pulp novels or amateur films?* Jarrod's attempt to be one of the guys was pathetic and transparent. Still, at least he was trying.

"Here's the thing," Alex said. "The seller agreed to meet with me tonight in Provincetown and bring a sample."

A mile-wide grin spread over Fuselli's face. "Just out of curiosity, where are you meeting?"

Alex tapped his iPad. "Someplace called the Crown and Anchor. In the bar area."

Fuselli's brows flew skyward. "Not in the Vault, I hope. I'm really not up for that."

Nik covered her mouth to keep from giggling. She'd once taken a tour of Provincetown with Jett. Although the Crown was a venerable establishment, the Vault was something else. It catered to a macho gay clientele with a sense of humor. She couldn't picture the lawyerly Dr. Lee, much less that stuffed shirt Jarrod Whitholm, at a leather bar. The U-Tube video alone would be priceless. He'd be expelled from the Federalist Society for sure.

"What's wrong? That's not the name," Alex said. He fumbled with a slip of paper. "Oh, yeah, I've got it. Forgot to transcribe the info. We're meeting in the Central House Bar and Grill. Anyone know it?"

"Oh, I've been there," Jarrod, said. "Danny liked their lobster cakes, although that whole scene's a bit edgy for me."

He looked at his watch. "It's almost eight thirty. When's the meet?"

"Ten o'clock. Everyone ready?"

Fuselli nodded and turned toward Nik. "Stay here. We can handle this thing on our own."

Anger, raw and pulsating, surged through her. Nik kept a leash on her temper as she faced Fuselli. "No way. I've been part of this from the beginning. I'll be there at the end."

Alex smiled at her, melting her heart like cheap chocolate. "It's okay, Sheriff," he said. "She'll be careful."

"Damn straight. Shelby counted on me, and I won't let her down." Nicole put on her game face. That quaking inside her was joy, not terror. She'd face the killer, watch his cowardly form slink off into the squad car, testify at his trial …

"We're waiting, Nicole. Change your mind already?" Jarrod smirked and headed for his Hummer.

"Whoa, partner. We'll blow our cover pulling up in that thing." Fuselli hesitated. "Sure can't use my squad car either."

Nicole wasn't fanciful, but at that moment she knew they weren't alone: Shelby Whitholm was with them. "It's sturdy, Cookie," she'd said, patting the door of her battered Jeep. "Not much to look at but strong enough to go the distance. Like me."

"Not a problem," Nik told them. "I have the perfect solution. We'll drive Shelby's Wagoneer."

Twenty-Two

Jarrod was livid. "No way. That thing must be older than I am. It won't even make it to Provincetown."

"It's a classic 1975 with bench seats and yellow interior, Just the type of vehicle a bunch of locals would use. It won't stand out either." Nik folded her arms and dared him to object.

Fuselli chuckled. "She's right, you know. Shelby kept that old doll humming. Always got it inspected, took it to the local garage for tune-ups and such. I'll contact the chief in Provincetown and read him in. They've got a good group up there." He pointed to Alex. "You better get going. We'll be right behind you."

"I insist on driving," Jarrod said.

Fuselli's scowl ended the discussion, forcing Jarrod to fume in silence. Alex squeezed Nik's hand and strode quickly toward his car. They waited silently while Fuselli made his arrangements.

"All set," he said, firing up the engine. "Remember, we're there strictly as observers. I'll drop Nicole off first, then find a parking spot. Jarrod and I will enter separately. Find the darkest area of the room, and get a table. I'll sit up at the bar where I can watch Alex. Don't say anything, and for God's sake, play it cool."

Cool? Nik considered that a relative term when her heart reverberated like a bongo drum. If the killer was local, he might bolt at the sight of Alex. She stuffed her long braid inside a baseball cap and hunkered down. Shelby's killer might be in custody by midnight. Could it possibly be that easy? What about her own life? Would Alex vanish like so many other people she had loved?

Nik considered the possibilities with an odd sense of detachment. Finding the murderer would expunge her debt to Shelby and free her to move on with life. Justice. Shelby was big on that. Even her excursions into blackmail had been focused on expiating sins. Compulsory atonement with a heavy dose of irony, that was Shelby through and through. The image of Amanda and Harris scrubbing the animal shelter brought a smile to Nik's lips. Mandy had practically gagged every time she'd eased a manicured toe toward Lifelines.

"Traffic's heavy for a weeknight," Fuselli said. "Guess I'll take Commercial Street and drop Nicole by the pier, okay?"

"Sure. Don't worry about me. I'll be fine."

"Huh!" Jarrod snorted. "We'll probably have to rescue her."

Nicole took a deep breath before speaking. "Bad attitude, Mr. Whitholm. Brush up on your social skills."

"Okay, kids, stop fighting. I can't drive and referee too." Fuselli maneuvered past a group of rowdy young men and stopped the Jeep. "Remember, Nik, play it cool. No heroics. This may all be a waste of time."

She hopped out and winked. "See you."

It was dark inside The Cove bar. Nicole stubbed her toe on a dense wooden table before she'd gone ten paces. Where the hell was Alex? She couldn't stare, and without her glasses she couldn't really see anything. The moment she got some cash she'd schedule Lasik surgery. Until then she'd have to squint, wrinkles be damned.

Most of the tables were taken, but Nik spied an opening against the back wall near the kitchen. *Blend in,* she chided herself. *Be inconspicuous.* Even though she loathed beer, she ordered a Sam Adams light. It seemed like a popular choice, if the empty bottles she'd seen were any indication.

Five minutes later Jarrod sauntered in, feigning indifference. Thank goodness he'd chosen law, not acting, Nik thought. He slouched at the far end of the bar, ordered a drink, and scarfed up a bowl of Beer Nuts. His body was angled away from Nik, giving him a full view of anyone entering the room. When Alex arrived, Nik's heart started those gymnastics she'd grown accustomed to. Instead of restraining herself, she reveled in it, luxuriating in every errant thud. *It means I'm alive,* she thought. *Involved. Obsessed. Doomed.*

Alex spoke with the waiter, handed him something and glided toward a small booth in the rear of the bar.

Where the hell's Fuselli? Nik wondered. Alex could be murdered without any of us seeing it. She gulped a lungful of beer and almost choked. *Ugh! How can anyone pretend to like this stuff?*

Without warning, the lights dimmed, and a jazz quartet fired up. The club was crowded now, full of pressing bodies, shrill sounds and clinking glasses. Nik focused on the only thing she could see, Alex's blazing white shirt. Out of the corner of her eye, she spied a man who might be Fuselli hunched over the bar clutching a drink. *Oh, God, please make it end!* She held her watch near the candlelight: ten-fifteen. Maybe it was a setup or a farce. Nik hunkered down, willing herself to be invisible. Jarrod turned toward the door as a tall, slim figure in black sweatpants and hoodie approached Alex.

He shook hands and pulled out a chair for his guest. Fuselli could hear everything, but Nik was flying blind. The quartet played Coltrane, exciting the crowd and causing some to rise from their seats. Nicole panicked. Was Alex in trouble? She drew a breath as she saw the flap of his jacket. His guest was gesturing wildly, as though ready to bolt. Suddenly Jarrod slipped off his chair and inched across the room. Fuselli easily beat him to the table. He moved fast for such a giant. Nicole threw down a bill and rose, refusing to become a mere spectator. The crowd erupted when the quartet started playing "Love and Happiness." A lout with a bushy beard corralled Nik, twirling her around like a marionette. A sharp elbow to his ribs left him howling and puzzled. She was almost there when she heard Fuselli's voice.

"Hello, Ms. Stevens. May I join you?"

Danielle Stevens lost her trademark poise, but only for a moment. She gave Fuselli a cool nod and turned toward Jarrod.

"Danny? How could you? What's going on?" The absurdity of his outfit and his shattered eyes stripped Jarrod Whitholm of any hubris. He had nothing left to say.

"Are you monitoring dates between consenting adults, Sheriff, or arranging a ménage a trios?" Danielle shrugged. "Either way, I'm game." She snorted when she saw Nik. "Oh, dear, this is family night. Little Miss Muffet is joining in."

Alex stayed very quiet, following everything with his bright eyes while his hands gripped a folder housing a Mylar sleeve.

"I heard everything, Ms. Stevens. Playtime's over." Fuselli nodded to a slim man in waiter's garb, who slid behind Danielle's chair and showed his badge.

"Provincetown police, ma'am. Best you listen to the sheriff."

"We have some things to discuss," Fuselli said. "Where we do it's up to you."

"Things?" Danielle raised perfectly arched brows.

"Criminal activities, I'm afraid. You know, felony theft, murder with special circumstances ... "

"Murder? You're delusional, all of you." Danielle shot a blistering glance at Nicole. "What's she been telling you? Or was it my fiancé, pardon me, my former fiancé? Unrequited love's a bitch, right Jarrod?"

"Enough of that. The deputy here will take you to the station house." Fuselli gestured toward the Provincetown cop.

"How stupid do you think I am? I'm not saying a word without my attorney."

Jarrod clenched his fist. "I'm your attorney, Danielle. Or at least I was."

The combination of music, chatter and emotion made conversation impossible until Alex stepped in.

"She can ride back to Goodhaven with me, Sheriff. After all, she's not charged with any crime yet. Ms. Stevens will be on her best behavior. Won't you, Danny?"

A slow grin transformed Fuselli's face. "Sounds like a plan. Take Ms. Nelson as your chaperone."

Alejandro Lee prided himself on navigating tight spots, but tonight Fuselli had outflanked him. He kept a firm hand on Danielle's shoulder while herding Nicole past the crowd and out the door. Alex wanted to touch Nicole, just to reassure her, but something told him to back off and concentrate on getting out alive.

He tried light conversation laced with humor. That bombed big time. Nik was noncommittal, and Danny ignored him. Both women sat stiff and wary, eyeing each other like spitting cats.

"You think you're so smart," Danielle sneered at Nik. "The big, bad college student."

"Doctoral candidate, actually. That means something to those of us in academia."

Alex tried hard not to laugh. Nicole was adorable in that baseball cap and tight jeans. Might be tough to take off those jeans, he mused. Good thing I'm up for a challenge.

"I'm curious," Nicole said. "Why did you do it? Murder seems out of character for someone like you. So messy."

Danielle snorted. "You don't know anything. I'll bet your boyfriend here didn't mention the nights we spent together. He went straight from you with your tight-assed ways to me." She sighed. "He's good isn't he? Pure bliss."

Color suffused Nik's cheeks, but she stayed silent.

Alex felt his world shifting and with it the promise of happiness fading away. He'd been stupid, risked everything he'd ever dreamed of. Time with Danny meant nothing. It was hollow sex, full of practiced moves and knowing grunts. A familiar world of physical release, nothing more. He'd tried using her as a shield to ward off his feelings for Nicole. It hadn't worked.

Making love to Nicole was special. Touching her skin, hearing her sighs as she found release, feeling complete for the first time in his life. He loved her. God help him, he did. He'd never felt that way before, and it was terrifying. From the frozen look on Nik's face, that might not matter anymore. Danny's poison may have found its mark.

"What's the matter, lover boy?" Danielle rasped. "Cat got your tongue? You're pretty talented with that tongue as I recall." She turned toward Nicole, licking her lips.

"It won't help, Danny," Alex said. "All your scheming won't count in a court of law. They take murder seriously, you know. Beating and torturing an old lady, that's going to cost you."

The word murder punctured her bravado. "Hold on! I never ... You've got to help me, Alex. I swear I had nothing to do with Shelby's death."

"Her *murder*, you mean." Nicole came out swinging. "You needed money, and you murdered her for that Ashcan." She curled her lip as she faced Danielle. "I knew you were venal but not vicious. I underestimated you."

"You've got to believe me, Alex." Beads of sweat formed on Danielle's forehead. "Fuselli likes you. He'll listen to you. Please."

This was his chance. Alex knew that if he played his cards right, he just might find the Holy Grail. He'd pay a price, though, a price that might include losing Nicole.

"You lied about the Ashcan," he said. "You never even had it."

A smug expression replaced her fear. "You're wrong. Maybe we could make a deal, cut out Mary Poppins and Jarrod and take off." Danny leaned forward, massaging his neck. "I could make you happy. You know that."

"Alex, no!" Nicole's eyes filled with tears.

"What would your partner say?" Alex asked. "I'm not good at sharing."

"Him? He's no threat. Believe me. We'll just pin everything on him after we get the Ashcan. With your connections selling it should be no problem."

Alex stared at Danny through the mirror and saw unvarnished greed. Funny, he'd once thought she was beautiful.

"My client still wants it. Naturally, he'll expect price concessions. Anything associated with murder loses value."

Danielle showed her most seductive smile. "We can work it out. I wasn't lying, though. We had nothing to do with Shelby's murder. The Ashcan was an unexpected bonus."

Alex reached under his seat and threw a length of tricolor rope to Danielle. "Tie her up good and tight. I think we've got a deal." He wrenched the car to the side of the road and stopped.

"Are you crazy?" Nicole elbowed Danny in the head and lunged for freedom.

"Sorry, Darling. It ends here." Alex leveled a shiny black handgun at Nik's forehead.

Twenty-Three

"Truss her up," he said. "Don't hurt her. Just make it good and tight. I figure we've got an hour before Fuselli sounds the alarm."

Danielle grimaced as the rough twine bit her fingers. "Damn! It's hard to tie."

Alex popped the trunk and leapt out of the front seat. "Oh, for Christ's sake. I'll do it." He dragged Nik, kicking and screaming, out of the car and slung her over his shoulder. The shock had worn off and she fought for her life.

"Bastard! I trusted you! I loved you!" Nik aimed her boot tip at his genitals and raked his cheeks with her nails. She drew blood and an anguished howl from Alex.

"Fuck!" He clutched his crotch. "Damnation!" He dropped her on the ground in a heap. "That hurt."

"Come near me again, and you'll get worse." Nik hauled herself up and assumed a wushu fighting stance. She had excelled during training class, but this was the real deal. Form an L. Right foot forward. Make fists. Her mind was a tangled mass of contradictions that would shame her beloved Sifu.

She glowered at Alex as he moved toward her. He was laughing! That lying, cheating bastard was laughing at her! He evaded her fists and grabbed her around the waist.

"You realize we probably can't have children now," he whispered. "That was some kick." Alex wrestled her into the trunk, gagged her with his tie and bound her hands. "Play along. Don't worry." He kissed her ear. "You can slip these things when we park."

It seemed like an eternity. Nik cuddled up next to the spare tire, praying that Alex hadn't lied. Was this a charade to trap Danielle and her partner, or just another in a string of deceptions? She wanted desperately to believe him, hated herself for tingling when he'd kissed her. She spent the time considering the identity of Danielle's partner. Only one man really fit the bill. One man who was wily enough to pull this off and ruthless enough to commit murder, an adrenalin junkie, yearning to recapture his days as a robber baron. It all fit.

The car slowed as they swung into a paved area. Nik heard the doors slam, Danielle's dreadful cackle and a hard thump on the trunk.

He'd said she could slip the ropes. Easier said than done. It took Nicole fifteen minutes of frantic rubbing to loosen her bonds and remove the gag. *Huh*, she thought. *That's the last time I'll slobber over a Hermes tie.* Fortunately, the trunk had an internal release, a child safety feature for which she was eternally grateful. She slowly raised the lid, peered left and right and extricated herself from her prison.

Nik checked her watch. Almost midnight. No wonder everything was dark. She crouched by the side of the car and gathered her wits. Of course. They were back in Goodhaven. She knew exactly where they were, and it sickened her.

A dim light shone in the building. Nik tiptoed around the back, focused on the rear door. It was seldom locked, even though insurance policies and a modicum of sense dictated otherwise. She carefully turned the doorknob and entered. From the outer room the rumbling of male voices was audible, punctuated by Danny's shrill laugh. Nik crept through the storeroom toward the sounds and the light.

She cracked the door and focused on Alex, sitting at a table, sipping wine, his long legs gracefully crossed. She flinched, imagining him wrapping those legs around Danielle Stevens. *Lovely,* she thought sourly, banishing the thought.

"I never dreamed you'd go for it, Lee." The man chuckled.

Danielle's voice was syrupy sweet. "I'm what he really goes for. We're taking off as soon as this is settled."

"What about Nicole?"

Alex shrugged. "Collateral damage, I'm afraid. She'll get over it. You can console her."

Big, salty tears trickled down Nik's chin. Hearing that pained her, even if he was just acting.

"I have to hand it to you," Alex said. "How'd you get hold of the Ashcan?" He slapped his drink down on the table. "Oh, now I get it. You and Danny impersonated Shelby and Jarrod. It was you on that tape at Rampart, wasn't it?"

Danielle Stevens interrupted. "We'd done a lot of community theatre. It was easy, especially since Shelby left her password here so neat and tidy."

Her partner sighed. "I spent half my childhood learning magic tricks. Sleight of hand works every time."

Bastard, Nik thought. *Shelby's trust meant nothing to you.*

"Stop torturing me," Alex said. "I have to see the Ashcan. If it's genuine, we'll consummate the deal tonight."

Nik crouched nearer to the opening. She had to see it. She had never seen five million dollars before. Just as she leaned toward the opening, a man's hand pressed hard against her mouth.

"Jesus, Nicole. I'll have to get a tetanus shot." Jarrod Whitholm examined the place where she'd bitten him. "I'm bleeding. You drew blood!"

She whirled around and faced him. "What did you expect? I've been kidnapped, thrown in a trunk and clobbered by your girlfriend. Your grimy paws seemed like more of the same."

He had dragged and half-carried her outside before slinging her into Shelby's Wagoneer. "Fuselli said to wait here, not barge in and complicate things."

"But Alex … "

"Can handle himself," Jarrod snorted. "If he gets the Ashcan, you realize what that means?"

"Big deal."

"Big bucks, you mean. Listen, I finally spoke with my dad tonight. He's a big fan of the Dalai Lama now, wouldn't you know." Jarrod shook his head. "Anyhow, I asked him about Shelby's kid."

"And?"

Jarrod hunkered down as a car approached. "Hold on. It's Fuselli."

Fuselli and two deputies leapt out of a squad car, guns drawn. They crept toward the building, prepared to breach the door.

"Back door's open," Jarrod said. "The three of them are inside."

"Be careful," Nik said. "Alex is in there, too."

Fuselli smiled. "I know. We've heard everything they said. Don't worry, Nicole. He's wired."

As the police entered the building, Nicole sprang up and followed them.

"Wait a minute! What's wrong with you?" Jarrod tugged her arm. "Stay put for once in your life."

"Forget that. I want to see that evil bastard's face."

She shook him off and scrambled ahead with Jarrod trailing. The lights were on now, exposing the building's secrets to the world. Fuselli's steady baritone rumbled through the Miranda rights recitation without a hitch as his deputies guarded the door.

Nicole inched into the room, watching as Jett Hall, her best friend and confidant, was handcuffed.

His composure floored her. The Jett she'd known was sensitive, a man who had cried at Shelby's funeral. This impassive stranger showed no remorse for his crimes. *Some judge of character I am,* Nicole thought. Naïve was the kindest description she could give herself, but dupe seemed more accurate.

She elbowed past Jarrod and confronted Jett.

"How could you? Shelby, of all people. She trusted you."

Danielle made a rude noise. "Oh, God, the prom queen. I'd rather do hard time."

"We can arrange that, Ms. Stevens," Fuselli chuckled. "Of course, cooperation would go a long way. You, too, Mr. Hall."

Danielle crossed her arms. "I didn't kill the old bag. I have nothing else to say without an attorney present."

"It's all on you, Mr. Hall."

Jett blinked his eyes and smiled at Nik. "Guess I blew it, right, Double N? You can take off these cuffs, Sheriff. Neither Danny nor I had anything to do with Shelby's murder."

Fuselli was an oasis of calm. Alex did his Sphinx routine. His perfect features showed no emotion as he sipped his drink.

"May I examine the Ashcan, Sheriff?"

His voice vibrated ever so slightly, and there was an odd gleam in those amber eyes. Nik watched him closely. The man was practically salivating. No wonder they called that thing the Holy Grail.

"I don't see why not," Fuselli said. "Remember, that hunk of paper is evidence in a homicide."

Jett Hall exploded. "Don't you listen? I—we—had nothing to do with that." He was twitching, taking deep breaths. "Look, I admit the Ashcan caper was wrong, but that's where it ended. Shelby left a folder here one day after our chess game. It had everything in it—passwords, inventory, the works. Keys to the kingdom. When she died, and word of this Ashcan came up, it seemed worth the risk."

"Shut up, you fool. Tell him nothing without an immunity deal." Danielle's eyes shot death rays.

Nicole glanced at Alex, gauging his reaction. While everyone else focused on Jett, Alejandro Lee was immersed in his own world. He caressed the Ashcan like a lover, gently stroking the cover, opening the pages with surgical precision. She'd seen that look before when he was in the throes of passion. It was lust, pure and simple.

Jarrod's flinty gaze reminded Nik of the hanging judges of old. Evildoers could expect no mercy from him.

"I get it," he said. "You two always loved doing amateur theatre. Clever, impersonating Shelby and me like that. Too bad greed got the better of you."

"Prove it," Danielle sneered. "You always were a pompous ass."

"Guess you've never heard of facial recognition software. The Feds use it big time." Fuselli grinned. "Hell, it's even used on Facebook. Bet I still have some good connections in D.C." He signaled to his deputy. "Let's take these folks down to the station. I'm going to need that Ashcan, too, Dr. Lee. You can authenticate it, I suppose."

Alex nodded. "Okay, but something this fragile requires special handling and storage. Luckily, they kept it in the Mylar sleeve."

"Come down to the station, and we'll figure something out. Can't break the chain of custody."

Nicole and Alex exchanged glances. "I'll be fine," she said. "Go on."

Without another word he sped off like a lovesick swain. Nicole knew she had a fighting chance against another woman. Competing with a seventy-year-old relic was impossible.

Jarrod clamped his arm around Nik. "Come on. I'll drive you home. Maybe you can rustle up two snifters of Shelby's brandy. It seems fitting. I have something important to tell you."

Twenty-Four

Despite her heavy jacket, Nicole shivered violently. As soon as they reached the carriage house, Jarrod lit a fire while she poured brandy and arranged snacks. After a night of rude awakenings, something more was coming down. Nik was confident of that.

Jarrod fidgeted with his glass, absently swirling the amber liquid back and forth. "I told you I spoke with my dad"

"Yes." Nik longed to shake him. Anything to speed things up.

"I finally asked him about Shelby's child. He hemmed and hawed and tried to evade the issue. Then he told me."

Another pregnant pause. Nik was close to biting her nails, but she powered down.

"He knew all about her son. It was a boy, you see." Jarrod took a healthy slug of brandy.

"What happened? Where is he?" If Jarrod stopped again, she'd scream.

"Right here." His haughty Whitholm nose pointed skyward. "I'm Shelby's son."

For the first time, Nicole felt compassion for Jarrod. He was somber but clearly shattered by the revelation. She hesitated. What if she said the wrong thing and hurt him?

"Such an old story," Jarrod said. "Shelby, my mother, fell in love with her married philosophy professor. Nature took its course, and she got pregnant. She couldn't keep me, society's taboos and all that, but she wouldn't give me up. My parents, that's how I still think of them, desperately wanted a child." Jarrod shrugged. "So they worked things out."

"But she was no kid at the time," Nicole said. "Why not keep you herself?"

Jarrod's sigh had a streak of melancholy a mile wide. "I think we need to cut Shelby some slack. She did her best. What more can we ask? I had two wonderful parents who loved me and a crotchety aunt who was always hovering in the wings. Not such a bad deal when you think about it."

"Will you tell anyone?" Nik asked.

"Nope. Shelby wasn't the only one who could keep secrets."

When Alex finally returned, Nik was grumpy, groggy and eager for comfort. Shelby had haunted her dreams, robbing her of sleep, ordering her to take some vague, unspecified action. Even the furry embrace of her pets couldn't exorcise the demons.

Alex held her in his arms, whispering sweet words and kissing away her fears. Nicole tried to be philosophical. Loving Alex was heavenly but evanescent. It couldn't last and probably wouldn't. He'd found the Ashcan. Once that deal was consummated, Alejandro Lee would jet back to California and be in the wind. She steeled herself for inevitable heartbreak.

"What's wrong, baby?" he asked, brushing aside her hair. "Still holding a grudge about your ride in the trunk?"

His touch was gentle, and Nik fought a sudden urge to wrap herself in his arms and never leave.

"Of course not." She cringed as she recalled Danielle's spiteful rant. Alex needed a woman, not a credulous girl. He and Danny must have yukked it up about that.

"My client still wants the Ashcan. Don't worry. I'll take care of everything." Alex raised her chin, touching her lips with his. "Jarrod already asked about it. Of course, Fuselli needs something for evidence, but I think we can work it out."

All he cares about is that damn Ashcan, she thought. *Shelby's murderer roams free, and Alex still obsesses about a comic book.* Nicole tried to concentrate, but it was impossible. How could Jett, her friend and steadfast ally, be a murderer? Danielle was another matter. Nik had pegged her as a stone-cold bitch the first time she'd caught her kicking Atticus. Danielle called it nudging, but she lied.

After mainlining espresso Nik formulated her plan.

"I'm going to the jail," she told Alex. "Jett didn't murder Shelby, and I intend to prove it."

Alex did the protective male thing. He glowered at her, hands on hips. "No way! Fuselli won't permit it, and neither will I."

His eyes softened as he moved toward her. "Can't you see? I want to protect you, keep you safe." Alex fingered the gold necklace that dangled from her neck. "You're so young. You can't possibly understand."

"Wait just a minute. Don't patronize me. You're only eight years older than I am, grandpa. I understand more than you think. I can take care of myself, too. I've had to learn."

The tension was unbearable. Nik gritted her teeth, determined to let him make the next move. She stood silent and unbowed as Alex absently stroked the chain he'd given her, staring at her as if she were a statue.

"I've tried fighting it ever since we met. I knew you were trouble." His voice was gentle, bemused. "That's why … I thought if I spent time with Danielle, I'd get over you. It only made me want you more." He put his arms around Nik and faced her. "I'm in love with you, don't you see? I can't imagine life without you."

The situation was absurd, impossible and incredibly hot. Nik stood on tiptoe, flung her arms around him and ignited a spirited exchange that ended in her bedroom. After some creative problem solving, they compromised on their differences. She sped off to the sheriff's office with Alex at her side.

Fuselli looked alarmingly like Mount Vesuvius. He slid his reading glasses down his nose, heaved a big sigh and glared at Nik.

"I'm not his social secretary, Ms. Nelson. Your dear friend is charged with murder. We'll be transferring him to the Barnstable jail this afternoon."

"Jett didn't murder Shelby. I'm positive of that." Nik tossed her mane of curls. "True, he was weak and greedy, but that's part of the human condition."

"Oh, spare me the liberal bullshit. I thought you had more sense. Dr. Lee, can't you control her?"

Alex gave a hapless shrug. "She has a point, Sheriff. Jett Hall is hardly Superman. Who knows? We might get something if she questions him."

Fuselli mumbled a really bad word and pointed at the cell. "Ten minutes, Ms. Nelson."

After allowing the deputy to commandeer her purse and pat her down, Nik scrambled through the door. Jett sat cross-legged on his bed's thin mattress, deprived of his belt and his dignity.

"Hey, Double N. Nice of you to drop by." His voice was soft but still vibrant. He gave Nik a cheeky grin and held out his arms. "Sit right down, unless your boyfriend objects."

"Thanks. I'll stand." Nik forced herself to meet Jett's eyes. It hurt, seeing him like this.

"I thought we were friends, Jett."

"We are." He polished his glasses on his shirttail. "I never touched Shelby. You know that."

"You were willing enough to steal from me and Jarrod." Nik unleashed the venom in her voice.

Jett hung his head. "Sorry, Nicole. Truly I am. I didn't know about you when we grabbed the Ashcan. It was just too good to pass up."

"Danny … she killed Shelby?" It sounded wrong even though she wanted it to be true.

"Nah. Danielle drove over there in the Hummer, but Shelby was already dead." Jett seemed amused by the thought. "It spooked her, I can tell you that. She's not so tough."

Tough enough to do whatever it takes, Nik thought. *I won't count her out as the murderer.*

"What happens to you now?" Despite everything, she still cared about Jett. Danielle, on the other hand, could rot in hell.

He shrugged with the insouciance she used to find charming. "It'll all work out in the end. Don't worry, Double N. Mindbenders is in good hands. Harris said he'd run the shop and feed Fagin. Even Amanda Haas offered to help."

"Harris Goldman hates cats," Nik said. "He hates all animals. Mandy's not much better."

"Maybe Shelby converted them. They went to Lifelines enough. Anyhow, I'll be out of here as soon as bail's set."

Fuselli strolled over, swinging his keys like a lariat. "Don't count on that, Mr. Hall. We plan to oppose bail. Murder with special circumstances and a flight risk, too. You had those tickets to L.A. in your pocket."

"Big deal. You'll have to do better than that." Jett seemed curiously untroubled.

"Whatever. Time's up, Ms. Nelson. Skedaddle." Fuselli's bemused expression followed her as she hustled up the corridor.

She found Alex sprawled on the hard plastic chair in the waiting room, snoring gently. He looked peaceful, a beautiful dark angel who could take her to heaven whenever he chose. There was another possibility, of course. Lucifer, the ultimate dark angel, had been beautiful, too, before his betrayal and downfall. She dispelled those thoughts by brushing her lips across his forehead. Her touch was whisper soft but enough to awaken him. His eyes flashed, then glistened when he saw Nik.

"How did it go? Are you finally satisfied?" Alex disguised a yawn with his hand. "Come on. Let's rustle up some lunch. Goodhaven oysters sound like just the ticket."

"Nope. You need to get some sleep. We can eat afterwards."

She ignored his raised brows and hopeful look. "Forget it, champ. Go back to your hotel and get some rest. I have things to do."

Alex straightened his tie, stood up and yawned again. "Okay, but don't do anything stupid."

"What could I possibly do? Shelby's murderer is in jail, remember?"

"Don't make me stuff you in the trunk again, Ms. Nelson. You're a magnet for trouble."

She danced away from his outstretched arms. "Get some sleep before you embarrass yourself. I'll see you later."

Nik was restive. She had plenty to do but couldn't settle down. Her career beckoned, deadlines loomed, and Alex loved her. He truly did. Nik's normal good sense fled in the face of that reality. Her joy felt almost obscene.

Jett's sad plight put a damper on everything. He was no murderer, even though he was a thief and a cheat. Nik resolved to do something to help him, no matter how insignificant. Wherever she now roosted, Shelby Whitholm would approve.

That brought her to Mindbenders just after noon. Everything looked normal: lights on, shades up, door open for business. Nik told herself she wasn't meddling, she was advocating for Fagin. The cat was sweet and loving, an easy mark for anyone who wished to harm him. He'd been one of Shelby's favorites at Lifelines, and Jett had to sweat blood to pass the adoption test.

"May I help you?" Amanda Haas sounded quite sure that she could not. Her voice quivered, and her speech slurred. "Oh, it's you, Nicole. What can I get you?"

There was something odd about her today, even by Mandy standards. Nik did a quick inventory of the skeletally thin woman standing before her. Amanda teetered on heels so high they seemed closer to stilts than shoes. Her makeup was askew despite an overly generous layer of foundation, shadow and blush. *Yikes*, Nik thought, *did the woman use spackle this morning?*

"Jett told me you were helping out," she told Mandy. "Is Harris here, too?"

Mandy's head jerked back as if she were a marionette. "He had to leave. I'm in charge." The thought seemed to please her, as if responsibility were a shiny new bauble.

Carpe diem was Nik's watchword. She seized the opportunity to quiz Amanda.

"How did everything work out with the sheriff, Mandy?"

The woman gave her an opaque look. "What?"

Patience, Nik told herself. Self-control. "You know, the encounter with the tourist. That hit and run?"

Mandy pasted a bland smile on her face and shrugged. "Oh that. Morgan took care of everything. People listen to him."

It took courage, moxie, chutzpah, but Nicole forged ahead, trampling over every social nicety in her path. "Jett never killed Shelby. I know that."

Amanda's eyes widened like those of a frightened mare as she took refuge behind the cash register. Her voice squeaked as it ascended to a higher-pitch. "Whatever do you mean, Nicole? He must have."

Nik took a giant stride toward her. "He had no motive. You did, and so did your husband."

"No, I swear." Mandy's frail body shook, generating a shiver of guilt in Nik. "Why are you doing this to me? I wasn't even here that day. Morgan knows that."

"What do I know, Darling?" Morgan Haas eased quietly into the shop and joined his wife. "Something wrong here, Nicole?"

Amanda flung herself into her husband's arms and sobbed. "Oh, Morgan. Help me."

Nik backed away and perched on the arm of the red velvet couch. She summoned every ounce of courage she possessed and faced the mayor of Goodhaven.

"I just visited Jett. He asked me to stop by and check on Fagin, but I don't see him." She gave Morgan her sunniest smile. "Any idea where he is?"

Morgan finger-combed his thick grey hair while leveling Nik with a look of executive distain. "Who the hell is Fagin, and why is it your business, Ms. Nelson?"

You're doing this for helpless animals everywhere, Nik told herself. *Be strong.*

"It's no big deal, is it Mr. Mayor? Fagin is Jett's cat. Mandy didn't seem to know his whereabouts."

Amanda wailed as if she expected a beating. "It's not my fault. Harris took him."

Her husband painted a politician's faux grin on his face and became Mr. Affable. "Well, that settles it. Harris probably wanted company. He gets lonely out there all by himself."

Nik knew he was lying. Blend a banker with a politician, and you get lies every time his lips move. She didn't trust Morgan. He'd shed his avuncular persona like a reptile's skin, replacing it with something more sinister. Mild Mayor Haas had been subsumed into a sharp-eyed adversary who took no prisoners. He advanced toward her, wearing a mile-wide smile full of deceit.

"What say we take that tour of my boat now, Nicole? After all, now that you're an heiress, you're my number one client. It's right down in the marina."

Mandy's lips said nothing but her frantic eyes spoke volumes. The woman was terrified. Nik was sure of it.

"I'll have to take a rain check, Mayor. It's important that I find Fagin." She strolled toward the door, doing her best to look confident while longing for Alex and the comfort of male muscle.

Morgan beat her to the door handle. "Let me drive you over to Harris's place. We have some details about Shelby's estate to settle."

Nik quickly adjusted to the new reality that was Morgan Haas. Years of squash and sailing had sculpted his body into a formidable weapon. He looked strong, easily capable of subduing an elderly woman who trusted him. Truth be told, he'd dispatch a twenty-four-year-old student quite handily, too, despite her black belt in tae kwon do.

"Sorry. Let's wait until Jarrod's available."

The heavy oak door closed behind her with a resounding thud. *Keep cool,* Nik chided herself. *This is Goodhaven, not the casbah. You're perfectly safe.*

She felt, rather than saw, Morgan Haas move behind her. A long forgotten self-defense move asserted itself as Nicole whirled around, confronting the town's mayor.

"Anything else I can do for you?"

His scowl would have scandalized his supporters. "Stay away from my wife. Do you hear me? Mandy's emotionally fragile."

Nik took a deep cleansing breath. She'd always battled her inner nice girl, that almost compulsive need to be liked. This was no time to regress, not when a bully was threatening her.

"Jett's fragile, too. He asked me to check on his cat, and I intend to do that. Mandy's your problem, not mine." She gave Morgan a brisk nod and strode toward home.

Twenty-Five

Despite his exhaustion, sleep eluded Alejandro Lee. Had he really opened his heart to Nicole? It was frightening, yet strangely liberating, to relinquish control for once. He had spent his life suppressing emotion, guarding his feelings like the emperor's tomb. His dad had taught him that.

Sylvester Lee had been a master of self-control even when it came to loving his son. A pat on the back or a fleeting smile was as close as he ever got to affection. Nei-Nei, his grandmother, was different. She'd rocked Alex in her arms, humming a tune with exotic words that captivated a young boy. He'd never really loved anyone else. When Nei-Nei died, Alex learned a cold, hard lesson: Giving your heart to another is a loser's game. The unbearable pain of her death stayed with him still.

Alex had let down his guard with Nicole. She had somehow evaded his carefully crafted defenses and opened the floodgates. Now he was totally exposed, vulnerable to a woman for the first time ever. He had never felt such abject fear or total exhilaration.

When his phone rang, Alex leapt to answer it. He had to hear her voice, if only for a moment. It was a flagrant show of emotion that roiled his blood.

"Nicole?"

"What? Have you been drinking?" Jarrod Whitholm snorted his disgust through the phone lines. "For Christ's sake, man, get a grip."

Alex forced himself into rational lawyer mode. "Never mind. What's up?"

"Everything. Fuselli released Jett Hall an hour ago."

"What?"

"You heard me. Apparently Jett has an ironclad alibi for the time of Shelby's death, playing chess with that desiccated Harris Goldman. The county DA said to release him on his own recognizance. Danny's not so lucky, though. She's still in the hoosegow. Good riddance to bad rubbish, I say."

A wave of fear swamped Alex. Nicole was alone at the carriage house. Suppose Jett confronted her?

"Are you still there?" Jarrod barked.

"I have to go. Meet me at Nicole's."

"She's not there. Probably walking that mutt of hers. I just knocked at her door."

Alex threw off the bedcovers. "I'll be waiting outside the hotel. Pick me up."

Harris Goldman was Nik's least favorite person in Goodhaven, and the feeling was mutual. He'd been surprisingly candid about it from the first time they'd met. After giving Nik a tepid handshake, he'd told her she behaved just like his former wife. In Nik's experience, channeling an ex-spouse never boded well. Since then she and Harris coated their dealings with the thin veneer of civility required by polite society, nothing more, nothing less. That civility would evaporate in a hurry if the old coot had hurt Fagin. She would tear him limb from limb and enjoy every minute. This new, bloodthirsty Nicole was a revelation and a release. No more saccharine smiles and unwarranted deference. She was empowered.

Nik reached her carriage house in record time, spurred on by a keen desire to avoid any more encounters with the mayor. He was probably okay, just overly protective. She wondered if that same instinct had made him a murderer?

As soon as she arrived Foo Dog flung himself at Nik, greeting her with the plaintiff howl of an abandoned pet. She hugged him, ruffling his silky coat and crooning all sorts of blandishments into his doggy ears. After feeding all three of her pets, she relaxed until guilt assailed her. Fagin was missing, and she couldn't rest until she found him. If that meant confronting Harris or Morgan, so be it. Things had changed since the comic book world transformed her into Wonder Woman!

Nik leashed Confucius and hopped into the Wagoneer. It was only two o'clock, but Harris probably went to bed at six. Waking him up was a grisly prospect no sane woman would even contemplate.

As she prowled the mean streets of Goodhaven, a scheme sprang to mind. Why not take a peek at Morgan's boat while he was occupied with Mandy? He might have taken poor Fagin there to dump in the ocean. It was a stretch, a total improbability. She hoped that the boat might yield some kind of clue linking Morgan to Shelby's murder. He was Nik's murder suspect number one. That old saying about making a killing on Wall Street raced around and around in her head. Ruthlessness was revered and rewarded there. Had Morgan Haas reverted to type?

Nik swung into the harbor lot, parked the Jeep and scanned the area. She gave Foo the down/stay command while she scoped out her target. The boat dock was deserted. That was both ominous and comforting. The last thing she wanted was another tête-à-tête with Sheriff Fuselli. Scratch that. The thing she really dreaded was coming face to face with Morgan Haas.

She knew nothing about boats, especially so-called sailing yachts. It was a sad testament to her work ethic, but in the eight months she'd resided in Goodhaven, Nicole had never been on any boat. To paraphrase a very bad joke, they all looked alike.

When a jaunty looking fellow wearing a nautical cap ambled toward the dock, Nik saw her chance. She applied a dollop of eau de girl next door and hailed him.

"Hi. I'm supposed to meet the mayor at his boat. It's called the Alger, I think." She ducked her head. "I'm afraid I can't tell one from the other."

"No problem, young lady." The man's dark tan framed a full head of salt and pepper hair. *Not bad for someone my dad's age,* Nik thought.

He pointed to a large sailboat. "There she is. I don't see Morgan, though."

"I'll just wait for him. Thanks for the help." Nik put her hands in her pockets and strolled toward the boat. Morgan's baby was opulent, even in comparison to those of other well-heeled yachtsmen. Mandy was right to call it a sailing yacht.

The thing was huge, easily fifty feet or more. What made her think she could snoop around something that big? Morgan Haas was no fool. He'd find a very secure spot in which to conceal evidence. She was certain of that.

"Beauty, isn't she? All fifty-five feet of her."

Nik's heart capsized at the sound of that voice. She slowly pivoted to greet the mayor of Goodhaven.

"Where the hell is she?" Alex was close to panic. That was a new and sobering reality for someone who always valued his composure. If anything happened to Nicole …

Jarrod Whitholm shrugged. "Calm down, for pity's sake. You're acting like an old lady. Come to think of it, Shelby was an old lady, and she was never hysterical. This is Goodhaven, not Manhattan. How far could she have gone? She has that dog with her."

Alex gritted his teeth. "Shelby died in her own living room, and for all we know, Jett Hall and your fiancée were responsible." He held his breath and slowly exhaled. Jarrod was right. Finding Nicole would require calm and logic.

"We can always call Fuselli. Let him unleash the team of bloodhounds they use to track down the feeble." Jarrod elbowed him in the ribs. "Must get a lot of practice in this burg."

"Nicole is not feeble-minded. She's brilliant and brave." Alex stopped right there before he made a total fool of himself. He was new to this love thing, and it was giving him fits. He'd had so many women, bright, accomplished women with looks and a future. None of them had ever touched him like Nicole. Not even close. He'd played his part for a while, enjoying the first flush of infatuation. Ultimately he'd left them without regret or recriminations. Not on his part, at least. All that had changed now.

Think, he told himself. *Where would she take Confucius? She dotes on that dog. Treats him like a child.*

"Swing by that store of Jett's. Who knows, maybe he lured her there. He gave her some sob story about his cat today at the jail. Nicole's a real sucker for animals."

Jarrod rolled his eyes and looked heavenward. "Have you checked the beach? I'm told cats love it. Just one big sandbox to them."

Alex eyed him up and down. "How good are you in a fight?"

"I boxed at Yale. You know martial arts, I presume."

"Yep."

Alex ignored Jarrod's assumption that every man with a drop of Asian blood was Bruce Lee. Even stereotypes have their uses, and in this case it happened to be true. He'd learned karate at his father's knee.

"What are we waiting for? Let's go for it." Jarrod clenched his jaw and stepped on the gas.

Fear causes brain freeze. Nik found that out when she came face to face with Morgan Haas. The mayor scuttled his friendly air, settling instead for unremitting menace.

"What are you doing here? Changed your mind about that boat ride?"

She forced herself to remain calm. After all, Morgan couldn't hear her heart thudding like a bongo drum. Candor was her enemy right now.

"I took my dog for a ride, and somehow we landed here." Nik nodded toward the Wagoneer. "It's lovely right on the ocean. You're lucky."

Praise worked wonders on Morgan. He summoned a ghost of his former smile and motioned toward his boat. "Perks of success, young lady. Hard work pays off. Come on. I'll give you the VIP tour."

Nicole was curious, not suicidal. She had no intention of joining him. "I wish I could, but Alex is waiting for me. Another time."

Morgan clutched her elbow. "I insist." He steered her toward the gangplank. "We'll take her for a little spin on the ocean."

"You can't take a young woman out alone on your boat. What about your reputation?"

He laughed as he surveyed the deserted marina. "Who'll know?"

"I will." Jett Hall appeared out of nowhere and joined them. "How's it going, Double N, Mayor?"

She'd always considered Jett more pest than angel. At that moment, however, he was a joyous combination of cherubim and seraphim.

"They released you?" She was almost afraid to ask.

"No sweat. I didn't bust out." Jett winked at Morgan. "I'm free as long as I don't leave Goodhaven. Hey, Nik, speaking of which, how about a ride home? I walked here from town, and my feet are killing me."

She didn't waste a second. "Of course. Thanks again, Mr. Mayor."

Nik took Jett's hand and sped toward the Jeep.

"What the hell was that all about?" Jett asked, fumbling with his seatbelt.

Nik focused on driving, letting the bumpy byways match the pounding of her heart. It wasn't much, but it beat hysteria. She took quick, even breaths before answering.

"I'm not quite sure. Morgan's acting very weird these days. Where to?"

Jett sighed. "Mind if we stop by Harris's place? I want to pick up Fagin."

"I was on my way over there when I got sidetracked. Are you sure he's got him?"

"Yep. Don't mind Harris. He's irascible at times, but he's been a good friend to me."

Jett's flirtation with larceny had changed him. He seemed more purposeful, less playful than before. Nicole missed her silly, old pal.

"Listen, Nicole," Jett leaned back in his seat, "I don't know how to act around you anymore. Are we still friends?"

She'd pondered that question. Jett had hurt her, but he hadn't killed Shelby. She was positive of that. "Still friends. That doesn't mean I'll forget what you did, though."

"Fair enough. I want to help find Shelby's murderer. Maybe … it might make up for what I did. Expiation. Shelby was big on that, wasn't she?"

Nik nodded. "Morgan is my preferred suspect along with Mandy, of course."

"Any proof?"

She shook her head. "None except for that hit-and-run conviction. Mandy finally confessed to Fuselli, but that doesn't mean she didn't kill Shelby. And Morgan's certainly tough enough to kill someone."

"But torture?" Jett shook his head. "I don't know about that. Takes a strong stomach. Turn here." He pointed toward the homey Cape with lush plantings. "Why don't I run in and get Fagin. That way you can avoid Harris if you want to."

"Good thinking," Nicole said. "Foo Dog needs some exercise anyway." She turned off the engine and freed her dog.

"Be careful," Jett warned. "Harris goes berserk if dogs touch his shrubs."

"Gotcha." Nik found Foo's ball and flung it toward an adjoining field. To her dismay, Confucius ignored his toy and ran directly into Harris Goldman's yard.

"Damn! Oh, shit!" Nik panicked. The old fart might attack them with a pitchfork! Foo ignored her commands and launched himself squarely into Harris Goldman's lush evergreens. Something about the place captivated him. Foo began digging, excavating was more like it. He was a furry fiend showing incredible zeal for his task. Dirt and greenery flew as he tunneled into the garden. Nicole tugged his collar to no avail. Instead of stopping Foo wagged his plumy tail as if inviting her to join him. Nicole had never seen him so obsessed even when food was involved. It made absolutely no sense. She'd never touched Shelby's garden or any other. The big dog made a final thrust into the loamy soil, emerging with a prize. Foo loved bones, and he'd found some worthy of his efforts. Nicole gasped as she spied the telltale phalanges of a human foot.

Twenty-Six

She didn't scream. She could barely breathe. Nicole grabbed Foo's collar, yanked the fetid trophy from his mouth and shuddered. Despite her panic, she heard the faint creaking of the front door as Jett emerged, cradling Fagin. He stood frozen on the front step, mesmerized by the bone dangling from her hand. If she could reach the Jeep, she'd have a fighting chance. Otherwise Harris Goldman would win.

"C'mon," she squeaked. "Run!"

He didn't move, even when she screamed at him. "Hurry, for God's sake!"

Harris Goldman edged out the door, brandishing a pointy metal rake. She'd seen one of those on the beach. Chatham scratcher, they called it, a clam rake with lethal prongs. If Goldman used it, Jett would die.

"Drop that thing and walk toward me. Your choice, Miss Nelson." Goldman teased the back of Jett's neck with the clam rake. "Keep that mutt away from me, or I'll stab him, too."

Jett's face was flounder pale. Nik couldn't abandon him. She had no choice.

"I'm coming," she said, "don't hurt him." She croaked a down/stay command to Foo and stepped gingerly toward the house. Maybe she'd get lucky. After all, she had youth and agility on her side, even without Jett's help.

Harris held the door open, keeping a firm grip on the clam rake, beaming a doorman's genial smile. "Now that you know my secret, you've complicated my life." He tsk-tsked and shook his head, motioning to Jett. "A shame, really. Tie her up. Good and tight. Put her on that chair."

"Secret? I don't know anything." Nik eyed the multi-hued rope on the sofa. Red, white and blue, the same kind that bound Shelby. *Oh, Lord!*

Jett's eyes telegraphed an apology as he fastened the rope. It was up to him now. If they had any chance at all, he'd have to tackle Harris.

"Come, come. You're much too learned to pull that off." Harris bared yellowed teeth. "'Shelby, I liked. This will be much simpler. Hmm, my garden needs more fertilizer. There's plenty of room for another corpse, right Jett?"

"Right, professor." He'd recovered quite nicely. He seemed almost perky as he cinched the ropes. "Sorry, Double N."

Goldman cackled. "You really didn't know. When my harlot wife had a little accident, Jett helped me dispose of her remains. All that digging was too much. I'm a senior citizen, after all."

"Jett?" Nik refused to believe it.

"The damage was done by then," Jett said, "and Harris helped me keep Mindbenders afloat with cash."

Nik felt the bile rise. She cleared her throat and forged on. "Shelby. Did you help him with her, too?"

Goldman laughed. "That was definitely a two-man job. She made quite a fuss about my wife's accident. And those stupid comics—guess you could say she died laughing."

Jett's eyes pleaded for understanding. "It wasn't supposed to be like that. Shelby put two and two together and threatened to tell. I just wanted to scare her, but things got out of hand."

He heaved a giant sigh. "You know me, Nik. I'm no murderer."

"Always an excuse. You're sickening." Nik angled her head away from him. "How will you explain me? Another disappearance in such a small town?"

Goldman's eyes sparkled with glee. "A murderess fleeing the scene, that's credible. We'll plant some evidence and let nature take its course." He motioned to the door. "Take her out to the shed, and do it. Strangling won't leave blood evidence. Much less messy."

"No way," Jett said. "I won't hurt Nicole. Do your own dirty work for a change."

Goldman stamped his foot like Rumpelstiltskin. "Just take her out there. I'll do it."

Nik wiggled her hands. The ropes had just enough slack to buoy her spirits. Her feet were free, too. The right kick could crack that cretin's head like a day-old egg.

"I hear something," Jett said, peering out the window. "Shit! That's Jarrod's Hummer."

Goldman's voice reached the upper octaves. "Gag her and put her in the bedroom. Now!"

"What about her Jeep? They'll know something's fishy." Jett's voice squeaked. It always did when he panicked. That might be a good sign, Nik told herself. Maybe he wasn't a total monster after all.

"Let me handle everything," Goldman said. "Just get her out of the way. If she makes one sound, I'll kill her boyfriend."

Jett threw Nik over his shoulder and staggered into the bedroom. He said nothing, but he seemed close to tears. Male voices rumbled in the next room as Nik strained to hear the conversation. Alejandro was there, no mistaking that voice. Jarrod, too. His preppy tones mixed seamlessly with Goldman's academic squeak. Jett cracked the door open a millimeter, just enough to catch the conversation.

"We found her Jeep, so where is she?" Alex asked.

"You mean she hasn't left yet?" Goldman sounded perplexed and very convincing.

Bastard, Nik thought.

"Her dog was with her. Shelby's dog, actually." Jarrod's tone was unfriendly.

"Ugh! That dreadful animal started digging and ran away. Ms. Nelson chased after him, and that was the last I saw of her. She dropped Jett off. Ask him, if you like. He's resting in the bedroom." Goldman called out. "Jett, wake up. We have visitors."

Jett rumbled his hair and stepped out. "Hi. What's this about Nicole?"

"We're looking for her. Where is she? It's getting dark." Alex's voice was strained.

"Damned if I know," Jett said, yawning. "She said she'd walk back to town with Confucius. Tossed me her keys and took off." He dangled the silver keychain under their noses. "She's around somewhere. No big deal. I'm going back to sleep. I'm bushed."

He closed the bedroom door and with it Nik's hope for rescue.

They made their move at dusk. Jett carried Nik to the weathered outbuilding that would serve as her tomb. She hadn't given up; she'd fight as long as she could draw breath.

Harris Goldman danced around the shed like a fire ant. Nik saw evil in his beady little eyes and something more. Bloodlust. He twirled a carmine scarf at his side, taunting her.

"I've never done this before, Ms. Nelson. My wife's death truly was an accident, and Shelby … well, that was unavoidable. Killing you, my dear, will be a pleasure."

They'd brought the clam rake with them in case they needed it. *Overkill*, Nik thought as Jett ducked his head. He was sweating, and his eyes had a feverish glow.

She'd managed to loosen her bonds just enough to make a fist. With luck, she could use her elbow to break Goldman's nose before he slipped that noose over her. Give the bastard a souvenir. She rehearsed her plan, hoping muscle memory would prove its worth. Success depended on split-second timing and lots of luck.

"Let's get this over with." Goldman tented his hands. "Say your prayers, young lady."

"Wait!" Jett said. "Hear that barking?"

"You're delusional. It's only a dog. So what?"

Jett leapt up and peered out the window. "It's Confucius. I swear it is. He'll wake up the whole damn neighborhood and tie this back to us."

Goldman spat. "Check it out, if it bothers you. I'll attend to Ms. Nelson. Be a man, for once, and kill that mongrel." He walked toward Nik as the door closed. "It'll be less painful if you don't struggle. I promise."

Nik bowed her head in faux submission, luring him closer, whispering. When Goldman bent over, she jabbed her elbow at his face. His screams of pain and rage were satisfying. Blood streamed from his professorial nose, as Goldman grabbed blindly for her. Nik tipped the chair and scrambled to her feet, ready to bolt for the door. Jett was waiting there patiently for her with the Chatham scratcher poised to strike.

"I abhor bloodshed, but you leave me no choice." Goldman's lips formed a thin, mean line as he wiped aside the blood pooling on his shirt collar. He took the rake from Jett and held it aloft, pointing its metal teeth directly at Nik's heart.

No tears. She felt curiously removed from the process, enough of a romantic to believe in happy endings even now. Play to his fears, she told herself. He's paranoid.

"Guess you never watched *CSI*, professor. All that blood evidence. Messy. They'll pin my murder on you in no time when Jett folds like a cheap fan."

He paused, considering her argument. "That's a risk I'm willing to take. You're a nuisance, Ms. Nelson. A pest."

She calculated her chances of dodging the prongs. Not good but worth a try. If only she could zig when he zagged.

"I'll go outside and keep watch," Jett said.

Nik curled her lip in disgust. He'd always been soft, cowardly. It's a wonder he had enough nerve to kill Shelby.

Harris Goldman, learned professor of philosophy, smiled as he twirled the rake. He taunted her, feinting left, then right. Nicole said a silent prayer and made her move. She veered sharply to the left, watching Goldman's mouth open wide as the door exploded.

Fuselli fired twice, ending Goldman's murder spree. Alex and Jarrod charged in behind him, armed with wooden baseball bats. The Chatham scratcher flew out of Goldman's hands, landing in the corner with a decided thud. Nicole froze in place, unable to speak or move. She felt distanced from the surreal scene, more observer than participant. Everything—the noxious smell of gunpowder, the perfect holes in Goldman's head and Jett's mournful wails—floated by her like a cloud. Then Alex scooped her up, checked for damage and cradled her in his arms, crooning softly.

"What about this guy?" Jarrod asked. He gripped Jett's shirt collar tightly.

Seeing Jett started her tears. "He murdered Shelby," Nik sobbed. "He and Harris."

"Piece of shit," Jarrod spat, shaking Jett like a ragdoll. "Burn in hell."

Fuselli used his cell phone to alert the coroner and the Barnstable authorities. His voice was strangely calm as he recited the facts. "Bring a forensic team," he said, "with shovels."

"Nicole needs a doctor," Alex said. "She's in shock."

"I'm okay, just cold." She huddled close to Alex. "Confucius. Where is he?"

"Fine. He's the hero of the day," Alex said. "When he trotted out with that foot bone, the game was over."

"Rather fitting," Jarrod said. "Shelby's instrument of justice. She saved that mutt, and he avenged her. It's almost biblical." He shot a look of utter contempt at Jett Hall. "I'll hang onto this guy until they bring the paddy wagon or what passes for it in the boonies. See you later at the house."

Alex caught Fuselli's eye. "Okay?"

"We'll wrap things up tomorrow. Plenty to do around here for now." Fuselli gave a half-smile.

As Nik and Alex walked by, Jett spoke. "Take care of Fagin, Nicole. Please. He's all alone."

She passed him without speaking and went to find his cat.

They gathered the pets and settled into the carriage house to wait for Jarrod. More waiting. Nik was tired of it. She'd spent her whole life doing that, erecting a slew of barriers to shield her from pain and loss. Now she could stop inventing what-ifs and embrace her future. As she'd waited to die in that isolated shack, Nik felt only one emotion, regret, for things dreamed of and undone, for opportunities squandered and lost forever. Thanks to Shelby's legacy, she now had options to explore and the money to fund them.

Her first order of business concerned Alex. Nik had no idea if they had a future, but for once in her bubble-wrapped life, she would take a risk and go for broke. He said he loved her. Okay, she felt the same way about him. No more tortured logic or dry analysis. She loved him, simple words with nuclear impact. Terror and joy fought for control of her heart as she practiced her speech. To ward off the chill in the old house, Nik readied the fireplace.

"Hey," Alex said, folding his arms in mock protest. "Fire-starting is men's work. You've upset the balance of nature, Ms. Nelson. Even cavemen had their assigned roles."

"Oh, I think you have other uses, Dr. Lee. You're a man of many talents, and I'm a very creative woman."

The surprise on his face pleased her. He'd just seen the new Nik. No more sober scholar or flailing ingénue. It was full steam ahead for Nicole Nelson, Wonder Woman in training.

She curled up next to Alex, watching flames lick the fragrant oak logs. At first she'd been uneasy about that fireplace, afraid that she'd burn the damn house down. Shelby taught her the tricks to laying a fire. Kindling, tinder and flues had been foreign terms before Shelby intervened. She now knew they were metaphors for other life skills requiring self-confidence and independence. Shelby's wisdom and caring had helped Nik to grow up. By avenging her friend, Nik repaid some of that debt. A worthwhile trade, all things considered.

Nik rested her eyes, cuddled up with Alex and the cats. She heard nothing but the peaceful sound of cats purring and the faint crackling of logs.

It took Confucius to jolt them out of their fugue state. He hovered around the door, ears alert, uttering a low growl. Alex leapt up, switched on the outdoor light and swung open the door.

"Lee, for Christ's sake, what's wrong with you? I spent the last five minutes battering down this door. My knuckles are raw." Jarrod burst into the foyer wearing a grimace that wouldn't quit. "Where's the cognac? No, make that Scotch. My friend Johnny Walker Blue, if you've got it."

Alex adjusted Grandma's quilt around Nik. "I'll handle it. Stay put." He filled a tray and beckoned Jarrod. "Help yourself, buddy. We're anxious to hear the latest."

"Fuselli said he texted you, but here's the color commentary." Jarrod clenched his jaw in the familiar Whitholm pose. "First of all, they locked up that slime bag Hall. He won't get out this time."

Nik leaned forward. "Did he say anything else?" Her voice quivered. "I don't need details about Shelby, necessarily, but I want answers. No hysterics. No swooning. Promise."

Alex and Jarrod exchanged glances, suggesting a conspiracy of silence. The steely look in Nik's eyes ended that. Jarrod cleared his throat and started.

"Jett's motive was purely mercenary. He knew about the Ashcan, and he wanted it. Greed, plain and simple. Shelby dropped plenty of hints about it, but she trusted the little bastard. Her chess buddy. Huh!"

"She thought she could judge someone's character. Always boasted about it." Nicole relived another Shelby moment. "No one outfoxes me, Pumpkin. I'm a shrewd judge of horseflesh."

"Typical," Jarrod huffed. "Hubris, the plague of the Whitholms. For once she was too clever by half. She snooped around Goldman's place, researched his wife and the imaginary chiropractor. Got it right, of course, but she made the mistake of tipping off her buddy Jett. He swears they went over to persuade ... beg ... Shelby to leave it alone. When she resisted, they tried harder. Shelby being Shelby, she wouldn't give an inch. Things escalated and got physical." Jarrod swallowed hard. "Naturally he swears

Goldman murdered her, but so what? Murder in the commission of a felony, he's equally guilty."

Nik shuddered. Despite the horrific outcome, at least Shelby had exited the world the same way she'd lived in it, on her own terms. Jett said things got out of hand. Bastard! If he couldn't accept the truth, Nik certainly could. Jett and Harris Goldman had gone to Shelby's prepared for murder. Shelby Whitholm, the woman who knew too much, had to die.

"You doing okay?" Alex asked her. "Had enough?"

"No problem. Please continue." Nik had to hear everything. She owed that to Shelby. Full disclosure. Words had no power to hurt her anymore.

She'd changed her mind about Jarrod, too. Underneath that jaded, preppy exterior, there was a deep vein of decency and compassion. Not surprising. He was his mother's son, after all. His composure was admirable, considering the grisly narrative he'd described.

Alex stood motionless, sipping his scotch as he drank in Jarrod's story. "What about Goldman? I realize we have only Hall's version of the story, but still ... "

Jarrod shrugged. "Apparently Goldman really loved his wife. When she tried to leave him, he freaked. He killed her and concocted that story about the chiropractor."

"He told me it was an accident," Nik said, "but I didn't believe him. He was evil, a real control freak. Misogynistic, too."

"If you've finished the feminist rant, I'll continue." Jarrod drained his scotch and poured more. "Forgive me, but my encounter with Danielle has temporarily soured me on women. Right now, misogyny sounds pretty damn good. Okay. Some of this you've heard. Goldman panicked, called Jett and bribed him into burying his wife in the garden. Naturally, he ponied up plenty of cash to seal the deal.

Somehow Shelby got on to him and forced him to work at that animal shelter."

Jarrod jumped as Fagin brushed up against him. "Egads! Where did that creature spring from?"

"That's Fagin," Nik said, "my newest family member."

"Ugh!" Jarrod curled his lip and faced Alex. "Are you going to allow this? You'll have a biohazard, for sure, if she keeps collecting animals."

Alex leaned back and grinned. "A small price to pay, my friend. Continue."

"There's not much more. Shelby never suspected Jett of any funny business until he slipped up somehow. Something to do with the sudden infusion of cash into his business. She spent half her life prowling around his store, and snooping was in her nature. Whatever. She got too nosey, and that sealed her fate. Big miscalculation on her part. No forced entry or breakage. They showed up at her door, and she let them in, even put her dog in the yard to accommodate Goldman."

Jarrod's voice broke as he concluded the story. *Not surprising,* Nik thought. *After all, he's describing his mother's murder.* She shivered.

"That explains it. Remember I told you that Goldman saw your Hummer at Shelby's that day? I'm so stupid. I focused on you or Danielle without thinking it through."

"Ah. To see that, Harris Goldman had to be there too. It was right in front of us all the time." Alex shook his head. "He incriminated himself."

They stayed silent for a moment, digesting the sad ending to Shelby's life. When Jarrod spoke, his eyes were suspiciously moist.

"You've got to hand it to her. Shelby, I mean. She was a tough old bird right to the end. Never gave in. Probably spit in their eyes."

"Lots to be proud of there," Alex said softly. "Shelby was one of a kind."

Jarrod ducked his head and gathered his keys. "My mother. Hard to think of her that way. Have to give it some time, I guess." He nodded at Nik and shook Alex's hand. "Fortunately, I've got plenty of time. My show's on hiatus for two weeks, so I plan to spend some time with my dad, get his take on baby sis."

"What about Danny?" Nik asked.

Jarrod bared a set of strong Whitholm teeth. "What about her? Bitch can grow old in jail, for all I care. In fact, even now I'm crafting a victim impact statement for her trial. With any luck it should add ten years to her sentence. I can't prove it, but I'm sure she knew more about Shelby's murder than she ever let on."

As Jarrod walked toward the door, Confucius wedged himself between Alex and Nik, baring his teeth.

"I told you that dog hates me," Jarrod said. "Oh, well. Watch the place for me while I'm gone, will you? Assuming you'll still be here."

"We'll be here," Alex said.

Nicole slept soundly for nine hours. She vaguely remembered the warm hug of Alex's arms, the furry embrace of her cats and the rumble of male voices. When Foo's moist nose awakened her the next morning, she thought she'd been dreaming.

Alex glided in the room carrying a breakfast tray. "Ready for nourishment?" he asked.

Nik blushed, realizing that he must have undressed her and popped her into bed. "Thanks for everything."

"For saving your life? Confucius gets that prize." He gently kissed her fingers. "I meant what I told you." He hesitated. "About loving you, I mean. Before we make plans, I have to tell you something."

She braced herself for the worst. *If he's married, I'll die,* she thought. *My heart will shred into little, bitty pieces and dissolve on the spot.*

"Still with me?" Alex asked. He took a deep breath and faced her. "I lied to you, Nicole. Misled you, actually."

Bile roiled the pit of her stomach, but she stared straight into his eyes. Those lying, amber eyes. "Okay. Tell me."

"I ... okay, there is no client for Shelby's collection. At least not the way I suggested." Alex touched her cheek. "I'm the client. The Whitholm Collection is for me."

Nik frowned. "I don't get it. Why pretend?"

"At first it was a negotiating ploy. You know, a way to win monetary concessions. Shelby was pretty damn sharp, and I wanted the best possible price." He turned away. "But afterwards, when I met you, I ... it was an excuse to stay near you. Jarrod found out right away from someone at Stanford." Alex grinned. "He didn't tell, though. I owe him for that."

"So you're a collector, not an agent. Big deal."

"It means I'm rich, baby. Wealthy even. Don't think I'm marrying you for your fortune. I inherited a bundle from my mom's family. Minor British royals."

"Wait a minute," Nik said. "You're a duke or something?"

Alex's eyes sparkled. "Nothing so grand. Just a baron."

"You mean I'll be a baroness? Cool!" Nik turned away, blushing. " I ... I wasn't presuming anything. About you and me, I mean. Come to think of it, forget about a title. I'd rather have my Ph.D. and be an American."

He took her hands and pulled her close. "I want you to presume, don't you see? I have big plans for you, Ms. Nelson. There are some conditions, of course."

Nik turned away. Could she give up the goal she'd been striving for so long, surrender a part of her soul? The rewards would be great, but at what cost?

"Hey," Alex said, touching her cheek. "Don't you want to hear my conditions?"

She pasted a smile on her face and nodded. It was do or die time.

"I fell in love with a feisty woman with lofty aspirations. I won't settle for anything less."

Nik felt confused. What was he saying?

He tried to hide the grin lurking at the corners of his mouth. "In plain English we'll defer our wedding plans until you get that Ph.D. Okay? Think of the dinner reservations we'll get with Dr. and Dr. in front of our names."

Her confidence melted like cheap oleo. Alex was toying with her, crafting a graceful exit strategy. He'd slip away, go back to California while she spent the next six months absorbed in her books. Nothing dramatic, just a genteel slide into oblivion. By force of will she kept her face blank. What a fool she'd been. Alex was an older, more sophisticated version of her former fiancé. The new, brave Nicole had met the same fate as her predecessor.

"How's that sound?" Alex asked. He shook his head in mock horror. "You didn't hear a word I said, did you?"

"Not really."

"I'll repeat. We'll stay in Boston while you finish up. My work's flexible enough to do anywhere, and I'll fly to the coast for the odd meeting when necessary."

"I don't understand," Nik said.

His amber eyes were alight with feeling as Alex took her hand and knelt in front of her. "This is a proposal. Will you marry me, Miss Nelson?"

"I … of course I'll marry you." She was stunned, reeling from shock and emotion.

"My pets ..."

"Not a problem. I love big families. You'll find out." Alex leapt up and twirled her around. "Shelby would be pleased, don't you agree?"

"She wanted me to be happy, and you're the best thing that's ever happened to me."

Alex raised thick black brows. "Come to think of it, knowing her as we do, it wouldn't surprise me if she planned everything. Not the tragedy, of course, but our meeting."

"Shelby said she was a good judge of character." Nik stood on tiptoe, kissing him. "That's one argument with her I never won."

Meet Author Arlene Kay

Arlene Kay spent twenty years as a senior executive with one of those alphabet agencies that strikes terror into the hearts of the average citizen. She found unintended humor in bureaucracy and discovered a world of quirky characters in the many offices in which she worked.

Since moving to Cape Cod, she strolls the beautiful beaches with her dogs, plotting murder and mayhem.

Arlene's mystery *Intrusion* was published by Mainly Murder Press in 2011. A sample follows. Both *Intrusion* and *Die Laughing* are available as e-books at www.Amazon.com.

Intrusion
Murder, passion and lip gloss
meet Boston high tech

by Arlene Kay

One

I was dreaming of Kai when the phone rang. Its harsh tone buzzed through my brain like an angry bee, stinging me awake. I pried open my eyes and stared blearily at the alarm clock. Midnight. Thank God for Lasik surgery. At least I could see the damn thing now. My fingers reached blindly for the cell phone on my nightstand. Who the hell would bother me at this hour?

"Hello." I mumbled into the receiver.

"Betts. Wake up. You've got to hear this."

It was Candy's voice, bright and bubbly just like always. No one else called me Betts, not even Kai. Lizzie Mae. That had been his name for me. I'd just settled into REM sleep, and she'd spoiled it. I hated her.

"Go away. I'm sleeping." I disconnected, burying the cell phone under my pillow. She'd done this before. Couldn't wait to thrill me with her latest conquest. Screw that. Girl talk should be mutual, and I had nothing to trade. Why else would I clutch my pillow on a Saturday night instead of curling up with him? Those days of cuddling and kisses were long gone. They say that abstinence is good for you, builds character. Phooey. If I really tried, I could feel Kai with me, holding me tight, whispering softly in my ear, lulling me to sleep. I drifted into fantasyland with a smile on my face.

The pounding wouldn't stop. It wasn't a migraine. It wasn't even in my head. Some idiot was battering down the front door. My mood was less forgiving than a mama grizzly's. Even my dog Della stayed sacked out in her crate to avoid my wrath. I grabbed a robe, belted it and lunged for the claw hammer. Not much of a weapon, but a woman couldn't be too careful. Boston lawmakers coddled killers, not vulnerable females. I took a chance and used the peephole. Killers cap you right between the eyes if you're not careful. All the books said so.

"Let me in. Come on, Betts."

I'd finally get the chance to use that hammer when Candy put her perfectly pedicured toes into my house.

I switched off the burglar alarm and flung open the door. Something was very wrong. Candy was shivering, oblivious to the mascara ringing her eyes. They were her best feature, those green cat eyes. Her legs weren't bad either. She wore a thigh-high silk dress with kitten heels. That didn't improve my mood any. I'd wear a burqa if it covered my bony legs.

"What the hell is wrong?" I asked. "You're a mess."

She staunched the tears coursing down her cheeks. "Oh, Betts, he's gone."

"Who? You're not making sense." I clutched my hands to keep from shaking her.

"Tommy," she cried. "He's dead."

We only knew one Tommy, Tom Yancey, our college buddy, confidant and court jester. He wasn't dead. Impossible. I'd spoken to him only last month. A wave of guilt assailed me. He'd left messages on my machine, sent emails, too. Nothing urgent, just needed to touch base. I'd ignored them, shuffled them off to my pending list. He'd understand. We had all the time in the world.

"It can't be," I said. "What happened?"

Candy hiccupped, an open portal to hysteria. She'd be incoherent soon unless I did something.

"Here, follow me."

I signaled Della to join us, since her people skills easily surpass mine. When Candy dissolves into a quivering mass, I get violent. Della licks her hand. Chalk it up to generations of herding instinct.

I filed into the kitchen and found the teakettle. British wisdom triumphed: nothing beats a nice cuppa when disaster strikes. Candy loved the soothing taste of Chamomile. Tommy insisted … I shook my head. No time for that kind of stuff. I blinked to keep from seeing him, long legs wrapped around the bar stool, sipping his mug of Earl Grey. "Real man's brew," he'd called it, making a muscle. "Strong like bull."

Candy grasped her teacup like a talisman. I didn't offer food; I knew better. That size two shape was no accident. She counted calories with nuclear precision.

"Got any Xanax?" she asked. "Or something stronger?"

"Later. Right now I need information." I found a bottle of Glenlivit tucked away in the cupboard and poured a dollop into her cup. "OK. Tell me."

Candy's cloud of hair gave up the ghost and escaped its clip. She raked her fingers through it, gulping. "They called. The cops. You never answer your cell phone, so they got me."

"When?"

She checked her watch. It was way too large for her, a legacy from her dad. "About an hour ago. Right before I called you. Someone, a detective I guess, said Tommy was dead." She sobbed. "They wanted an ID, Betts. Like at the morgue. I can't do that."

Morgue? Just the thought gave me the willies. I'd seen that hellhole once before. Just once. My skin felt clammy, and my breathing slowed. *Not again. I can't do it either. Not again.*

Candy gulped her tea and looked for more. I made this one stronger. Half the cup was pure scotch. She didn't even notice.

"Maybe they're mistaken," I ventured. "Tommy might be fine." Candy's grim face called me a liar. She shook her head.

"They have a picture from his wallet. You know the one. Us three and Della."

How could I forget that day? It was three months ago. I'd been cowering in my bedroom, missing Kai with all my heart, praying he'd come back. Back from the dead. I saw his cheeky grin and sparkling eyes, felt his strong arms holding me.

Just like that, they'd invaded my space. Tommy was a mess in torn jeans, sloppy tee and sandals. He'd stuffed his thick crop into a Red Sox cap just to annoy me. Candy looked much better. She'd paid good money for her torn jeans and faded blouse. Those honeyed blonde streaks cost her plenty, too.

Since Kai's death, I'd seldom ventured outside except to work and walk Della. Couldn't recall my last meal or decent night's sleep. Didn't really care.

Tommy dangled a key under my nose. "This is an intervention. Get dressed, Mrs. Buckley."

I flinched. Hearing that name, *his* name, made everything surreal. Elisabeth Mae Buckley. Mrs. Kai Buckley. Aren't there naming conventions for widows? Can I still use his name?

They camped out on the bed until I surrendered. With ill grace, I snatched an outfit from my closet and stomped into the bathroom. Tommy chattered nonstop until I reappeared.

"Well. That's much better." His smile was just short of a smirk. "Now, grab your things, leash Della, and follow me."

"Where are we going?" I sounded peevish, unlike the vibrant Betts of old. "This seems more like an intrusion, an invasion of privacy."

Candy tugged my arm. "It's a secret. Come on. Take a risk. Live a little."

That's what Kai always said. Climbing Mount Washington exhilarated him. He couldn't understand my reluctance, called me a chicken. I could still see him and Tommy strutting around the room, arms flapping, clucking like fools. Oh, God.

"What should we do?" Candy moaned. "He's expecting us." She pinched her skirt into a sodden mess, hiking it up to an alarming level.

"Who's expecting us? You're not making sense."

She fished a tattered card out of her pocket and thrust it at me. It was an unimpressive government issue with name, rank and organization: Sergeant Mark Andrews, Homicide Division.

I shook Candy like a rag doll. "Homicide! Tommy was murdered? Why didn't you say so?"

She cowered beside Della, whimpering. "I thought I did. The cop said someone ran Tommy down. Didn't stop. Right outside his office." Her tears aroused my guilt and a sneaky sense of pleasure. I'd morphed from dishrag to bully in five minutes flat. Kai would be proud.

"I'm not leaving now. Forget it." I folded my arms and stared Candy down. Della hovered around her, eyeing me. "Besides, he's probably gone home. Best to wait until tomorrow." That seemed to placate her. Deferred action but a glimmer of hope.

I found a Xanax in my pocket and held it aloft. Candy's eyes gleamed as she reached for the magic pill. Midway through she stopped, hiding her face under a mass of tangled curls.

"Maybe I shouldn't," she said. "You need it more than I do."

"Don't worry. I have plenty." I'd stockpiled enough pharmaceuticals to pacify all of Cambridge. Those capsules had been my boon companions since Kai died. I'd had to hide them from Tommy. He didn't approve of masking pain and threatened to flush every one of them down the drain. "Face reality. Let it all hang out." Tommy was big on slogans.

Candy washed down the tranq with an alcohol chaser. To hell with consequences, desperate times called for bravery. She curled up on the couch, pulled the cashmere throw around her and sacked out with Della at her feet. I envied that childlike sense of detachment. Sleep claimed her like a lover, while it only flirted with me.

I set the alarm, slipped into my bedroom and snuggled back under the sheets. Maybe if I closed my eyes he'd find me again.

Sunlight filtered slowly through my solar shade. I lurched out of bed, wondering if it had really happened. Had I dreamed it? Maybe it was just another convoluted nightmare. I checked my clock. Nine o'clock. Jesus, Lord! Della would be desperate by now. I tore into the living room and saw my best friend calmly reading a paperback. No more hysteria. Candace Ott, beauty guru and confidante of the stars, was in the house.

"It's true then," I said, scanning her perfectly groomed person. She'd shed the minidress for one of mine and smoothed her French braid. No mascara trails today.

Candy nodded. "I called Sergeant Andrews. We're meeting him at noon." She pointed toward the kitchen.

"Espresso over there, and don't worry about Della. We already took a run around the Common."

I staggered toward the caffeine. "Nothing's changed. I won't go to the morgue. I can't."

She waved her arms dismissively. "Not a problem. He's coming here."

"Here!" My synapses weren't firing yet. I couldn't bear that police presence, the bland, meaningless phrases like, "We're so sorry for your loss, Mrs. Buckley," invading my home again. "No," I sputtered. "Call him. Cancel everything."

Candy masked pity with a mile-wide smile. "Sorry, Betts. No can do. He's on his way now." She checked that ridiculous watch again. "Oops. Better get in gear. Your hair could use a shampoo."

My hair! I'd always pampered it, obsessed about it actually. Not many natural redheads around these days, Kai always said.

"You're right," I said. "After all, I'm supposed to be a makeup maven, aren't I?"

"Exactly. You have time to deep condition, too, and a face masque wouldn't hurt." Her smile never wavered. "Tommy would approve. You know how he was about appearances. Kai, too."

Did I ever. The three of us had shared a college flat in Georgetown. Money wasn't plentiful, so Candy whipped up mayonnaise hair masks, oatmeal facials and God only knew what else. Tommy was a good sport about it. We'd slopped that goop all over him, too. Whenever he brought a girlfriend home, we flaunted pictures of him wearing our handiwork. He swore that's why he'd never married.

Armed with a dizzying array of products, I stepped into my shower. It boasted a collection of knobs, nozzles and gadgets that I'd never quite mastered. My birthday surprise, a sybaritic combo of marble, bronze and river stones fit for a monarch. Kai's queen. I stemmed the tide of self-pity, applying myself to the beauty rituals I loved. There's comfort in the scent of lavender and the soothing glow of honey cream. I emerged, scrubbed, perfumed and pampered, an almost believable visage of city chic. Candy's amazing camouflage cream masked the circles under my eyes. Vanity aside, my eyes were my best feature. Deep hazel. My auburn locks looked shiny again even though I didn't blow them dry this time. Let Johnny Law see me *au naturel*.

One spritz of Creed and I was ready. I chose his favorite, Silver Mountain Water. Every time he used it, Kai heaved a giant sigh, closed his eyes, and swore he was back in the Alps. He'd loved the mountains, loved them to death.

Candy nodded at my buffed-up image. "You clean up nicely, Mrs. B."

My smile was wan at best. "Thanks. Listen, Candy. Just one thing. Cops can be ruthless. Nothing's off limits when murder's involved. Stay on your guard."

She cocked her head. "Why? I certainly didn't kill him. I loved Tommy. So did you."

The buzzer ended our sparring. Della charged the door as I let in the law.

Available in trade paperback and e-book for Kindle
at www.Amazon.com

www.ingramcontent.com/pod-product-compliance
Lightning Source LLC
Chambersburg PA
CBHW061556170626
46811CB00001B/225